The Blasphemers

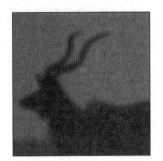

The
Blasphemers

Annamaria Alfieri

FELONY & MAYHEM PRESS • NEW YORK

*All the characters and events in this work are either products
of the author's imagination or are used fictitiously.*

THE BLASPHEMERS

A Felony & Mayhem mystery

ISBN: 978-1-63194-125-2

Manufactured in the United States of America

First edition, 2018

Library of Congress Cataloging-in-Publication Data

Names: Alfieri, Annamaria, author.
Title: The blasphemers / Annamaria Alfieri.
Description: First edition. | New York : Felony & Mayhem Press, January 2018.
  Identifiers: LCCN 2017053586 (print) | LCCN 2017053811 (ebook) | ISBN
  9781631941269 () | ISBN 9781631941252 (pbk.)
Subjects: LCSH: Ex-police officers--Fiction. | Women missionaries--Fiction. |
  Race relations--Africa, East--Fiction. | Africa, East--History--20th
  century--Fiction. | Mystery fiction.
Classification: LCC PS3601.L3597 (ebook) | LCC PS3601.L3597 B55 2018 (print)
  | DDC 813/.6--dc23
LC record available at https://lccn.loc.gov/2017053586

In loving memory of my brother
Andrew Puglise,
who gave me my sense of adventure

ACKNOWLEDGMENTS

I am deeply grateful to:

Maggie Topkis, my publisher and editor, whose sure and guiding hand is a boon to me as a writer.

Adrienne Rosado, my ever-encouraging agent.

Stanley Trollip, for his continuing inspiration and advice as I seek to give the marvel that is Africa its due.

Risa Rispoli, midwife, healer, and great fan of crime fiction, for helping me get the childbirth scene right.

My tribal brothers and sisters at Mystery Writers of America, New York Chapter, and my splendid blogmates on *Murder is Everywhere*. They feed my soul.

The skilled and caring people who look after David and give me the peace of mind I need to do my work.

The staff and supporters of the New York Public Library, the most democratic place on earth. Free knowledge for everyone! Without its splendid collection, none of what I write would be possible.

SUPPORT YOUR LOCAL LIBRARY!

Other "Historical" titles from

FELONY&MAYHEM

ANNAMARIA ALFIERI
City of Silver
Strange Gods
The Idol of Mombasa

FIDELIS MORGAN
Unnatural Fire
The Rival Queens

KATE ROSS
Cut to the Quick
A Broken Vessel
Whom the Gods Love
The Devil in Music

CATHERINE SHAW
The Library Paradox
The Riddle of the River

LC TYLER
A Cruel Necessity

LAURA WILSON
The Lover
The Innocent Spy
An Empty Death
The Wrong Man
A Willing Victim
The Riot

The Blasphemers

Thou shalt not take the name of the Lord thy God in vain.

I will confess that, travelling in East Africa for the first time in my life, I learned what the sensation of land-hunger is like.

The Right Hon. Winston S. Churchill, M.P. quoted in *The Handbook of British East Africa,* London, 1912

The Masai are…picturesque, brave to a degree, boastful, quarrelsome, comparatively faithful and honorable, and yet economically useless…and as far as anything can be humanly certain, it is certain that they too will lose their birthright.

Lord Cranworth, *A Colony in the Making,* 1912

We blame colonialism as a whip horse but it is colonialism that eventually offered the beacon of light of women's western education and exposure which propelled us to the outer world and recognition of the commonality of women's subjugation world-wide.

Helen Chukwuma, "Women's Quest for Rights: African Feminist Theory in Fiction," *Forum for Public Policy,* 2006

Nairobi, Nakuru,
and Their Environs
British East Africa
1913

Justin Tolliver looked with joy upon his son in the arms of his sister, Constance, who had come all the way from Yorkshire to be baby Will's godmother. The child wore the family's christening gown, as had all the Tolliver offspring—beginning with Justin's older brother, John, then Justin himself, and then Constance. All three had been taken to the ancient font in the sturdy gray stone church at the edge of Tilbury Grange, their father's estate. Constance had brought the outfit with her when she traveled to Africa for the baptism of the newest Tolliver, the second of his generation.

Justin's mother, in anticipation of the babies she hoped to have, had purchased the elaborate dress while honeymooning in Florence. That was in 1875—the year the British explorer Verney Cameron became the first European to cross equatorial Africa from sea to sea. Papist, their father called the gown, but in deference to his wife he had allowed his children to be christened in it. And now here was the seven-month-old Will, sleeping in his auntie's arms, waiting to be photographed.

The man with the camera fiddled with his lens. Tolliver posed beside his wife, lovely in her best daytime frock. They stood in a line—he and Vera, flanked by Constance and his father-in-law, Clarence McIntosh, still in clergyman's garb after performing the ritual. Looking on from the lawn were the gentlemen and ladies of the Protectorate, nicely turned out. Many had traveled from Nairobi for the occasion—more, Justin imagined, to make the acquaintance of Lady Constance than to honor the child. They had teased her about her hat, which was designed to frame her lovely face rather than to protect her from the dangerous African sun.

Several of the Reverend McIntosh's Kikuyu converts, in their dark orange *shuka*s and necklaces and bracelets galore, watched the proceedings from the edge of the coffee field, blooming this day in May, after the late long rains.

The family struck several poses. The photographer finished his work and made off with his equipment. The guests arrayed themselves in the shade of the veranda, their conversation heartened by sips of everyone's favorite Sunday-morning libation—an effervescent concoction they called "waters of the Nile."

While the ladies cooed over his son, Tolliver stood aside and wondered about the boy, born here in Africa, baptized in this Scottish Mission enclave in the wilderness. Little Will would spend his childhood seeing the beauty and majesty of this place every day: the acres of bittersweet scented blossoms, the cows grazing on the hill beyond, and across the silver ribbon of the river, a vast sea of green dotted with acacias and lovely creatures—giraffes, zebras, varieties of antelope. A London boy would see such animals only in the Zoological Park. As he grew, would Will recognize the glory of it? Or would it be so familiar that it would seem to him nothing special at all?

A gnat of doubt troubled Tolliver. Would Will then grow up as Vera had, not quite British, not really African, but always halfway between the two? As if she had read Justin's thoughts,

Vera gave the child to Wangari, his Kikuyu nanny who had also been hers. She came to Justin, went up on tiptoes, and whispered in his ear: "The ladies are full of advice and conversation for me. Seems I have finally earned my place among the settler women by giving birth to an English gentleman." The statement was ironic and tinged with more than a little resentment. These were the very wives who had, until this day, judged his light-footed, African-born sylph of a wife as "more than a bit wild."

Constance approached with a half-empty glass in her elegant hand. "I am tipsy," she said, though she looked completely steady on her feet. "What is in this drink?"

Vera giggled. "Champagne and brandy. The waters of the Nile do creep up on one, don't they? It's a good job nearly all this lot arrived in carriages or on horseback, rather than in motorcars. Their horses, at least, will be sober enough to get them home."

Constance handed her glass to a passing servant in a white *kanzu* and red fez. "This is all very lovely," she said, "but next Wednesday cannot come soon enough for me. I must say, though, my expectations of my first safari are so high that I fear I will be disappointed."

Vera shook her head and loosened a dark curl. "Wait. You'll see. It will capture you as it did your brother."

"I agree," he said. "There is not much chance of a letdown."

Wangari returned with Will, now in a blue cotton outfit with a sailorish cut. Vera took the child who immediately grabbed at her pearls. As if some sort of signal had sounded, the crowd out under the shade trees moved to the veranda and began to take their leave.

Much more than on baby Will, they centered their attention on Constance as they bid their hosts adieu. Since her arrival, she and Justin and Vera had been the recipients of dinner invitations from several of the Protectorate's toniest socialites. Lord and Lady Delamere had even invited Vera's father along to dine with them—a missionary at their table, unprecedented as far as Tolliver knew.

Last in the line of leave-takers was the most sought-after companion of all, Denys Finch Hatton. Tolliver had resented him mightily two years ago when he had paid too much attention to Vera. Now the man's bright eyes were resting on Constance in a way that threatened to rekindle Tolliver's indignation.

Vera Tolliver kissed little Will's hand and removed it from her pearls. She turned him so that he faced outward, away from that temptation, and she breathed in deeply the sweet smell of his hair, so pale that from a distance he looked completely bald.

How would she do without him for the twenty days she and Constance and Justin were about to spend on safari? There had been a time when she wanted nothing more than to travel through the wilderness. Now she could barely bring herself to leave her father's mission because it meant she must leave her baby behind. She hardly recognized herself anymore.

She carried the little one into her father's house, kissed his sweet head once more, and handed him over to Wangari.

"You will want to rest, *mwari*," Wangari said, calling Vera "my daughter" as she always had. There was no word in Kikuyu for "nanny," so Wangari had always referred to herself as *nuyukwa*—mother—to Vera and her brother. She had spoken of them and to them as she would her own children.

Aurala Sagal, a young Somali woman, standing behind Wangari, placed an elegant hand on her pregnant belly and smiled indulgently. "We will take very good care of him when you are away." Aurala spoke in Swahili—the language of the coast where she had met Tolliver and Vera the previous year. Soon to give birth to her first child, she was hardly more than a child herself. She had fallen in love with Tolliver's tribal lieutenant, Kwai Libazo, and had come here to hide from the wrath of her father and brothers who sought to take her life in exchange for her having insulted the family's honor by running away from home.

Kwai, her child's father, was on duty up in Naivasha, serving with the Protectorate's police force.

Vera touched Aurala's shoulder. "I will be back before your baby comes, and I will have news of the farmland we have chosen. It will be a lovely place for all of us to live—including you and Kwai and your child." She caressed Will's cheek and forced herself to turn away from him and go back out to do her duty to the straggler guests.

The following day, Tolliver, Vera, and Constance took the up-train from the Athi River Station to Nairobi, just an hour's ride. Scores of Europeans coming from Mombasa on the coast crowded the first-class cars, most of them too pale and starched to be anything but new arrivals. The two engines also pulled eight goods cars that were no doubt stuffed with their belongings.

"We must not lose another minute selecting our land," Vera whispered to Justin as they left Nairobi's inelegant corrugated-iron-and-wood station. "Look at all these people flooding in, hungry for a new start. They will all be applying for land and grabbing up the best places. We'll be left with some scruffy desert fit for nothing but a few miserable goats."

Out in the town, the tremble in her heart quickened. Nairobi had not even existed when she was born twenty-one years ago, barely twenty miles east of here. She first knew it as a helter-skelter village of convenience for the railway builders, but

England had opened "the healthful highlands" to settlers, and they were gobbling up all the available territory.

Constance looked around, bemused. "I must say that I never pictured Nairobi as such a bustling place." She swept an arm, taking in the black wires strung on poles. "Or one with electric lighting. I am impressed."

Justin wrinkled his nose. "To my way of thinking all this modern paraphernalia is an eyesore."

Vera shook her head. "I like the electric lighting," she said. "It's the growth out of control that I find troubling. Father told me there is a huge tent encampment beyond Government House for the newly arrived who can't find hotel rooms or can't pay the inflated prices. And they are all looking for farmland."

"Really, dearest," Justin said, his tone not at all in keeping with his term of endearment. "We will make our tentative choices today. That will reserve them for us until we decide. No need to be so distressed. Please try to be calm."

"Calm?" she said. "I'm glad you can be calm. Look at this street!" They were threading their way through the throngs shopping at open-air stalls along Biashara Street. "It's turned into a madhouse."

"Really, Vera, this is not like you. Why are you so emotional?"

She wanted to tell him the reason why, but she could not think how to explain it. The thought of losing out on having their own place jangled every nerve in her body. "I don't see why you are not every bit as anxious as I. Suppose we end up with the wrong sort of place and our farm fails and we lose everything."

He took out his pocket watch. "Look. I think you need to eat and drink something to calm yourself. We are a bit early for our appointment. Let's stop at the Carlton Lounge for a bite before we proceed."

He exasperated her. "I insist we go directly to the Land Office before the whole of Africa is taken over by these Johnny-come-latelies. Frances Bowes told me her brother had to settle for a place more than ten miles from the rail line on bad roads. He can barely get his crop to market before it spoils." She heard a tremor in her own voice.

Justin harrumphed. "Very well," he said none too pleasantly.

"Once you have made your choice, we can celebrate at luncheon," said Constance, ever the peacemaker.

They spent the next hour with Mr. Evans, the Protectorate's land officer, poring over maps of vast areas of wilderness that had been sectioned into parcels. Desperate as Vera was to be settled into a place of their own, the sight of the divisions gave her pause. For the first time, she saw straight lines imposed on the gorgeous expanse of her birthplace. They brought to mind a drawing she had seen in a butcher's shop in Glasgow, of a cow with lines on it showing the locations of the different cuts of meat. Her Africa was a living thing like the beast in the butcher's picture. She pushed away the thought that dividing it would kill it.

Justin was pointing to a large section on a chart and explaining to Constance that there were already designated forest reserves and tribal areas. Vera was of two minds about that too. She wanted to call some of Africa her own, but it rankled that the British acted as if all of it were theirs to use as they wished.

"Taking into account your intention of starting a fruit orchard," Evans was saying, "I think that one of these two parcels in Ngong—" He pointed out two sections on the top chart. Then he pulled another chart from the bottom of the stack and, with his thumb and forefinger, indicated two irregular sections on it. "—or one of these two up near Nakuru, at the edge of a Maasai reserve, will do very nicely. All relatively close to the railroad and along small rivers to ensure a supply of water."

Vera, contrite at having been cranky earlier, looked to Justin for approval.

"All four seem to meet the criteria we set," Justin said.

She nodded as if she were sure, but she felt more anxious than ever. It was such a big decision. She worried that he was overrating her judgment. She was born here, but she was not all that confident when it came to a choice as critical and irreversible as this. "Yes," she said, despite her doubts. "Let's concentrate on those four." She prayed it would all turn out well. Wherever they landed up, she told herself, she would be happy. She prayed it would be so. She and Justin and Will would live there and be happy together. *Please, God*, she begged.

They arranged with Evans to inspect all four parcels while they were on safari in the following weeks. Justin paid their deposit, took the provisional receipts, and agreed they would make their final decision within the thirty days allotted.

Justin seemed satisfied. Vera forced herself to believe.

They exited the office into the glaring sunlight. "I say champagne with luncheon," Justin declared.

"It surprises me the quantity of champagne that is consumed in this country," Constance said with a laugh.

They had moved only a few steps toward their goal when they happened upon Denys Finch Hatton standing in the shade of a blue gum tree. He was chatting with an elegant man whose clothes were better tailored than any Vera had seen in these parts.

"Tolliver!" Finch Hatton called. "Come meet Giovanni Lorenzo di Savoia." He raised his brown slouch hat to the ladies. "Lady Constance Tolliver, Mrs. Justin Tolliver, Justin Tolliver, may I present His Grace the Duke of Sulmona."

The duke removed his pith helmet, stood erect, and bowed. "*Enchanté*," he said in French. He was as tall as Finch Hatton, but more slender of frame. His eyes were hazel and his hair a shade of brown that confessed it had been blond when he was a child. He was handsome and elegant, as would be expected given his title, but the stiffness of his posture was softened by the warmth of his smile. Vera caught him glancing at Constance's ring-less finger.

"Very pleased to meet you," Justin said. "Have you just arrived in the Protectorate?"

"No, no," the Italian responded. "I have been climbing mountains up in Abyssinia and Uganda and then I came here to scale the Ruwenzoris and to do some hunting. I have come to town to deliver my trophies to the taxidermist." His English was perfect, if spoken with a soft Latin accent.

"We were about to drop in at the Carlton for luncheon," Finch Hatton said. "Would you like to join us?"

"We were about to do the same," Justin answered. "Shall we all go together?"

As they made their way along the bustling street, they separated into two groups, with Justin and Vera walking before and Constance following behind, flanked by the duke and Denys. The threesome paused to examine safari gear on offer in a shop window.

Vera and Justin waited at a small distance. She put her arm through his and squeezed. She forced aside her doubts and made her words light. "I am sorry I was agitated earlier. I worry so that we will not have the future we both so desire. But now my head is full of lovely imaginings of our first real home," she said. "I see foals running after their mares in a paddock. I see pear and apple and peach trees flowering in the spring." She had to believe that everything would be perfect.

"And my brain is full of worries," he said, "about blight, and failed rains, and rinderpest killing off our best horses."

Tears came to her eyes. She needed him to be lifting her up. "How can you be dwelling on such nasty thoughts at this moment?"

Tolliver's heart sank. He was sorry for her and angry with himself. Why did he so often erase her joy? Why could he not keep mum about his worries? He was a dolt.

At that moment, District Superintendent of Police Jodrell, the man who had been Tolliver's superior officer when he first joined the police force, crossed the street toward them. He wore the serious expression of a man with news to impart.

Tolliver felt his spirits sink further. He looked down at Vera and prayed the D.S. would not say something that would heap more worry on her.

After a bare minimum of pleasantries, Jodrell said, "I've gotten word. Your discharge has been approved. You will have to come to my office and sign the papers. They arrived in the dispatch pouch on today's up-train. Come in tomorrow morning."

"Very well, sir," Justin said. His hand moved as if to salute, but he stopped it.

Vera felt something between relief at Justin's coming release, and guilt that, largely at her instigation, he would lose the satisfactions of the work he had done for nearly three years.

"The effective date is not until the first of July," Jodrell said. "They are always on the halfyear, but you won't be posted anywhere, as that is less than two months away. Failing any crisis, you may go about your business."

"Thank you, sir."

Failing any crisis, Vera thought. *Failing any crisis.* Those words chilled her spine.

While they were all at luncheon, Vera invited Finch Hatton and the Italian duke to come to the Mission for dinner—an event that turned out to be quite festive.

That evening, the visitors arrived in time to watch the sunset. Then, after two hours of good conversation and laughter at the table, they settled into the parlor, where Tolliver and Vera played a Schubert sonata for piano and cello.

It was then that Tolliver began to prickle. Vera invited the duke to sing. She accompanied him in a Neapolitan art song, and the man, it turned out, had a lovely tenor voice with a silvery ring to it. He directed his performance at Constance, whose eyes turned starry, triggering Justin's big-brotherly protective impulses.

The party then went to the veranda to sip brandy and look at the night sky. Gian Lorenzo, as he insisted they all call him, walked a little distance away from the lamplight and pointed out to Constance how different the constellations were here at the equator, how many more stars one saw than up north. To Justin's consternation, Constance looked at the duke's face in the starlight as much as she gazed at the firmament. He told himself that this encounter would come to nothing.

The Blasphemers

None of them seemed to want the evening to end, but the brandy ran out, and that signaled bedtime. The guests, for whom there were no spare rooms in the mission house, had had their tent pitched under the rain tree at the bottom of the lawn, near the edge of the coffee plantation. It was well past midnight when they all turned in for the night.

All the champagne, claret, and brandy from the night before prevented Justin from getting an early start the next morning. It was close to noon when he left his horse at Afghan Ali Kahn's stable near the Nairobi Station. By then, his headache was dulled, but his emotions began to roil as he approached Government House. He stepped smartly in his uniform, but he was aware that he was wearing it for the last time. In a few minutes, he would sign the papers that would free him. But it would also cut him off from his service to the king, a duty that had been his since he joined the Yorkshire regiment and was then seconded to serve on the British East African police force. Tradition had required him, as the second son, to go into the army. From boyhood, he and his brother had had their futures settled: John would be the eighth earl with all that entailed, and he would be a soldier and then find an heiress to marry and make some sort of upper-class life for himself.

His future had started off as expected, but then his life turned into something completely unforeseen.

He had gone to South Africa with his regiment and, while posted there, had visited and fallen under the spell of these splendid highlands. All he had wanted was to stay here in BEA. Lacking other means, he had chosen to become a policeman so that he might have his heart's desire. And soon afterward his heart's desire included being married to Vera.

It was time he settled down. He had a son. His time for youthful adventures was past. He was ready to leave the force. He was sure of that. He had certainly had enough of having to enforce what masqueraded as justice in the Protectorate of British East Africa.

Vera's opinion was absolutely right—the word *protectorate* was a sham. It was supposed to mean that they were there to protect the local cultures and improve the lives of the natives. Hardly any such thing ever took place.

Then again, as much as he wanted to embrace his future life as a settler on a farm, thoughts he could not dismiss warred with those convictions. He still craved the satisfaction of solving riddles in his investigations, of eking out the truth and then finding a way to arrive at some semblance of justice. Though often frustrated by the way his cases turned out, he had managed, from time to time, to deliver something approximating his idea of law and public peace.

A camaraderie had developed between him and his sergeant, Kwai Libazo—the only man he had found to trust in BEA. This was a strange thing for an English son of an earl to admit to himself. There were many men much more like himself in the region, who had gone to similar schools, been brought up in nearly identical ways. Why was it that he preferred to make himself into an outsider among them and to ally himself so closely with a man they regarded as a savage?

Kwai was off up-country now, serving in Naivasha, and Tolliver was on his way to end his obligation to his king. Their days of shared adventures were ending. Justin promised himself that, on balance, he would be relieved once his resignation was complete.

He entered the great stone Government House, the most elaborate building in the highlands of the Protectorate, and pressed his way through a crowd waiting at the registrar's office to put themselves on the list for permanent residency. Ever since the completion of the railway, the British government had been advertising to bring in people to settle the high country, luring them with promises of cheap land and a healthful climate. They had even opened an office in Trafalgar Square where people could go and be talked into coming here to get rich.

As Justin mounted the stairs to the second floor, he met one of that get-rich promise's greatest proponents, District Commissioner Cranford. The big man in his perpetual gray suit smiled, shook Justin's hand, and clapped him on the shoulder. "Good to see you, my boy," he declared. Cranford had either forgotten or was pretending to ignore how the two of them had locked horns over Tolliver's investigation into the murder of Vera's uncle. Tolliver pretended warmth too, as was only proper, gentlemanly, and politic.

Tolliver found Jodrell alone in his office, pen in hand, chewing on his mustache and frowning down at a report he was writing. "Come in, come in," he said heartily. "You know how I hate composing these bloody things. Any interruption is always welcome. Tea?" He indicated the seat opposite and, before Tolliver had a moment to accept his offer, called to the hall boy to bring a tray.

District Superintendent Jodrell was typical of His Majesty's better colonial administrators, knowledgeable and confident, but without arrogance or self-importance. He had a big head and a leonine brow that elicited jokes from the men on the force whenever they were called upon to deal with a lion on the streets of Nairobi—an event less frequent than in the past, but still not all that unlikely.

While Justin and the D.S. waited for the tray, they traded gossip about the pedigrees of the newly arrived safari hunters and settlers. Jodrell was taking a great interest in everything Justin could tell him about the Duke of Sulmona, who was—by virtue of being first cousin to King Vittorio Emanuele—the talk of the town.

Once the tea had been served, Jodrell took a sheaf of official-looking documents from the left-hand drawer of his desk and laid it between them.

He gave Tolliver a disappointed smile. "I suppose it was inevitable that a man like you would not want to stay long." He drained his cup. "You might have risen to the highest levels of the force."

Tolliver had never considered such an eventuality. It was one thing for a man like him to take temporarily a position that amounted nearly to servitude. That could be chalked up to a whim. But committing to the work? Rising in the ranks? That was out of the question! Not that he could ever explain that to Jodrell without sounding like the worst sort of snob. "I doubt that very much, sir," he said instead, with a smile. "Rather than receiving promotions, I might very well have been drummed out for refusing to follow orders. You know how often I pressed for one desired outcome when the administration wanted another."

"Mmm, I suppose. There are many of us who agreed with you more than we said. That was your strength. You cared more about what was right than about making rank." He blew out his breath. "Ah, well. You have two months' leave coming to you. I hear you are going to use it to look at land."

Grateful for the change of subject, Tolliver chuckled. "The Protectorate's gossip mill is functioning with its legendary speed and accuracy, I see. Yes, sir. We have only thirty days to make our final choice. We are going off day after tomorrow to look over the possibilities and do some shooting along the way. I must say it is a daunting decision I have ahead of me. Once we commit, we will be wedded to the place."

"That's one of the better things about government service," Jodrell said. "If you don't like where you are, you can wait a while and they will send you somewhere new."

Tolliver sipped his tea and remained silent. He didn't want his heart to regret the choice he had made. He was committed to his life with Vera. He was. He indicated the papers lying between him and Jodrell. "Shall I, sir?"

The D.S. nodded, and Tolliver withdrew his pen from his breast pocket and signed three copies each of two different forms. A lump came to his throat as he watched Jodrell countersign the documents and place one of each in an envelope, which he handed over. "Your copies," was all he said.

Tolliver placed it in his inside jacket pocket.

Jodrell picked up his teacup, saw it was empty, and replaced it in the saucer. "I say again how sorry I am that you will not—"

A sharp rap on the door interrupted him, and District Commissioner Cranford barged in. "Ah! You are still here, Tolliver."

Tolliver stood "I was just about to leave, sir." He took his sun helmet from a table near the door, hoping he might get away without having to engage with the D.C.

Cranford waved him back into his chair, but Tolliver did not oblige.

Cranford took a chair for himself. "I am glad you are still here. Save me the trouble of sending for you."

Tolliver glanced at Jodrell who gave a quick, almost imperceptible shake of his head. "Actually, Tolliver has just signed his discharge papers and is about to go off looking at land possibilities."

Cranford raised his bushy eyebrows. "Yes, I know that. I understand that two of the tracts you are considering are near Nakuru. When do you expect to arrive up there?" he demanded, as if nothing Jodrell had said had any relevance.

Tolliver did not want to become embroiled in whatever Cranford had up his sleeve. "In about a week, I imagine. We have two parcels to visit in Ngong."

"Sit down, please," Cranford commanded, as if Tolliver's standing was a personal affront.

Tolliver wished he could ignore the soldier inside of him, trained to obey orders. He could not. He perched back on his chair. Obviously Cranford wanted to rope him into something. It would be best to cut him off before he made an actual request. "Sir, I will be going out there on family busin—"

The D.C. made a gesture as if he was shooing a gnat. "Now hear me out." His tone was authoritarian in the extreme. "We have an operation about to start there. We are moving some Maasai from that area—just down to Narok on the other side of the Mau Forest. I have a detachment of the King's African Rifles up there, but it will be very useful to have an officer like you on standby while the move gets under way."

"But sir, I am taking my wife and my sister with me. If there is going to be trouble…" He couldn't think what else to say. He looked at Jodrell for support.

"Perhaps a more thorough explanation of the situation would be helpful, sir," Jodrell said. "And pardon me for saying so, but is it quite right to impose this on Tolliver when he is traveling with his womenfolk?"

Cranford made a characteristic gesture of cancellation with both his big hands. "You two are talking as if I am sending school-girls into a war zone. It is not that at all. It's those lily-livers in the Home Office who are on tenterhooks. They are dealing with that ridiculous lawsuit the Maasai have brought over their grievance at having to move. If it were up to the Maasai, they would share the land with no one at all." He twisted his big body on his chair and faced Tolliver. "We don't expect any real trouble. I just want you to understand that we may need you to give advice to the local man. One small last service to king and country." Tolliver expected that next Cranford would be quoting Admiral Nelson—"England expects that every man will do his duty."

The D.C. turned back to Jodrell. "Tolliver's the best man we've ever had for getting on with impertinent natives. He doesn't have to do anything in particular. He may need to watch the Maasai men jump around in those silly contortions they call dancing and tell them how generous we are being. That sort of thing is all I am talking about. I dare say Lady Constance would enjoy seeing the buggers do their dance."

He rose and clapped a meaty hand on Tolliver's shoulder. "Surely since you are going to be there on your own business, it's a small thing for England to ask of you, my boy."

Tolliver was about to object again about how vague Cranford was being on what might be required, but the D.C. pointed one of his sausage fingers at the paperwork on Jodrell's desk. "Besides which, that decree does not take effect until the first of July."

Vera was the first of the party on the veranda to see Justin approaching. She stood and crossed the lawn to meet him at the stable. Something told her that she should warn him about the visitors before he saw them.

The light of the lowering sun had turned the river gold and the coffee blossoms a lemon yellow. The hippos in the pool beyond the coffee factory snorted and splashed, a sound that always seemed to come up the incline of the land as if it were amplified.

Justin cantered toward her, dismounted, and handed the reins to Haki, a waif they had brought here from Mombasa, who now styled himself a stable *toto*. When Justin kissed her, their embrace lasted longer than either of them expected.

He swept the hand holding his riding crop over the golden vista before them. "Look at that! It never ceases to thrill me."

"I think half of your falling in love with me was your infatuation with that panorama," she said with a laugh.

He chuckled, patted her backside, and kissed her again. "You may be right. But only half."

She wriggled away. "I came out to warn you. Finch Hatton and the duke are still here."

"Still?" He was about to express annoyance, but a more amenable thought occurred. "Do you think that Denys might be forming an attachment to Constance?" It would be a decent match perhaps, if Denys had any money. Which perhaps he did not. Constance had none to speak of.

Vera pulled his arm across her shoulders and curled hers around his waist. "I rather think it is the duke who is falling in love."

His mind went back to its original big brother's automatic disapproval of the duke as a suitor. "I got a glimpse of her when he was singing last night," he said. "Surely my sister is not giving her heart to him so quickly." His feet stopped moving. "Good God! He's probably a Catholic."

"I would think that a certainty," Vera said. She felt his body tense and understood what must be going through his mind. His father would never approve. Even worse, his older brother, John, would go daft. John, who never said the word *Catholic* without making it sound like a pejorative, as if they were still in Tudor times and anyone of that faith was a spy for Rome.

Justin started them walking again. "That is not the sort of match I would ever hope for her. An Italian? No. Not right at all."

She turned to him. "Be careful. You are beginning to sound like an awful bigot."

He felt the rightness of what she had said. He was sounding too much like Father or the insufferable John. Still, he could not banish the shadow of disapproval at such an outcome as Constance and an Italian. He softened the opinion for Vera. "What troubles me is the rancor in the family that would come from such a union. If she falls for him whilst she is visiting us, my father and John will blame me." He wanted to talk more about this, but by then they were rounding the corner and everyone was standing to greet him.

Without being asked, Finch Hatton poured him a quinine water and gin, as if he were the host. The man had an ease about him that almost everyone found irresistible. He seemed the natural inhabitant of any place he went.

Justin, completely at odds with Denys's relaxed air, was even tenser than usual, given what was developing between his sister and the duke. He looked over at Constance, who was drinking white wine. As was the Italian. "You are taking your quinine, Consty?" Justin asked her. He was back to being the three-year-old protector of his newborn baby sister.

"Yes, I am," she answered.

"Is there malaria at this altitude?" The duke's hazel eyes widened.

"Not as common as on the coast or down near Lake Victoria," Vera answered, "but it is better to be safe than sorry."

"I have heard that you are going off to choose the property for your own farm," the duke said. His English was nearly perfect, except for that accent, which Tolliver was sure his sister found enchanting. Two girls he had known growing up had wed Italian nobles. Religion didn't seem to come into it for them, and those marquises and barons of this and that were not as well-connected as this member of the Italian royal family. But that would not matter to John and his rigid wife, who never stopped reminding everyone that *her* father was an archbishop.

Denys turned to look across the river. "No matter where you decide to settle down, it's going to be hard to find a place this wonderful," he said.

"It is very beautiful here," the duke said, but he was looking at Constance, not at the view.

"I hope our place will be beautiful too," Vera said, her heart going back to her same niggling worry. "All the more reason why we must make our decision quickly. Otherwise, we'll have to settle for some sandy bottom, where nothing will grow."

"I hate to think of it all divided up and deeded as if it were some parish in Suffolk or Surrey." Finch Hatton was still looking at the view, but now he was frowning at it.

"We will hunt as we go along," Constance said, deftly smoothing over any unpleasant turn in the conversation, as was her wont. "I am over the moon about experiencing the wilderness for the first time."

"I say," Denys declared. "Gian Lorenzo and I are planning on going hunting in a few days. Do you have a chart of where these properties are? We could try to meet up with you. I hear you'll be near Nakuru. I know some lovely places to hunt thereabouts."

"How is it that everyone in the Protectorate knows precisely what we are planning when we have hardly decided upon it ourselves?" Tolliver's voice came out more harshly than he had intended. He was not at all sure he wanted these men tagging along with them. The more he thought about it, the more sure he was that the Duke of Sulmona was not the right man for his sister.

Denys laughed. "You know very well, Tolliver, that other people's business is to social transactions here what the coin of the realm is to paying one's tailor in London. We all pay for our dinner invitations by passing on the latest juicy news."

Constance put her hands together and shot Justin a pleading glance. "Oh, let's show them the land charts and see if we can hunt together. It would be lovely, don't you think?"

Tolliver didn't, but how could he say so without insulting the men who were looking to him to agree?

The Tolliver party's first days on safari gave Constance something other than the duke's handsome countenance to fall in love with. Now her eyes glowed when she exclaimed over the expansive scenery, the colorful birds, the thousands of animals.

On the hunt, they came upon a kudu. Justin and Vera stepped back and gave Constance the first shot. She made a clean kill and delighted in being the one to provide meat for the camp for three days. That evening at dinner, she declared that she never wanted to leave.

Vera became a bit dispirited each evening, longing to hold her baby and hear his giggle, but she cheered up visibly once they got to the land sites in Ngong. She hiked all over the properties, tirelessly going up hills to find new perspectives and point out the best locations for orchards and views from imaginary houses.

Once they parted from the Ngong land officer, they made camp near a gently rolling stream. Open grassland rose behind their tents. At the crest of the hill stood a lone acacia with a single giraffe under it. "He looks as if he is posing to be photographed," Constance declared.

That evening, at sunset, after tea, Justin brought out the chart and spread it on the table in the light of a hurricane lamp. Vera and Justin put their heads together over the map to decide which of the two local possibilities they preferred. Constance, across from them, seemed to be taking as intense an interest in the decision as they did.

Justin pointed to parcel 29. "It has the river boundary we require and is quite near the railway—so it meets those criteria," he said. "And it is a nice regular shape. It's the smaller of the two, but not by much. I quite like the fact that it abuts a forest reserve."

"It also has the nicer site for your house," Constance added. "I could almost see how the prospect would look from your veranda."

Vera knit her brows and tapped on the number 28. "This one is longer and narrower, but it is a bit larger and has a river on each side which could make quite a difference if the rains are sparse one year. And it is that much closer to the railway line. With fresh fruit, we will need to get it shipped as quickly as possible, before it goes off. If we site the house at this end, once the fruit trees are mature enough to bear, we will have a lovely view, especially during the blooming season."

"But it won't have those lovely blue hills that we saw in the distance," Constance said wistfully.

Vera sighed. "True. Neither is perfect."

Justin looked at his sister. "I put a lot of stock in Vera's opinions about this sort of thing. She grew up on the successful coffee plantation that is part of her father's Mission. She knows more about what is important."

With the courage his words imparted, Vera spoke more forcefully. "We have Granny's wedding gift to work with, so we can take on the larger piece." She did not add that one day they would have her grandfather's entire fortune, a fact that had not been true until her uncle's and mother's deaths and her brother's disappearance. Under the circumstances, it would be beyond crass to speak of herself as a newly minted heiress. "In future," she said instead, "we may be very glad of the second water source and the extra acreage."

"That's what Papa would say—the more land the better," Constance put in.

"And abutting the forest reserve is a detriment, I believe," Vera said. "That might seem like a wonderful thing in Yorkshire, but here it would conceal hyenas that would threaten your calves and foals, monkeys galore that will help themselves to your apples and pears, and the occasional pride of lions intent on bringing down your prize bull."

Justin folded up the map. "You see, Consty. Thinking like an African is very valuable here. Number 28 it is."

"At least until we see the properties up at Nakuru," Vera said. "We may find—" A sudden noise distracted her.

"Oh, my." Constance pointed and with a happy grin said, "Look who is here."

A safari party neared, with porters attired in Tarlton Outfitters navy-and-brown livery, about twenty of them, nearly twice as many as the Tolliver party's and much more elegant. They approached from the northeast with Denys Finch Hatton and the duke in the lead. With the late-afternoon sun shining on their faces, they looked every bit the golden boys the world thought they were.

Constance was waving to greet them and walked a few yards in their direction.

When she was out of earshot, Vera whispered to Justin, "Stop being so sour. You look as if you have been sucking a lemon."

"Surely, you don't think there is a happy future for my sister with him. Now, if it was Finch Hatton who was paying court to her…"

"You are sounding like a bigot again," Vera said. "Besides which, I think Denys would be a far more dangerous choice. From everything you have told me about your father's finances, Consty will not have a large dowry."

"Hardly any at all—"

"Well," Vera whispered, "Finch Hatton is here in Africa. That is either because his family can't keep him in luxury in England or because he rejects the mores of English society. I imagine it is some of each. Which certainly means your sister might become something to him, but I very much doubt it would be his wife." Vera took his arm and urged him on toward the approaching visitors. "If you ask me, I have never thought of dear Denys as the marrying kind. I think he loves women, perhaps even only one at time, but I very much doubt he wants to be anyone's husband."

Justin gave her a wry look. "Is that why you chose me over him?"

"Luckily for you, my heart gave me no choice."

"Halloo," the duke called. He strode up and bowed to each of them in turn. Vera found herself curtsying and felt embarrassed until she saw Constance do the same. "Finch Hatton said he knew about where you would be camping, and he was right. We saw the smoke from your fires as soon as we crossed Dagoretti River."

Whatever Justin thought, Vera liked the Italian. His manners were courtly in the extreme, as one would expect from a man of royal blood, but even if his posture was a bit stiff at times, his smile was ready and his words always warm and friendly. What he said next won her over completely.

He came to her and said, "Mrs. Tolliver, I have news for you. We stopped at your father's Mission when we left Nairobi. I want you to know that all is well there. We have spoken to your esteemed father, and he reports that everything is as it should be with the child. It seems to me that he is enjoying his role as grandpapa."

Vera put her hands together in front of her face and thanked him profusely. "This is the time of day I miss my son most," she said, "it is so good to hear that all is well with him and my father."

The duke's smile broadened. "When we last saw them"—he looked up to his left, figuring in his mind—"three days ago, your father was dandling the precious boy on his knee."

She burst into tears and shocked everyone by taking the duke's hand into both of hers in gratitude.

"You see, Denys," the duke said. "I told you that Mrs. Tolliver would want this news of her child."

Justin looked away. He loved Vera with all his heart, but he could not help recalling a snide remark his sister-in-law had made, that there was "something Italian" about Vera, with her impulsive outbursts of emotion.

He went and took her hand. "Thank you, Your Excellency," he said to the duke, using the proper honorific to restore some distance between them. "My wife and I are very grateful to you for bringing us news of our son."

The duke's handsome eyes twinkled. "I would like to ask that we men, at least, need not be so formal. Please call me Gian Lorenzo. It is what my friends all call me."

Over the next few days, Constance continued to declare herself "over the moon" about being in the wilderness, clapping her hands and laughing aloud at the antics of monkeys and exclaiming enthusiastically whenever they spotted a herd of zebras or a family of warthogs. She took to referring to Gian Lorenzo as Savoia and told him he could drop the "Lady" and call her Constance.

The duke impressed Tolliver by not taking such liberties at once. Only after a few days did he drop his formality with Constance, but then he called her "Cara Lady Costanza," as if she were halfway to being his wife already.

It was about then that Constance began immediately drawing to his side if there was the least chance of danger. All of which was not exactly improper, Justin reminded himself. He wasn't going to have Vera scold him for snobbery again.

Justin wanted to speak to his sister of her growing infatuation, but he was unable to say anything. He was afraid she would start to cry, and then everyone in the camp would know he had upset her. If Finch Hatton got wind of it, when he went back to Nairobi the settlers at large would be chuckling over the whole business. Tolliver had no choice but to stew in his own disapproving juices.

On the fourth day that they were all together, as they neared Nakuru they came upon another trekking party led by someone Vera knew—Arthur Ramsay, a missionary from Naivasha who worked closely with Vera's father.

From the looks of him, Justin would have guessed that Ramsay was not a missionary at all, but a member of Finch Hatton's profession: an ivory hunter. He had a rugged physique, a shock of unruly brown hair, and sported the sort of breeches, boots, and worn brown canvas jacket that said adventurer rather than pastor. Only his demeanor bespoke his vocation—a determined and confident aspect underlying a gloss of serenity, and a clear and gentle voice. His gray eyes were those of a man looking at the far horizon. He was traveling with a retinue of Kikuyu Mission boys as porters and a Swahili gun bearer and tracker.

"I am on my way to the Maasai Reserve," he said over dinner on the first evening after they had joined their parties. "An American missionary there has asked me to support her as she tries to right a wrong that is about to take place."

Vera thought she knew what he was talking about. Justin had mentioned something vague about the Maasai being moved off their land. "Is it about the Protectorate relocating the Maasai? I don't think that's at all right."

As she so often did, Vera had said aloud what at least half the people at the table were thinking but were reluctant to bring up. In the interests of peace and privacy, Justin bit his lower lip and suppressed his exasperation. Constance opened her mouth as if to speak, but then closed it. Arthur Ramsay assented with a slight smile. His eyes told Vera he approved both of her opinion and of her willingness to express it. As for Finch Hatton and the duke, their reactions were more amusement than anything else.

Finch Hatton spoke first and was oblique, as was often his wont. "Cattle raising is in your plans, no?"

Though he addressed his question to Vera, Justin answered. "Yes. Partly. Most of our acreage will go into growing fruit."

Denys chuckled. "Well, for once the Protectorate's grapevine has erred. At any rate, I was about to say that if cattle were your goal, your herd would be safer without the Maasai nearby to steal them."

Arthur Ramsay leaned forward, his expression dark. But knowing—from overhearing discussions between him and her father—how argumentative he could be when it came to tribal rights, Vera cut him off. If the conversation continued in this vein, Justin and Arthur would be at odds, and she would have to stand up to both of them. It would not do, in front of the duke, to have Constance's family appear to be a raucous bunch. "I understand what you mean, Dr. Ramsay. We need to have more respect than we often do for the rights of tribal people, but I must say that the Maasai attitude toward cattle is entirely extreme. Why, it ignores not only British ideas of justice but also the rights of all the other tribes that have been here every bit as long as they."

Constance looked apprehensive. She glanced toward Gian Lorenzo. "What do they do with the cattle?" She seemed ready to wince at an answer involving some satanic ritual.

Vera giggled. "It's not horrifying. Their religion teaches them that their god gave them the right to own every cow on earth. They have an ancient creation myth that says so. According to them, if they find cows with another owner, they have a God-given right to take them back. Surely, Dr. Ramsay, you don't think it right for them to take the cattle of the Kikuyu around your Mission?"

The serenity in Ramsay's eyes disappeared momentarily. His voice took on a sonorous and grave tone. "I see your meaning, Miss McIntosh—excuse me, Mrs. Tolliver—but I do not think it at all right that we interfere as much as we do with how the natives lived before we came here. When it comes to the land, for instance, we British use the excuse that we have the knowhow to make much better use of its agricultural possibilities than the tribes who were here before us. It's the height of arrogance to say that, because we can produce more product per acre, the land ought to belong to us and not to them." He pointed to Finch Hatton's gun bearer, who was standing near the bonfire the porters had built to stave off prowling animals. "I daresay that if we put District Commissioner Cranford's dinner jacket on Kinuthia over there, it would look a sight better on that lithe body than it does on the D.C.. Does that mean we should take Cranford's clothing and give it all to a man who would sport it more elegantly?"

Finch Hatton and the duke laughed merrily. "I'd like to see that," Finch Hatton said.

Ramsay harrumphed. "We built a railroad through their territory and then because we can benefit more from the railroad than they can, we think we have the right to move them away so we can live near our 'iron snake.'"

Vera saw Justin frowning, and though she agreed heartily with Dr. Ramsay, she knew she had better change the subject. "You know, Finch Hatton," she said, "Constance has yet to see a lion." At which point everyone around the table looked relieved to have something less serious to discuss.

It was not until later, when she and Justin were alone in their tent, that she had the opportunity to ask him the reason for the intensity of his displeasure.

He kissed her shoulder and stroked her hair. She was sure he meant to distract her from bringing up the subject again. "Stop it, Justin," she said, pushing him away. "Tell me what is going on in your mind. I can smell that you're upset. It's about moving the Maasai, isn't it?"

He sighed in resignation. "You know as well as I," he said, "that Arthur Ramsay is going to Nakuru to stir up the natives and make trouble."

Her scalp prickled. He was hiding something from her—something that would upset her. "Why do you care what stand Arthur takes on moving the Maasai? You surely agree that the administration is extremely high-handed."

Her voice was rising. In a minute it would drown out the din of the cicadas. If he was going to keep this between them, he would have to confess. "Promise me you won't shout," he said.

"About what?" she demanded.

"Please, dearest," he whispered. "I will tell you, but we don't need to let the others hear us. Please. Promise."

She sat on her camp bed and pulled him down next to her. "Tell me!" Her whisper was closer to a hiss.

"I haven't said anything until now, but I met D.C. Cranford at Government House when I went in to sign my discharge papers. They are filed, but they don't take effect until the first of July."

"And?" Her voice was sharp as a thorn.

"And with the business of moving the Maasai—"

She grabbed his wrist and squeezed it so hard it stopped his words. "And you let Cranford talk you into resuming your role of policeman?" Her eyes glowed hot in the lamplight. She let out an exasperated breath.

"Not really," he said, intent on keeping his tone soft. "Cranford swore to me that all he wanted me to do was say fine words to placate the Maasai. And to advise the local assistant district superintendent. He said I would not have a role other than that."

"And you agreed?"

"No," he said with a sigh. "I swear to you that I did not agree to anything. Cranford pointed out that I remain part of the force for several more weeks. There is nothing I can do about that."

"You should have told me."

"I didn't want to spoil the fun of our land selection and Consty's first safari."

"Well, it's spoiled now anyway, isn't it?" she said.

She knew they could not have this out here, where not even the insistent music of the African night would sufficiently cover their voices.

He knew that too. He lay down on his cot.

She sighed, blew out the lamp, and lay down on hers, reaching for his hand in the darkness. "Will you get all cross if I say something?"

"I promise not to," he said.

"If you get involved in any trouble with the Maasai, we will miss our due date for choosing land. We will wind up with a place where all our fruit spoils before it gets to the railroad."

She suffered through a long pause.

"I will not let that happen," he said.

She did not press her point. They both pretended that all danger of a row had passed, but it took a very long time before either fell asleep.

When Constance left her tent the next morning, the sun had not yet risen. She had become accustomed to awakening in the half-light, taking a quick cup of tea and a biscuit or two, and beginning the hunt. When she left her tent, she pulled her shawl around her against the damp chill of the early-morning highland air and started across the semicircle of five tents. The flap on Denys's was still closed, meaning he was still asleep.

She crossed toward the fire just visible in the gloom, hoping the boys there were ready with the teapot. She spotted the duke just on the other side of Vera and Justin's tent, the last one on the right. He and his tracker were squatting and examining something on the ground. She would not have noticed but for Dr. Ramsay standing behind them shining a torchlight on whatever they saw.

Constance went to see. "What is it?" she asked.

The duke leapt up and came to her side. She looked into his face, but as soon as she saw his eyes, her smile faded.

"Two big lions were here in the night, quite recently we think," the duke said quietly. He took her to look and pointed at their footprints, deep and clear, in the ground softened by dew. "From the looks of the spoor, they could have passed here within the hour. See how their paws disturbed the insect tracks all around."

Vera emerged from her tent. "Did I hear 'lion'?"

At that second, there came a low, almost imperceptible growl. Constance took in a quick, shaky breath. "Did you hear that?"

The duke pushed her behind him. "Yes, I did," he whispered. "I can't tell the direction." He looked to Ramsay. "Do you know which way?"

Ramsay pointed to their left, behind Vera and Justin's tent. The tracker pointed slightly to the right, to the tall grass beneath an acacia tree, about fifteen yards off.

Constance gripped her shawl and shivered. She felt suddenly how tiny they were in the vastness of the wilderness that surrounded them. No one made a sound.

Then it came again. A low, throaty noise, just a hair louder. All their eyes focused on the high grass.

Vera backed very slowly into the tent. Constance turned to follow her.

"Don't move," the duke ordered under his breath.

Constance's heart beat out the seconds against her ribs.

A huge male lion stood up, so tall that his head and his back emerged from the grass. He made no sound, but cocked his head as he appraised them. He took two steps in their direction.

Silently, Justin emerged from the tent, wearing only breeches and a loose shirt, with a rifle in each hand. He tossed one to the duke. The lion began to move toward them, slowly at first. Then it charged. Justin and the duke fired simultaneously. The lion fell.

A female lion stood and bounded off so fast it was hard to believe she had ever been there. Vera was suddenly next to Constance, with an arm around her. Denys Finch Hatton emerged from his tent wearing even less than Justin.

Without a word, hearts still pounding, they walked cautiously toward the fallen lion.

"It's dead," Ramsay said. He knelt beside it and touched its head as if he were giving it blessing. "One of you hit the brain and the other the heart."

"I aimed for the head," the duke said.

"As did I," Justin said.

Denys laughed. "We will never know which of you is the better shot." He looked down at himself and bowed low. "I beg your pardon for my dishabille, ladies," he said without any sign of remorse, and turned and marched his statuesque physique back to his tent.

"*Moi aussi*," Justin said with a grin, and slipped back into his tent.

Constance looked down and saw her hand in the duke's. She did not remove it.

Ramsay stood and walked off without a word.

Gian Lorenzo squeezed Constance's hand. She blushed and took it back.

Vera took her arm and smiled up at her in that kind, affectionate way of hers. "This calls for tea," she said.

"Or coffee," Gian Lorenzo responded.

Justin experienced the next few days as the least satisfying he had ever spent in the bush. Two years before he had been rushing along, ignoring the beauty around him, focused on nothing other than rescuing Vera and finding a murderer. This was worse. Those anxious days had ended with tragic news, but with Vera in his arms. He could not think of one good thing that could come out of the events now dragging him down.

This trek was meant to be a shooting safari in honor of Constance's first visit to the Protectorate, something that should have been entirely pleasurable. Instead his blood was seething.

He disliked himself for it, but his temper regarding the Italian interloper heated up daily, made worse by the fact that he could not express his displeasure to anyone. How could he say what he felt without sounding petty—like the bigot Vera had warned him not to be. He was a fair and open-minded man. Even so, how could he stand by and watch his sister heading for a pool of sorrow and not try to stop her from falling in.

Blithe and enchanted, Constance had begun to act as if an engagement between her and the duke had already been proposed and received all the necessary family approvals. None of which was at all likely. That business would end in uproar, a scandal, a broken heart for his sister. She had always been the one family member he could count on to be kind and understanding. He loved her. He wanted her to be happy. Now all he could think to do was issue a warning that he was sure would bring tears to her eyes and anger to her lips. He held his peace and rankled.

And then there was the thorn called Arthur Ramsay. At the moment, after dinner on a lovely starry night, Ramsay was standing and singing "Jerusalem." A hymn totally inappropriate for the occasion. Justin was sure he was doing it to be provocative. The others around the fire, sipping whiskey, seemed to be thoroughly enjoying his basso profundo. All Tolliver was able to take in was the lyrics, which Ramsay was performing with great passion: "*I will not cease from mental fight, nor shall my sword sleep in my hand.*" Aggressive words that for Justin presaged only one thing—the missionary was here to prevent the government from carrying out its intentions of moving the Maasai out of this area. Ramsay's opposition would do no good. The administration would not relent. Attempting to prevent it would only embroil Tolliver in a quagmire of arguments and recriminations. In the end it would mean that even though he did not totally agree with the Protectorate's administrators, he would very likely end up arresting Vera's father's colleague.

Tolliver was ordinarily more sympathetic to the native point of view than most of his fellow Englishmen. On the other hand, the Maasai were unruly, and if he and Vera did take land near here, they would certainly not want their cattle to be at risk of capture by a people who believed they had a divine right to every ounce of beef on the planet.

If Ramsay meant to stir up trouble, Tolliver would inevitably be drawn in. He must continue as a member of His Majesty's police force until the half year. He was duty bound to carry out orders. And how could that end well for him? He would be caught between the missionary and the Maasai on one side and the Protectorate's administrators on the other. Worse yet, Vera would side with Ramsay. The King's African Rifles were camped not far away, ready to swoop in if any real trouble started, and Tolliver knew full well what tack the K.A.R. would take. A show of force was the only one they knew. They could and likely would be brutal. How could he—the man he had become—let himself be part of that?

Vera would be appalled at such an eventuality, and rightly so. On top of which, if he took any active part as a policeman, she would see it as a betrayal. He had promised to give absolute priority to their land investigations. Unalloyed on that score, her anger at the administration would pour out on him.

Now here was Constance, playing her flute, which she had not brought out since the duke arrived on the scene, and there was the Italian nearly swooning over her. No music of Pan's pipes could have created more of an atmosphere of desire. Gian Lorenzo's chiseled, regular features softened into a look of pure pleasure. Tolliver had to admit that the man had a hero's face, but that only made him more dangerous.

Justin roused himself from his reverie and rose as Constance finished her rendition of a Puccini aria. He had to do what he could to interrupt the flow of these events. If Ramsay could sing a hymn to make a point, so might he. And he would have Vera help him. "A Balm in Gilead" was what he had in mind. A song about the "sin-sick soul" was just the thing to take the stars out of his sister's eyes.

He bowed to Vera and took her hand. "Let us take our turn, dearest," he said. The smile she gave him was beautiful in the firelight, and before he knew it, she started with "Let Me Call You Sweetheart," a song guaranteed to make matters worse. In a few minutes, they were all standing and singing it, even the Italian, who had no right whatsoever to know an American song in English, nor to sing it in such a beautiful tenor voice.

They applauded themselves, toasted the day with the dregs of their drinks, and made for their tents, all delighted with themselves except for Tolliver who wondered if he shouldn't stay up the night and stand guard over his sister.

Vera's worries about Constance had taken an entirely different path. The few intimate conversations she had had with young English wives had told her that upper-class British maidens learned next to nothing about what their mothers called the "facts of life." Separately, three young women had come to the Mission, ostensibly to congratulate her on the birth of her son. Once they had cooed over the baby and settled on the veranda with tea and cakes, they had, hesitantly and with many blushes, asked Vera the most basic questions about having a baby. One of them, the daughter of a top administrator, could not even bring herself to say those words. "In the family way," she had called it. All three confessed that their mothers had spoken up only on the eve of their weddings, and then had said precious little about what would actually happen on their wedding night, and nothing about the birth of babies. The advice they had received tended more toward what Vera's granny in Glasgow had said to her on her honeymoon visit.

"I know," that stiff, distant old lady had said, "that it is too late for this now. You have been married for many weeks, but I also know that your mother was...was gone when you were wed. Is there anything you want me to tell you...about what a wife needs to know?"

If Granny had had the slightest inkling that Vera and Justin had made love before they were married, she might have died of apoplexy on the spot. As it was, Vera had learned more than her granny probably ever knew from the Kikuyu girls she grew up with, and from Wangari who had no Victorian repressions. Except for Vera's mother, all the females she had grown up around were frank and unembarrassed about sex. Vera had managed to put on what she hoped was a convincingly demure expression when her grandmother counseled her that she must put up with "the act" in order to have children.

When Vera had talked to those settler women, she had tried to speak carefully and not shock them by using words they could not tolerate hearing. She was sure that Constance had grown up in typical British ignorance when it came to lovemaking. Having seen the stars in Consty's eyes, and in Gian Lorenzo's too, she thought now was the time to inform her dear sister-in-law that there were other ways for human women to think about their bodies and the beauties and joys of the sex act.

She invited Constance to stay behind in camp on their last afternoon in the bush before they reached Nakuru. The men all went off to try their luck hunting birds for their dinner. She and Constance sat together over tea, watching the shadows lengthen on the plain before them.

Trying her best not to sound shockingly improper, Vera broached the subject. "You are falling in love, Consty. I can see it."

"Oh, Vera," she said with a tinge of fear in her voice. "You aren't going to warn me off, the way Justin seems to want to, are you?"

"No. No," Vera said. "Not at all." She paused, casting about for the right words, but afraid any opening she chose would make her sound like Granny. Finally she launched in. "Not at all. It's just that—um—um—" She was sputtering and she hated it.

Constance stopped staring into the distance and turned to her. "You needn't worry. I know what I am not supposed to let him do until we are wed."

"That's just it," Vera said, sounding to herself more exasperated than encouraging. "I know that sort of warning is the only thing girls brought up like you ever hear. You wouldn't believe what my granny said to me six weeks after Justin and I were wed."

Constance giggled. "Let me guess. It's the same thing John's prissy wife said to me."

"Not your mother?"

"Eleanor said she was saving Mother the trouble of telling me. She said my husband would know what to do and that it was my duty to let him so that we could have children."

"She spoke that way and you were not even engaged?"

"There was a schoolmate of John's who was coming around often and playing up to me at the time. He was good-looking in a pudgy sort of way, had all the right bloodlines, but boring in the extreme. Eleanor started out telling me that with my money situation, I should consider him my most appropriate choice."

"What intolerable cheek!" Vera blurted out.

Constance sighed. "What else would you expect from her? I let her go on. I think she took my silence as sincere interest."

Vera could picture the scene vividly. "And that's when she spouted all that drivel about allowing it in order to have children?"

"It was like a scene out of a play," Constance said.

"A farce," Vera said, which made them both laugh.

Once Constance had stopped sputtering protests about her intention to guard her virginity, Vera explained.

After they started giggling, it was very hard for them to stop, but Vera managed to get out the most important thing she wanted to say: "Love between a man and woman is not something we need to tolerate, Consty. It is really quite thrilling and lovely. You will learn to—to—to savor it. To want it for its own sake."

They fell silent.

As the light of the sunset turned red and they spotted the men in the distance, coming in from their hunt, Constance took Vera's hand. "Thank you, Vera," she said. "I have known from the first time I saw you two together that there was something very special between you and Justin, that I had never seen with any other married people I knew. Now I think I know why. Am I right?"

"Yes," Vera said. "Justin and I have many differences. We often have our rows. But what we have together—it trumps everything else."

"I want to be myself, Vera," Constance said, "not a twentieth-century version of my mother."

"I don't think there is any danger of that," Vera said. "And I don't think Gian Lorenzo would have fallen in love with your mother."

They were in danger of falling back into the giggles, which neither one of them wanted to have to explain to the approaching men.

They stood as the hunting party neared with their catch of at least a dozen guinea fowl. Constance embraced Vera. "I have always wanted a sister," she said. "I am so glad she turned out to be you."

There were tears in both their eyes. "I too," Vera said. "I too." Then she quickly whispered, "Please don't tell your brother about our talk."

Constance laughed. "There is absolutely no danger of that."

Tolliver, overhearing, asked, "No danger of what?"

"Of our starving to death," Vera said quickly. "Look at all these lovely birds you have brought us."

Justin knew she was lying, but he let it pass. It seemed, though, that there was something new in the way his sister looked at the duke, something that spoke decidedly of a danger that she was completely in love.

Trouble started the next day, as soon as they reached Nakuru, and none of it was the sort Tolliver expected.

The township hardly merited that title. The railway station was the typical serviceable but unlovely affair. It had one all-purpose room that was both a shelter for travelers waiting for the train and a dining room, where first-class through passengers could descend and have a meal. The tiny second room served as a ticket window and the telegrapher's office. The outside was painted a brownish yellow and the inside a somber blue on the bottom half of the walls and on the upper part the same muddy ochre as the outside.

The rest of the town was a motley collection of flimsy shacks and hastily constructed corrugated-iron-and-wood eyesores common in all parts of the Protectorate. The only exception was the Midland Hotel, stone-built and impressive, which looked as if it had been snatched up from Nairobi or Mombasa and set down here to embarrass all the other structures.

Nakuru's position of surpassing beauty, made up for the general lack of grace in the town. At this elevation, a thousand feet higher than Nairobi, the air was clear and the views of the mountains superb. Below, Lake Nakuru glistened gold in the light of the African sun and stretched out to the horizon.

The first sign of turmoil greeted them as soon as they entered the town. Ruth Van Slyck fairly ran to them. When he spotted her approaching, Arthur Ramsay explained who she was. "An American, a missionary of the Congregationalist Church. Came up from South Africa with a small group from her country to start a Mission among the Maasai."

"She's a glutton for punishment then," Finch Hatton whispered as she came near. He had no idea how prescient his thoughts were.

The woman looked to be somewhere in her forties—simply dressed in a white shirtwaist and a long, perfectly plain dark blue skirt, very like the uniforms upper-school girls had worn twenty years ago. She was slender and small of stature with dark hair and light brown, gold-flecked eyes that made her otherwise ordinary face captivating.

They were barely introduced when she turned that gaze on Ramsay and said, "It's all arranged. The girls are being made ready. I have done what I can alone, but I fear we cannot stop it."

Tolliver's skin prickled. It was as he had thought. They intended to oppose the government's moving the Maasai. Now for certain he would have to walk a tightrope between pacifying Vera and preventing these missionary do-gooders from starting an all-out war. He should do something, say something to nip this in the bud, if he could. But for the life of him, he could not think what to say that might succeed in deterring them.

The first thing he needed to do was settle his companions here, where they had expected to spend several days getting to know the area and inspecting the land choices. He had imagined they would make camp at the edge of the village, but it turned out there was a lovely guesthouse, run by a Belgian couple,

Madame and Monsieur Gillet, that could accommodate him and Vera and Constance. The duke and Denys took the porters and equipment to a field nearby and set up their tents there.

As soon as their party could, they broke free of Ramsay and the American woman. While Vera and Constance were settling themselves in their rooms, Justin slipped off to the police *boma* to meet Oliver Lovett, the assistant district superintendent for the Naivasha-Nakuru District. He congratulated himself—at the very least, his troubles over his sister were in abeyance. The Italian was now camped away from where Consty would be sleeping.

Tolliver knew Oliver Lovett from having served with him in Nairobi when Lovett had just come from army service in India. He remembered him as an eager, skinny, rather unassuming sort. The man he found was quite different.

While being in Africa had opened Tolliver's soul, it seemed to have shriveled Lovett's. His body was toughened, but the look in his eyes was hollow. Tolliver got the impression the man was already slightly drunk, though it was barely noon.

"I've heard you arrived with that bloody missionary Ramsay," Lovett said practically before he shook hands and said hello.

Tolliver had to give Lovett his due—the man was facing some dreadful possibilities. "Yes," Justin said. "We met out in the bush and have trekked together for a few days."

"Then you know what he and that meddling American woman are up to."

"They are supporting Maasai resistance to the move." Tolliver thought that went without saying.

"I wish that were it," Lovett said, and scratched the stubble on his chin. His formerly pleasant baby face showed only anger and disgust.

"What is it then?"

"They are satisfied that the Maasai court proceedings will stop the move. Now they are trying to stop some fool ceremony for the girls. What possible business is it of theirs what the Maasai do to their womenfolk?"

Tolliver was completely nonplussed. "I can't imagine. What kind of ceremony could possibly stir up such feelings and how could it be such a bone of contention?"

Lovett waved his hand in front of his face. He took out a steel-cased pocket watch. "Time for my quinine. Can I offer you one?"

"No thank you. I usually take mine just before luncheon and dinner."

Lovett's grunt seemed to say, "Just as I thought. You are a prig." He turned around to pour himself a drink. It occurred to Tolliver that the man kept his alcohol within reach.

"When I tell you what this is about," Lovett said, "you will be sorry you didn't take me up on my offer." He gulped his drink before speaking. "You have heard of the Maasai circumcision ceremony for boys?"

"Yes, of course." Lovett was the first European man Tolliver had ever heard call it by its right name without wincing.

"Well, they have one for girls."

For a second Tolliver was not sure he had heard right. "Ahem. Ah. Assuming their girls are made more or less the way ours are, what do girls have that they can—er—remove?" Tolliver realized that what he was saying was more a question for himself.

Lovett shrugged. "Damned if I know," he said, "but that Van Slyck woman and Arthur Ramsay are determined to stop it. That woman tried to describe it to me. It was appalling how she actually wanted to talk to me about the parts of the female body. Can you imagine? I would not have wanted to hear it if I were a doctor. The gall of the woman." He gulped his drink.

Tolliver knew he was more sympathetic to the missionaries than most of his fellow members of the administration, but from what Lovett was saying, this all sounded like a tempest in a teapot. The next thing Lovett said, though, gave Tolliver pause.

"It's supposed to cut down on a woman's sexual appetite. Damn good thing if you ask me, considering how half the white women start behaving when they come here. Must be the air here that does that to the female. Englishwomen don't act so wild at home. And they don't do that in India either, I can tell you. More buttoned-up there than in Devon or Derbyshire."

"Let me see what I can find out about this from Ramsay," Tolliver said. "Is all in order when it comes to the move?"

"Not by a long chalk," Lovett said, his tone funereal. He drained his glass and poured himself another. "It's got to happen before the next rains. Supposedly the Maasai chief, the one that the High Commissioner put in charge, has agreed, but what choice did he have with the King's African Rifles standing by? There is a small but very noisy splinter group still resisting, and you know what grief we'll take from the Home Office in London if we have to use force. Then there is that bloody legal challenge. I can't see how the tribe will get anywhere with that. Bloody mess if they do."

Unable to take any more of Lovett's moaning, Tolliver stood to leave.

Lovett raised himself an inch or two, sank back down, and picked up his drink. "You must stop Ramsay and that insane American woman. The movement of the Maasai will turn into a powder keg if we don't watch out. And those two missionaries could be the fuse."

Vera's clean clothes felt lovely on her body after a nice hot bath. Much as she loved the wilderness, civilization—if Nakuru could be characterized as such—had its compensations. The luncheon the Belgian couple gave them was a perfect example thereof— poached lake fish in a buttery cream sauce. Afterwards Vera was ready to stretch out on the chaise on their back veranda with a book. Justin intervened. He wanted her to go with him to visit the missionaries. Not the sort of postprandial invitation she was used to receiving from him. Whatever he had on his mind, it so distracted him that he did not even frown when the duke came to take Constance away for a stroll.

On their way to Ruth Van Slyck's bungalow, Justin told her what he had heard from Lovett, which sounded more like a deal of drunken rambling than anything Vera knew about African behavior. For one thing she could not believe that Arthur Ramsay, the missionary who had successfully organized a coalition of all the sects with installations in the Protectorate, would be against a tribal tradition. Not he, the most articulate crusader for native rights. He was the last person she would have suspected of such a thing.

Until she confronted him.

Ruth Van Slyck welcomed them into a parlor sparsely furnished but attractive and comfortable. The upholstered furniture was draped with Manchester cottons in the bright prints the English sold to the tribal women. The walls were hung with handwoven native baskets. The only thing that revealed anything about the lady herself was a large American flag pinned to the wall at the end of the room, opposite the door.

Arthur Ramsay sat on an armchair beneath it, sipping tea. He stood and greeted them. "I am so happy to see the two of you without the company of the others, charming as they are," he said, in the most cordial voice she had heard him use since they all met in the bush.

Once she and Justin had accepted tea, they passed as many pleasantries as Vera could stand. She took a deep breath and broke the ice. "Just after we arrived, my husband had a bizarre conversation with the local A.D.S. of Police. What can he possibly have meant about what the Maasai are doing to their girls?"

She had addressed her question to Ramsay, but Ruth Van Slyck answered immediately. "It's an abomination. We must stop it at all costs."

Vera glanced at Tolliver to make sure he was not about to explode. He was still breathing normally, so she went on taking the lead. "Is this a Maasai tradition we are talking about?"

Ramsay answered. "The Kikuyu mutilate their girls too."

"Mutilate?" she asked.

Justin leapt to his feet. He opened and closed his mouth two or three times before he managed to say anything. "I am not sure I want my wife to hear any of the details about this."

Vera stood too. She looked only at Justin. "I am not sure I want to hear this either," she said, "but I think I must."

Justin objected, but she insisted. Whatever it was would have to have happened to her playmates when she was a child, and if it had, she would have known. With Justin vehemently defending her sensibilities, however, she would never learn the first thing about what Ruth and Ramsay were so vehemently against.

Justin was looking more determined than ever to stop the conversation. "I fear it is a filthy secret, Vera," he said. "It could upset you horribly."

It grated on her, this instinct of his to protect her from herself, but she would not say so before these relative strangers. "Perhaps it would be easiest if Miss Van Slyck and I were to discuss it separately from you and Dr. Ramsay."

He relented.

"Why don't you and I go into the garden and talk privately," Vera said to Ruth Van Slyck, who immediately started for the door but then turned and pointed across the room. "Dr. Ramsay, there is whiskey in that cupboard. Mr. Tolliver may want some."

Vera followed her out, hoping she herself wouldn't need some whiskey too.

The description Miss Van Slyck blurted out was as ugly as her garden was beautiful. Vera stared at the profusion of vivid flowers and took in facts that made her moan. Half-disbelieving, half-nauseated at the very thought of what Ruth described, she voiced her doubt. "What can they hope to accomplish by doing such a thing?" But she knew. She knew how her own desire for Justin had caused her to break the most important taboo for a woman like her.

"The men believe it subdues a woman's sexual desire."

"So doing it to the girls makes them stay faithful to their husbands." Vera's words were half-statement, half-question. She thought about women like Lucy Buxton and Lady Gresham, married seductresses who had targeted Justin.

"The men think it does, but the women know it does not."

A horror surpassing any she had just heard flashed on Vera's mind. "Do the men then do it to the girls by force?"

Ruth clenched her arms over her ample breasts and clamped a hand over her mouth, suppressing what would surely have been a scream. "No. No," she said when she had recovered. "A woman does it. It's a special role in the tribe. The mothers willingly prepare their daughters. In fact, the mothers insist upon it. Women shun any woman who is not cut."

"But why?" Pouring through Vera's head were images. Her Kikuyu playmates giving her detailed descriptions of the acts they had performed with boys older than they, when they were only eleven or twelve. They were gleeful about what they had done. Then seriousness overtook them when they prepared for the ceremony that would make them women. She knew about that. Her mother had told her it was a "welcome to womanhood." She had made it sound benign—like the sacrament of Confirmation in the Anglican Church. "Why do the women do it to one another?"

Ruth Van Slyck indicated a bench at the back of the garden. "Let's take a seat." It was a command, not an invitation. Vera did not resist.

At this altitude, flowers common in English gardens thrived in profusion even here at the equator—peonies, irises, roses were all blooming and filling the air with their heady scents, their joyful colors painful against the black dread in Vera's mind.

"This is the obstacle we must overcome," Ruth said. "The practice has become so lodged in the way of life of the tribes that they cling to it unreasonably. If a woman refuses to have her daughter submit to it, she and the child become outcasts. No man will marry such a girl. If she has a child, the others of the tribe will not honor her with the title of 'mother.'"

Vera blurted out another evil the Maasai men would see: "Her father will not be able to sell her for a good bride price." Vera's conscience had always prickled when she congratulated her Kikuyu friends on the bride price they had commanded. It had felt too like they were being sold into slavery by their own fathers, happy as they might seem about it.

"No bride price at all."

Vera could not imagine the life of a tribal girl who could not find a husband. A British old maid might suffer, but an African girl who could not find a husband? By the time she was sixteen she would have no identity within her tribe. A girl either became a wife or she was nothing. There was no shortage of available men here, since a man could take many wives. English old maids were a pitiable lot, poor if their fathers died and left them without means, dependent on their brothers, if they had them. Or forced into servitude. Or prostitution. Unwed African women might starve to death.

Ruth broke the silence that had fallen on them. "Dr. Ramsay is calling for the British government to outlaw the practice. A letter was sent to Parliament last year, but I do not think that will stop it. How would they enforce it? We have to convince the women not to inflict it on their daughters."

"But how, if refusing will make their daughters pariahs?"

"It causes unspeakable pain."

"They give their sons to pain when they go through the male ceremony." Vera saw in the shocked expression on Miss Van Slyck's face, that what she had said sounded like an excuse for the inexcusable.

Ruth pounced on it. "They told me that you thought like an African. I did not think your indoctrination into their ways would extend to condoning mutilation."

Vera was nonplussed. She could not think how to defend herself.

Ruth plowed on. "That is exactly what *they* say—men and women. It is exactly what they tell the girls and what the girls believe. And they make them believe they are giving them a great honor. They dress them up in finery. They give them gifts. They make them the center of attention, something not one of them has ever been before nor will be again. It has all the trappings of what it feels to be a bride in the United States. And what it ends in is pain, suffering. Some of them will become infected. Some will never bear children. Some die."

Tears came into Vera's eyes—from the horrid images the woman's words called to her mind, and from the shame and frustration she felt at being so misunderstood.

Ruth stood and put her hands on her hips "So you can weep, my girl. Are you weeping for yourself or for the women of Africa?"

"I think you are right," were all the words Vera could get out.

"Yes, but what will you do about it?"

Justin and Vera walked back to the Belgian guesthouse slowly. "I mightily resent the fact that that woman told you those lurid details in a way that brought you to tears. What right has she to hold her sanctimonious principles over you?"

Vera put her arm around his waist and pulled his arm over her shoulder. "Oh, dearest," she said. "I wept for many reasons—for those girls, for my ignorance, for the fact that people keep women like me in ignorance. They say they are protecting us. But they are protecting us from the power knowledge would give us."

"I want to protect you from people like her. People who will only upset you."

"I don't want to be protected. I want to be able to do something about the things I care about." Her tears flowed again.

He handed her his handkerchief. "I care that over your shoulder I see my sister practically in the arms of that Italian."

Vera spun and saw them, at the edge of the town, gazing at the hills in the distance. Only their upper arms were touching, but Vera remembered precisely how she had felt when she and Justin had stood like that—in the Kikuyu Reserve, when a hyena had invaded their peaceful picnic. "Would you deny them what we have?" she asked. And she thought of all those girls who were about to undergo a ceremony that would rob them of their natural right to such pleasure.

"Do you really think Constance can find a life such as we have, married to a man so different from her?"

She reached up, put her hand on the side of his face, and looked into his eyes that matched the highland sky. "They are both aristocracy—he even a higher rank than she. They have every bit as much in common as you and I did when we met— more, actually."

"He would want her to convert to Catholicism."

"You sound as if that would be like asking her to paint herself green and live in a tree."

"I'd like to see that," he said, and laughed. "Imagine my mother going for a visit."

"Along with John and his prissy wife," she said. They had started to walk again. "From what you have told me, Consty won't have much of a dowry. He on the other hand seems rich enough to marry whomever he chooses."

"I don't know about the royal family of Italy, but in England anyone within a few steps of ascending to the throne would have to ask permission of the king." He realized he was hoping Gian Lorenzo's family would stop it so he would not have to.

Vera was not giving up. "It's not as if he is next in line for the throne."

"No, evidently not, as far as Denys knows, but it might be an issue. Whatever the Italians say, my family will try to prevent it, I am sure. You know they will. It will cause a lot of strife."

"You did not think about that when you married me. You didn't need your father's permission, but I imagine he tried to talk you out of it."

He could not keep his expression from giving away the truth. He had not given his father the chance, but she was right. His father had said as much after the fact, and his brother was livid at the family being forced into "such an unlikely connection" and told him so.

She sighed. "Suppose she did convert? Would that be so horrid?" She hadn't seen anything very religious in any of Justin's family when the two of them visited Tilbury Grange on their honeymoon. Oh, they took their pews at the front of the village church every Sunday morning, but for a girl used to prayers before every meal and family prayer before going to bed and a father worrying over his Sunday sermons even though they were spoken in Kikuyu, Justin's people's religion did not seem much of an impediment to marriage between people who were falling so in love.

"Really, Vera, if it doesn't work out for whatever reason, it will break Consty's heart. I think, for her sake, it would be better to nip it in the bud, and spare her such pain."

"Look at her," Vera whispered when they were within ten yards of the veranda. "It's already too late. That flower has bloomed."

That evening they all dined together on hare, which Denys had shot and delivered in time to be braised. When the men had gone off to their cigars, Constance moved into a chair next to Vera's, bringing her glass of claret with her. "What is it?" she said without preamble. "I can feel it. Have you and Justin had a row? There is something strange going on between you—not anger. But you are both—I don't know—distressed, withdrawn."

Vera did not know how to begin to tell Constance what was troubling them. Certainly she could not tell her the wretched details of what she had learned from that Van Slyck woman. She reached for the claret decanter and filled her own goblet.

"I am sorry," Constance said. "Mama would scold me for prying."

Vera sipped the wine. "It's not something between Justin and me. It's a disturbing tribal practice." She intentionally sat up straight and brightened her expression. She looked into Constance's expectant gaze. "It's not a part of native life that I think you need to hear about. I've lived here my entire life, and I never knew about it until today."

Constance put down her wineglass and shifted in her chair and looked away from Vera. "Are you protecting me from life—the way my parents always do?"

Vera could not suppress a sigh. "Let's just say that the natives have their own way of discouraging their girls when it comes to their...their desires." She forced a smile. "You really ought to see some of the more picturesque parts of tribal life before you learn that the noble savages can be just as set in their ways as the British."

Constance looked skeptical, but she demurred. "Very well. But if your mood worsens I shall ignore my upbringing and insist you treat me like a fully fledged grown-up."

Vera took Constance's hand. There really was a bright and determined young woman under Constance's satin veneer of gentility. "I am sure you will. I think it's time we went and sipped some of that brandy before the men drink it all."

They rose.

"Speaking of native life," Constance said, "Gian Lorenzo says that tomorrow we might go onto the Maasai Reserve and see how they are living. Can we, please?"

"Certainly," Vera said, relieved. "One of our potential land parcels is just on the edge of that reserve. We won't be going to see it for a day or two, however, because we have to wait for the land officer to show us exactly where it is."

"Will *you* ask my brother if we can go? He is being so contrary with me these days. You would think he was John or Papa."

Vera gave her a reassuring look. "I promise you that I am entirely on your side."

That night, with the moon throwing shadows of lace curtains on their walls, Vera and Justin did not speak of what they had learned during the disturbing day. "Oh my darling, my darling," were the only words he spoke. He drew her nightdress over her head, took her in his arms, and lifted her onto the big feather bed. He kissed her all over. Kissing over and over those parts of her that they were both so thrilled were whole. She drank in his warmth, his passion, his joy in her, the intensity of their hunger for each other. More of him. All she desired was more of him. And to be all this to him in return.

The vow they had taken, the most wonderful one to keep, was the one she reveled in. That night it rang in her blood. "With my body I thee worship."

When she whispered those words to him as they lay still in the small hours, he began it again. More slowly. Erasing all thought.

The next day neither Justin nor Vera was willing to let the other out of sight. They did not speak of it. They wore the bond between them as if it were a garment to keep out the cold.

That comfort became more and more necessary as the day drew on.

Breakfast was a bit late that morning. Before they and Constance had finished, Monsieur Gillet announced the arrival of the duke and Denys Finch Hatton and showed them into the dining parlor.

Vera noted that Justin did not harden his face at Gian Lorenzo's arrival, a first in many days.

The duke bowed to everyone, went to the ladies and kissed their hands. Denys went to the sideboard and helped himself to a brioche and a cup of tea. The duke, after being invited by Vera, took a coffee. Both the visitors wore expressions that Vera could only describe as cautious.

As soon as they were seated, Denys reported what they had observed from first light on. "Another group of Maasai have arrived. My tracker, Kinuthia, said they are coming in to bring their girls for this ceremony. Gian Lorenzo got his first glimpse of *ilmurran*."

"*Ilmurran?*" Constance asked.

"It's what the Maasai call their warriors," Denys said. "They are done up in their handsome best. Evidently, these gatherings are the Maasai equivalent of the coming-out balls in London, where the eligible men and women get to size each other up for the first time."

"I must say," the duke added, "they have an elegance one rarely sees anywhere. Such style in their dress. If I were an artist, I would want to paint them."

The women smiled, Vera nodding agreement, and Constance said, "I so look forward to seeing them. Their fame has spread all the way to Yorkshire."

Justin's policeman's instincts perked up at what Denys and the duke reported. This influx of warriors might also mean that objections to the government's impending move were intensifying. A protest could be brewing, and he was not at all sure Lovett was the right man to deal with such a situation.

"Oh, do let's go out and have a look at them," Constance said.

Justin drained his teacup and rose. "I agree. Part of the whole circus will be their dancing to show off to one another. Why don't you ladies go and get your hats. We will wait for you here." One glance into Vera's eyes told him she understood that he wanted a moment to speak with the men alone.

She took Constance's arm and ushered her out.

He sat back down. "I want you both to know what I have learned about how the situation here might unfold. I am sure it is perfectly safe for us to go to the village this morning. It is when the start of the move is officially announced that there might be trouble."

"I've seen it in the newspapers—this business of the lawsuit," Gian Lorenzo said.

"The Maasai don't read the papers," Denys said and refilled his teacup.

"No, they don't," Justin said. "Nevertheless they are waiting for word of the lawsuit. All will be well until the move is ordered. *If* it is ordered." He looked into his empty cup and pressed on. "As I explained to you as we approached Nakuru, it might get touchy. You both know what the district commissioner has asked me to do. I visited the local police official yesterday, and I am sorry to say that I have very little confidence in his..." He hesitated. It would be one thing to admit Lovett's shortcomings to Finch Hatton, but he did not want to reveal anything to the foreigner. "Let us say that the local man is inexperienced and may not be up to anything on a massive scale."

"Might you have to take charge?" Denys asked at once.

The duke knit his brows. In their casual chats over dinner, Justin had learned that he had served in the Italian Admiralty, so he knew something of military issues. The duke stiffened his back. "Our first concern must be the safety of the ladies."

"Let's not overreact," Tolliver said. "There is no immediate cause for alarm. Evidently, this ceremony for the girls is distracting the local people from the larger issue for the moment. We can go about our business as usual for the time being. I just want us to be on our guard for any change in the mood of the place."

"How will we know?" the duke asked. He was keeping his cool, which was more than Tolliver would have expected of an Italian.

"We'll know," Denys said. "One can pick it up on one's skin. Besides, Kinuthia will have his finger on the pulse of it."

It flashed in Tolliver's mind that he needed to send for Kwai Libazo, who was in Naivasha—this district—and only three railway station stops away. He wondered why he had not thought of it before now. "All we need to do for the moment is to take logical precautions. We must make sure our weapons are guarded by people in whom we have absolute trust, and that they are ready at hand."

"I have already seen to that," Denys said.

"I am afraid I will have to ask you to stay in or near the town all the while, Denys. Pleasant as it has been to have the game you have been supplying, I think we should forego hunting until we have a better sense of what's ahead."

"Certainly."

"If the situation heats up suddenly, we will meet at your camp and leave well before we end up in the fray."

"Will Mrs. Tolliver and Lady Constance have to know that they are in danger?" Gian Lorenzo asked.

"They are in no actual danger at this moment," Tolliver said. "We merely need to have a plan. It may very well turn out to be an excess of caution, but better safe than sorry."

There was a rustling of movement outside the door. "They are here." He lowered his voice. "We needn't alarm them."

He opened the door and suggested that they walk down the hill for their first close view of the lake. It was also in the direction of both the Mission school where Ruth Van Slyck taught the local girls and the Maasai village beyond, near the edge of the lake. No doubt that was the place for all the most colorful parts of the ceremony.

As they passed the Mission, Arthur Ramsay called out and joined them. They went through a small wooded area and emerged onto a low rocky promontory overlooking a huge expanse of water. Hundreds of flamingos were feeding in the shoals of the near shore.

"Oh, how very wonderful," Constance exclaimed.

"I so wanted you to see them," Vera said.

Constance came and took her by the arm. "Isn't it the most magnificent sight? Africa is magnificent. I do not wonder you never want to leave it, Justin."

They all stood for several moments in silence. Then Arthur Ramsay picked up a large stone and heaved it out into the midst of the birds. As one being, they rose up and flew, low to the water, away. The effect was dramatic, but Constance gave a little groan of disappointment. The spell was broken.

Ramsay pointed off to their left, at a Maasai kraal, a wide circular enclosure built of thorn-tree branches and set back about a hundred and fifty yards from the edge of the water. It contained a collection of mud-and-stick huts, some with flat, some with conical thatch roofs. Wisps of smoke rose above them. Within the circle, a group of men lounged under a thorn tree. Children played on the bare ground between the squat houses. "There is to be a *ngoma* today," Ramsay said.

"What is that?" Constance asked.

"It will be a treat for you," Vera answered. "They will sing and dance."

"I have never seen it either," the duke said.

"Where is Miss Van Slyck?" Vera asked. "Does she not want to see the dancing?"

"Oh, she has seen it many times. She has stayed behind to pray. They have moved up the ceremony. They told us it is to take place tomorrow. She says she has done all she can to convince the mothers and the girls not to go through with it. Now she says she can only appeal to the Almighty to stop this travesty. I announced to this Mission's converts last evening that they will be barred from worship if they allow their girls to be mutilated."

Constance gasped at the word.

"Please, sir," the duke said. "It is untoward to speak of such things before the ladies."

"Perhaps you and Denys might walk a bit ahead with Constance," Vera said. "I am the daughter of one of Dr. Ramsay's colleagues. I would like to speak to him about the Mission's role in this."

The duke bowed and gave Constance his arm.

When the others were out of earshot, Vera, Justin, and Arthur Ramsay followed along at a quiet pace. "How did the converts react when you gave them that ultimatum?" Vera asked.

"To be honest, the Congregationalist pastor here has had to divide his time with their Mission in Nyeri. The number of faithful here has dwindled. I come to do what I can, but there have not been any new converts in some time."

Vera waited to see if he would answer her question. She had taken Justin's arm. She squeezed his forearm to prevent him from interrupting.

"Dr. Ramsay," she said, "I know that my father cooperates with you on many issues. I do not know his opinion on this one, but—"

"He was signatory to a joint letter to Parliament from the Council of Christian Missionaries. We sent it last year, demanding that Britain outlaw the practice in all of His Majesty's territories."

"And?" Justin asked.

"And nothing. We received a reply thanking us and telling us that it will take some time for the matter to be investigated and discussed."

"And what about your converts? I ask this because perhaps my father will want to take the same stand, but if I urge him to do so, I also want to tell him what the risks are."

"All but one of the converts walked out," Ramsay said. "I doubt that we will see them again." He sounded as if he were angry at Vera for asking.

She wanted to say something in her own defense, but she also knew how heartbroken her father would be if his hard-won little congregation abandoned him for making the same announcement. She was about to speak when Justin expressed exactly what she thought. "That does not make your position the wrong one."

The silence that descended on them was broken after only a few minutes by loud rhythmic singing and shouting coming from a meadow on the other side of the Maasai settlement.

"The dancing is going to start," Ramsay said.

"Hurry," Constance called over her shoulder. "We don't want to miss it."

Vera chuckled and caught her up. "Do not fret, dear," she said. "This dance might easily last until tomorrow morning."

Scores of Maasai men milled around a green sward about the size of a cricket field. They all wore *shukas* tied at the shoulder, most of them in the vivid red of a valentine heart, but some in rosy pink. Constance remarked on how amusing it was, seeing tall and very strong-looking men decked out in a shade she had favored when she was four. Their clothing was cinched around their slender waists or hips with belts of leather or metal, decorated with bright beads or baubles. They all sported many necklaces, bracelets, anklets, and earrings dangling from large holes in their earlobes. They jingled when they moved.

The younger men had long hair, braided with bits of cloth or tied at the nape of the neck. Some wore circlets around their heads, a few of which held ostrich feathers. They all carried spears, making their rather girlish getups all the more incongruous. Eight or ten in single file began to circle an old man whose close-cropped hair and beard were salt-and-pepper gray. He too wore the common red *shuka*, but his upper body was wrapped in a cloth of red-and-blue plaid. A man with a shaved head appeared next to him; he carried the spiral horn of an antelope.

"The horn is from a kudu," Vera whispered to Constance.

The man raised it to his lips like a flute, and when he blew into it, it made a beautiful sound, low and rumbling, that might have been the voice of a huge tree.

With that signal, three drummers on the far side of the field began to beat on tall drums, and the old man began to call out words. The circle of men, which now included all the spear bearers, shouted a response. As the tempo increased the singing became louder, and the men moved faster, skipping now in a circle that nearly filled the space. Older men, whose *shukas* were of darker reds and browns, stood at the edges of the field and looked on.

"Where are the women?" Constance asked, her voice hardly audible above the drumming and chanting.

Ramsay answered through clenched teeth, "They are off in a separate women's village, built especially for the ceremony. They are preparing those poor girls to be cut to pieces."

The duke stiffened. "Please, Father," he said, "have a care for the ladies."

Ramsay's expression hardened. He did not apologize. "I think I had better leave." He stalked off without offering even the minimum of niceties by way of a good-bye.

Justin pulled Vera a few feet away and whispered, "Is Dr. Ramsay always this overwrought?"

Vera shook her head. "He has always been a cordial colleague of Papa's. I have never seen him this hard and determined. You know he is a physician as well as a pastor. Perhaps the doctor in him is so appalled he has lost his perspective."

"Evidently," Justin answered.

The drums stopped and the men ceased their circling, but the volume of their chanting increased. They opened their circle to an arc facing the gathering of older men. At this point the dance consisted of standing in place and bobbing their bodies from their hips and their necks. Then they began, in turns, to take a few steps forward and to jump straight up into the air. Some went up more than two feet. They continued this for several minutes.

"It is not graceful, what they do," Gian Lorenzo said.

"It is more a physical stunt than an art form, I admit," Finch Hatton offered, "but I daresay it prepares their legs to run all day long without tiring. In the Mara, I have watched groups of them appear on the horizon and run at a steady pace to the opposite horizon, moving for four or five hours at a stretch."

Their little group continued to watch the dance for longer than any of them were actually amused by it, each of them unwilling to break away if the others were entranced. Vera spoke first. "If you don't mind, I think I would like to go."

"I would too," Constance said. "As for the dancing, it is curious, but rather repetitive."

Justin turned to Vera. "Perhaps we should walk to the railway station and see if there is any news of the land officer's arrival?"

"Why don't we all come along?" Denys said. "There is a native and Indian market near there. Miss Tolliver might find some trinkets to take home as souvenirs of her visit."

"Africa is the most fascinating place I can imagine," she said. "I feel as if I never would be bored here. Not ever."

"I understand that very well," Denys said. "Africa does beguile one."

"I am beguiled," the duke said, but of course he was looking at Constance.

Vera glanced at Justin, who surprised her by seeming perfectly in accord with what had been said. She was sure he was only being polite.

They started uphill in the direction of the station but decided to stop at the guesthouse to refresh themselves before going on.

Madame Gillet invited them to take tea and put out some of her excellent madeleines. They had barely taken their seats in her front parlor when a loud knock came at the front door. Within seconds, a police sergeant, a Goan by the look of him, was shown in. He went to Finch Hatton, stood at attention, and saluted crisply. "Mr. Tolliver, sir, A.D.S. Lovett sent me to fetch you. There has been a murder, sir."

Justin rose. "I am A.D.S. Tolliver," he said.

The man performed a perfect right face and saluted again. "Begging your pardon, sir."

"Tell me who has been murdered, Sergeant."

"The woman who performs the *emuratare*, sir,"

"Woman?" Vera took in a breath. "*Emuratare* is the Maasai word for the rite in which boys become men."

"It's only for boys," Finch Hatton said.

"Also for girls," the sergeant said with a grimace.

Tolliver reached for his pith helmet, certain Vera would see his leaving as a betrayal. Their land inspection was supposed to come first, and she would balk at having to look for that message from the land officer by herself, but he felt compelled to answer Lovett's call.

Vera took her hat too. "Let's step outside a moment." Her voice was determined. Justin was relieved that it wasn't harsh.

When they went out the front door, the sergeant stepped off a few feet and looked away.

"You must go and find out what happened," Vera said at once.

"But the land officer," he said.

"He is not here yet. He said he might be here by today, but that it would most likely not be until tomorrow, perhaps even Saturday. You must go and find out what happened, Justin. I am very afraid."

"You don't think Ramsay—" he started to say, but he saw anxiety in her eyes. Her fears were the same as his. "They are *missionaries*," he said. "Do we really think they would do such a thing?"

"No," Vera said vehemently. "But given how he and Miss Van Slyck have been acting, they will be suspected. You must do whatever you can to help them clear their names."

"I want to," Tolliver said, his blood up, more, if he admitted it, because of the challenge of a crime to solve than in any hope of clearing the missionaries' names. The game's afoot, he thought. Once more into the breach. He felt fully alive.

She gave him something between a smile and a smirk. "Of course you want to." And he saw in her eyes that she read his thoughts. "Go ahead, A.D.S. Tolliver. I will go to the station and see to the land officer."

He squeezed both her hands in his. "You must be careful. Stay with the others. Keep close to them. Promise me."

"I certainly will."

He gave her a quick kiss and followed the sergeant down the hill.

The sergeant, whose name turned out to be Marcal, led Tolliver along a path that paralleled the shore of the lake. Scrubby bushes on either side hemmed in their view of the lake below them. From down near the shore came the voices of men talking, occasionally shouting.

"News of the murder has spread?" Justin asked Marcal.

"Nothing remains secret around here, sir."

"I take it A.D.S. Lovett is at the scene."

"Yes, sir, and the missionary doctor too. But the woman was very dead when they arrived. The doctor could do nothing for her."

"We had better hurry." A worry prickled Justin's conscience. This situation could turn very ugly, very fast. His first duty was to protect Vera and Constance.

He walked quickly forward, warring with himself about whether he should go back and get his wife and sister out of the area as quickly as possible. After half a mile or so, he and the sergeant emerged into a clearing in a wooded area, separate from the gathering of huts where the men were still dancing. Amid a circle of rough, mud-colored Maasai dwellings, about thirty brilliantly clad women milled around, many weeping. A few of the oldest seemed to be chanting a prayer.

In front of the third dwelling on the left two askaris holding rifles stood at attention on either side of a low opening. Six more native policemen were arrayed around the tiny building. Tolliver thought again that he needed to get Lovett to bring Kwai Libazo up from Naivasha immediately. No one could be more useful than Kwai in a situation like this. And being half Maasai, he spoke the language.

Tolliver would not bother enlisting the help of any of these native policemen at this point. He would wait for Kwai.

He practically had to fold himself in half to get inside the hut.

"In here," Lovett called from an inner room.

After the bright sunlight outside, it took a moment for Tolliver's eyes to adjust. He found himself in a small, low-ceilinged, smoky room. In the middle of the dirt floor a banked fire smoldered in a circle of stones. The roof was held up by a mismatched collection of wooden poles, nothing more than tree limbs with the bark removed. The air was acrid. What smoke that managed to escape went out through a small opening at the top of the thatched roof. The place smelled also of goat dung and something like stewing beef, though nothing was cooking over the fire.

Lovett beckoned from the doorway to a separate, tiny space where the other odors were joined by the sweet smell of human blood. Ramsay knelt praying next to a wooden pallet raised only a few inches above the packed-dirt floor. The bed, if one could call it that, was strewn with a motley collection of blankets, and on them lay an old Maasai woman. One of her wrinkled, thin arms hung off the side and carried ten or fifteen wire bracelets.

Ramsay stood and removed a handkerchief, undoubtedly his, from the dead woman's face. She had close-cropped gray hair; her eyes were closed. Otherwise, to Tolliver, she was indistinguishable from any other old Maasai woman he had ever seen. Ears and neck festooned with native jewelry. Her body covered with draped cloth in shades of red and blue. There was a large, browning bloodstain in the middle of her chest.

Ramsay held up a small iron native knife. "She was stabbed with this. It is the instrument she used to perform her atrocities on those girls."

Tolliver didn't know why, but he blurted out, "Is the ceremony over then?"

Ramsay hung his head. "It was not supposed to take place until tomorrow, but they moved it up, I am sure to foil our attempts to convince the women to withdraw their girls. The poor victims are with their mothers and grandmothers, writhing in pain, no doubt." Tolliver's suspicions were aroused. But he realized that if Ramsay were guilty he might play down his disapproval of what the dead woman had done. Ramsay's attitude lent itself to conflicting interpretations—for and against his having murdered the woman himself.

Tolliver took the knife, which still showed traces of blood. He had solved a murder in Mombasa last year using the science of fingerprints, a new approach for Africa. But there was no such technique available up-country, not in Nairobi, certainly not here in Nakuru. There was no way to ensure that, if he sent the knife to the coast to be examined, it would be kept properly so the evidence would not be contaminated with the prints of everyone who handled it along the way. It already had his own and Ramsay's on it. And if Ramsay was the murderer...?

He turned to Lovett. "This is your case," he said. "I am not in this area on official business. I should leave this to you."

Lovett grimaced. "Please don't. I will gladly defer to your greater experience. I would not know where to begin."

Tolliver bowed. His "greater experience" amounted to having been on the force just over a year longer. Lovett was the younger man, one or two years younger than Tolliver's twenty-six years. Yet Lovett was the one with the cynical, disinterested air. He had arrived in the Protectorate from service in India with the Queen's Own Corps, the most prestigious regiment in the Imperial service. Last year in Nairobi he had been enthusiastic and determined. Tolliver wondered what could have happened to Lovett to rob him of his spirit.

"I take it you have notified Jodrell," Tolliver said.

"May we walk outside to talk? The stink in here is killing me."

"You go out and wait for me," Tolliver said. "I want to take a closer look at the corpse. I'll join you outside in a moment."

Lovett beat a hasty path to the door. Ramsay remained in the room but stepped aside to allow Tolliver to approach the bed.

Closer examination told him nothing more. There were no other marks on the body, no sign that she had struggled. "Was the knife still in her chest when you found her?" Tolliver asked him.

"Yes it was. I pulled it out instinctively. There was nothing I could do for her. She was obviously dead." The man spoke as if he were talking of a broken chair or a torn shirt. It was all Tolliver could do not to ask him outright if he had killed the old woman. "Come outside," he said.

"What will happen to the body?" Ramsay asked.

"I don't imagine we can learn anything more by looking at it." Tolliver knew that the Kikuyu left the bodies of their deceased out in the bush for the carrion eaters to deal with. He had no idea what the Maasai did with theirs. "We can turn it over to her relatives."

"I believe," Ramsay said, "that the women who perform these atrocities do not come from the tribe itself, but come from outside the immediate group. More proof that, on some level, they know what they are doing is horrifying."

Tolliver moved away to the main room. "I do not see how continuing to make such statements can be helpful at this point, Dr. Ramsay."

The missionary glowered. "Exactly what do you mean by that?"

Tolliver shrugged. He knew what he was about to say would rile Ramsay, but he said it anyway. "Your hatred for what the woman did might suggest that you became overwrought and were the one who stabbed her."

"That is outrageous," Ramsay sputtered. His eyes—gray when he was calm—flashed blue anger. "How dare you insinuate such a thing? How dare you?" He elbowed Tolliver aside, slipped out of the building, and marched off. By the time Tolliver reached the sunshine and his eyes adjusted to the glaring light, Ramsay was halfway out of the settlement.

"What was that all about?" Lovett said mildly, as if a schoolboy had just walked off the playing field in a fit of pique.

Tolliver thought it best to let him believe that nothing important had transpired. "Do you have a notebook and pencil? Out of uniform, I am without mine."

Lovett reached into his breast pocket and produced them. "To answer your earlier question," he said, "I have not yet reported this death. I usually report to the D.S. once a week on Monday. And I don't put in a special report every time a native dies. Besides, this woman died only a few minutes before I arrived. And I have been here ever since."

"True enough," Tolliver said. "We should report it before long, though. With the move of the tribe imminent, it's a touchy time. This murder could spark wild fire."

Lovett blew out a breath of resignation. "Perhaps *you* should report it to Jodrell." He was issuing a challenge.

Tolliver flipped open Lovett's notebook. The last entry in it was dated 1 January 1913, more than four months ago.

"Tell me exactly how the news of this killing reached you." He poised his pencil.

"A woman came screaming into my *boma*. The whole place was up in arms before my boys could calm her enough to tell us what had happened. I have only a handful of Maasai-speaking askaris here, and most of them were not on duty at the moment." He wrinkled his nose. "They had taken their half day off to go do their silly dance with their brothers. As soon as I understood what had happened, I took a squad of boys here and when I saw the corpse I asked Marcal to fetch you. That's everything."

It was not even a good start. Lovett was not answering like a policeman at all. More like an ordinary witness. People told policemen what they thought was important, or what would keep themselves out of trouble, or what they thought the policeman wanted to know, or what would get them out of spending their time in answering further questions. He was not sure which of these tactics was Lovett's. Perhaps none. Perhaps he had just lost his taste for police work and was doing the minimum, even at a moment like this.

"What is the name of the woman who reported the murder?"

"I have no idea."

"Who took her testimony?"

"Marcal was the one who wrote it down."

"Very well. I will get that from him. Was Ramsay already here when you arrived?"

For the first time in this conversation, Lovett looked as if he was taking an interest. He paused to think and then shook his head, more it seemed to settle its contents than to communicate a negative answer. "To be certain, I do not know. There was such a commotion when I arrived."

"Please describe the commotion."

"Well, we came along the path, we found our way—"

"Excuse me. What path was that?"

Lovett gave Tolliver an annoyed glance. He pointed to the opening through which Marcal had led Tolliver not half an hour ago. "That one. It is the most direct from the town."

"Go on." Tolliver poised his pencil.

"As we came along the path, we encountered a group of Maasai warriors. They told us that we were not allowed to visit this village. That it belonged to the women and that no men were allowed in this place. We told them there had been a report of the murder of a Maasai woman. They got pretty agitated. I had to remind them that my squad had weapons."

"And Ramsay was not around while this was going on."

"You suspect him, don't you?" Lovett said, proving that he was not exactly fast asleep.

"Not really," Tolliver replied. "But knowing who was exactly where at the time of the crime is always helpful. It can help us find witnesses and lead us to the killer."

Lovett looked disappointed. "Well, I honestly do not know where Ramsay was while we were having our little tug-of-war with the native boys."

"What happened then?"

"They relented and let us in. The woman who came for us brought us here." He indicated the hut they had just left.

"So the woman who came to report the crime was with you when you came back."

"Yes, of course. At least she had given up her horrid screaming."

With his hand, Justin described a circle, indicating the open area between the dwellings within the circular kraal of thorn-tree branches. "Tell me what was happening here when you arrived."

"The place was still occupied only by women, but there were few of them about. I think most of them had retreated to their own places. And don't ask me again about Ramsay. I only remember one thing about him—he came into the room just as I was approaching the body, and glad I was to see him. He is a medical doctor, you know, as well as one of the faith. Saved me from touching the corpse. He was there to grope for a pulse and declare her dead. Not that there was any doubt. Her unblinking eyes told me that. He said she was quite warm, so dead likely less than an hour. Can you imagine?"

Tolliver could. Twice in his life he had arrived at the scene of an accident in time to witness the moment of death. It gave even the strongest man pause. And Lovett was not the strongest man.

"Where was the murder weapon when you arrived?"

"Sticking out of her bloody chest," he said. He snorted. "Bloody in both senses of the word. And what a bloody mess the whole thing is. I think I had better send a runner to Hobson out at the army encampment. I think the King's African Rifles had better move in closer and be at the ready."

Tolliver nodded. Lovett was a better soldier than a policeman. And that might prove the more valuable skill before this episode was over.

Constance was both happy and sad that her brother was not with them on their little excursion to the station and market. Happy because he was not there to frown every time Gian Lorenzo paid her a compliment.

She liked those compliments. They were unlike the ones she had gotten from boys she knew in Yorkshire and London, who were looking for a girl with a pedigree and would bolt, she was sure, the second they found out about her paltry dowry. Gian Lorenzo was sincere. And gallant too, but not in a way that seemed forced. Had Justin lightened up a little on his scowling this morning? Or was that only wishful thinking on her part?

Her brother had no call to disapprove. He had come to Africa and married into a missionary family. Now, with all his pretensions of fair play and modern thinking, he was being a prig when it came to her choice. If he had the right to marry Vera, why shouldn't she be allowed to marry an Italian, who just happened to be a duke. A duke!

Vera had told her why Justin was so disapproving. Religion, of all things. He was worried about how Papa and John would react. Well, she could see to that.

The only thing that John really cared about was having enough money to maintain Tilbury Grange without selling every last Van Dyck and Fragonard in the place. She was certain that once she told him Gian Lorenzo had offered to forego her dowry, John would brave the wrath of his wife, the archbishop's daughter.

Justin was Constance's favorite in the family, the only one who cared more about her than about appearances. He had stood by her when Mother and John became all uppity, like that time she brought home a girl from school who had no family and whom everyone suspected was someone's illegitimate child. Constance could not think of losing her connection to her best brother. She so wanted Justin to take her side now.

Vera, standing next to her at an Indian stall in the market, made a sibilant sound and threw her an impish grin. "You have been staring at that sari silk for a full minute, Constance. What is on your mind? As if I didn't know."

"Shush," Constance said for effect. Gian Lorenzo was fifteen feet away, chatting with Denys. They were in no danger of being overheard, except by the chubby stall owner. Constance put down the length of cloth. "Thank you," she said to the Indian vendor. "It is lovely, but it is not the color I am looking for." She walked away before he had a chance to protest.

Vera took her arm. "I never thought I would say this, but I am glad for the land officer's delay. It will give you and Gian Lorenzo another day. I know he and Denys want to get on with their hunting once Justin and I make our detour to look at the possible farmsteads."

"Actually, I think they are not going to go off, at least not until we start back to Athi River."

Vera put a twinkle in her eye. "Oh, good," she said, pretending all she wanted was for Constance and the duke to remain together long enough to strengthen their bond. That would be lovely, of course, but what Vera welcomed most about this news was that Gian Lorenzo and Denys and their men would remain with them to act as extra protection. She was certain that the missionaries would be suspects in the murder investigation, and from what Justin had told her about Lovett, he would not even bother to try to find out who had actually killed the woman. Trouble could easily be brewing among the Maasai over this. Lovett—and his superiors in the administration for all she knew—could very well leap at the easiest response and call in the army. All hell could break loose.

The whole matter was so very disturbing. The African ceremony was horrific, and she understood full well why Dr. Ramsay was so determined to stop it. How could he not be? Unlike her mild father, many missionaries who offered medical treatment exuded a nearly fanatic devotion to their work. Some were men of God first and men of medicine after. Others were the opposite. Ramsay's passions for both God and medicine were so strong that they bordered on zealotry. Where his emotional state might lead him did not bear thinking about.

A train whistle sounded to the north. She glanced at her watch. The down-train was more or less on time. Oh, how she wished she could board it right now. To have it carry her away from all this turmoil, back to her baby boy.

She did her best to shake off her longing. "It is nearly one," she said to Constance. "Let's collect your men and make our way back to see what the talented Madame Gillet has in store for us for luncheon."

"They are not my men," Constance protested with a hint of glee.

"Oh, I think one of them is."

At that moment, as Denys and Gian Lorenzo started toward them, a boy of about ten approached Vera from the direction of the station. He handed her a cable. "Oh, it's the answer to the message I sent my papa when we arrived." She opened it, full of apprehension. Then she smiled and read it out: "All well here."

"Is that everything?" Gian Lorenzo asked.

Denys laughed heartily. "It's all she can expect from a Scot paying by the word."

Justin scribbled a quick note to Vera saying he would not be back for luncheon, tore the page out of Lovett's notebook, and signaled to an askari. He handed the paper to the boy. "Do you know the Gillet guesthouse?"

"Yes, Bwana."

"Take this there. And call me sir." Justin watched him run off, recalling how often he had said that phrase to Kwai Libazo. He looked around for Lovett, but the man had gone off, most likely to his gin bottle. As soon as possible, he would ask Lovett to send for Kwai.

Justin thought with regret about what, if anything, he might find to eat in place of Madame Gillet's delightful fare. He was starving. His best bet for something decent, he supposed, was at the American Mission, and he had plenty of reasons to go there as part of his investigation. He might get a decent bite to eat into the bargain. "Marcal," he called out.

The sergeant was a wiry man of medium height who smiled too much but seemed competent. Given Lovett's drinking, he was very likely the one keeping things together.

"Yes, sir?" he said with his ever-ready salute.

"Have you found the woman who reported the murder?"

"Yes, sir. Do you want to interrogate her?"

"Yes, but first I think I will go speak to Dr. Ramsay. What have they done with the body?"

Marcal shrugged. "They have taken it, sir."

Tolliver dug his watch out of his pocket. "Very well. I will be back in about three quarters of an hour. Have the woman ready to speak to me. What is her name?"

"Simu."

"Just Simu?"

"I think that's enough to find her, sir."

"Have her here when I return. Keep a close eye on things. Send a runner at the first sign of trouble." Tolliver looked him in the eye.

"At the very first sign, sir."

Tolliver returned Marcal's salute and set off up the hill to the Mission, feeling a bit strange to be acting in such an official capacity out of uniform. Even dressed as he was, he had fallen immediately into his role. He was grateful that Vera agreed with his taking this on, rather than wanting him to keep his promise to focus only on their land acquisition. It troubled him that this felt more right to him than he could imagine farming ever would.

He recalled a conversation he had had with Vera when they went on that picnic, the day he knew that she was the only woman for him. She told him that, having been born in Africa of Scottish parents, she always felt herself a person between two worlds. Not African. Not British. Neither. And both. He too had always felt a bit at odds with the world around him. Perhaps it was because he was a second son. His brother, John, had known from the outset that he would one day be the eighth earl of Bilbrough. John's upbringing had pointed him only in that direc-tion, with the lion's share of the family's money to be used to keep intact the estate and the great house that went with the title. John's life and that of his progeny would certainly follow those old traditions.

For Justin, there had been only enough to pay his way through the proper schools and to buy him a commission in the army. After that, as a second son, he was on his own. It was that uncertainty, he thought, that left him feeling disconnected. In comparison to John, he certainly was. That day of the picnic, he had told Vera that it was only on the playing fields that he felt he belonged, but his work as a policeman gave him that same sensation—of being part of something larger than himself. Men working together, with a clear goal, and knowing in the end whether or not they had achieved it.

He would soon withdraw completely from such work. He wondered what would become of his need for it.

The American Mission and school in Nakuru stood on a promontory overlooking the lake. Vera's father had sited his Mission in Athi River with a wonderful prospect. Evidently the founder of this place had had the very same inclination. Justin knew the missionaries had started coming in during the final quarter of the last century. It was quite possible that they had grabbed up all the best panoramas before they converted their first Christian. He was joking with himself, but he was not sure Vera's father would think this idea very funny at all. Certainly, Arthur Ramsay seemed completely devoid of a sense of humor.

Tolliver found him in the Mission office, papers before him on the desk, a pen in his hand, but a blank expression on his face.

"I wonder if I might speak to you for a moment, Dr. Ramsay."

"Are you here as a private citizen or a policeman? You look like the one and act like the other." The death the man had witnessed that morning had not at all softened his arch attitude.

"I was just thinking about that myself." Justin offered him a smile, which accomplished nothing at all. "I came into the area on a personal trip, but I am still a member of the police force and clearly there is a need for such service here today."

"What about Lovett?"

"We are working together."

Ramsay sneered, but said nothing.

"May I take a seat and ask you some questions?" Tolliver did not wait for an answer. He pulled a rickety-looking wooden chair from the corner and perched gingerly upon it. "This is not your Mission, I believe. My wife tells me that your Mission is among the Kikuyu, closer to Nairobi." He paused, but Ramsay did not take up the subject. "Can you tell me what brought you here?" Tolliver thought to take out his notebook and pencil but he decided that would only put Ramsay further off.

"We spoke about this in the bush on our way here."

"Please tell me again."

Ramsay pulled himself up straight. "I see. This is part of an official investigation."

"Yes, sir, it is—an investigation into the murder of—" Justin realized he did not know the dead woman's name.

For a moment, Ramsay looked as if he would laugh at him, but he folded his hands and sat back and said, "Well, this makes for a nice change. In my experience, His Majesty's government takes no interest at all in the death of an African tribesman. Ordinarily, their deaths are totally ignored."

"Not in this instance, Dr. Ramsay," Tolliver said as evenly as he could. "Given your approval of our undertaking this investigation, I am sure you will want to cooperate fully. Shall we begin in earnest?"

"Yes, but I do not see what my being here has to do with your investigation."

"The typical police investigation begins with gathering general information. So the officer in charge can get an understanding of the background of the crime. Much of that information turns out to be useless, but one never knows which little tidbit might complete the puzzle and lead to the truth. So tell me what brings you here to a Mission of a different denomination, so far from your own installation." At this point Tolliver did take out the notebook, which had its intimidating effect.

Ramsay's tone turned to that of a man defending himself in court. "As I told you out in the bush two days ago, the Christian missionaries have taken a stand against—'that native practice,' shall we call it?"

"Yes, let's call it that," Tolliver agreed.

Ramsay went on. "The Church Missionary Society, sponsored by the Church of Scotland—your father-in-law's organization—began condemning the practice as long ago as 1906."

Tolliver failed to hide his surprise. "But my wife has lived here all her life and she knew nothing of it."

Ramsay's indignant tone turned completely frosty. "You don't imagine that Clarence McIntosh would speak to his womenfolk about it, certainly not to Vera. What was she then, thirteen? Twelve?"

Justin had no choice but to believe him. Vera's father certainly was the sort of man to take such a stand, but he would never burden Vera with such knowledge. Not when she was so young. Not ever. "Very well," he said, "but why come here and now? It's a particularly difficult moment, what with the move and the lawsuit."

"Do you really think we should time our work for the convenience of the administration? I certainly don't. It is an unusual situation. By chance, we learned that a ceremony involving the practice was about to take place here. Ordinarily we would have no idea of when it would occur. Evidently, this land is a kind of sacred place for the Maasai. It was mentioned specifically in an earlier treaty the British signed with them. The Maasai were determined to perform the rite here before they were forced to leave this place. I came straightaway to prevent the mutilation of those girls."

"Is there not a missionary here who would be able to fulfill such a role?"

"Augustus Warner, who founded this installation in 1904, took his wife home to Boston for treatment six months ago. I had diagnosed her with cancer. While under surgery, the dear lady died. Mr. Warner is on leave for another month. It is believed that he will return. In the meanwhile, this Mission has been left without a head."

"What is the role of Miss Van Slyck?"

"She acted as secretary to Mr. Warner. She has also acted as a teacher in the girls' school here. Of course, she could not take over the pastoral duties."

"Of course not." Tolliver let that bland remark hang in the air. Ramsay had gotten into a rhythm of calmly answering questions. Before he got too comfortable, it was time to put him a bit off balance. "Given your very strong objection to the procedure, do you not think the dead woman may have gotten her just deserts?"

The question was barely out of Tolliver's mouth when Ramsay slammed his fist on the desk. "How dare you make such an insinuation a second time! I had hoped you had thought better of insulting me! I am a medical doctor and an ordained minister. It has been my life's work to heal people's bodies and their souls. I have never—I would never harm a person, much less murder one." He pressed his mouth closed—the picture of a clergyman holding in a curse. Or a threat.

Tolliver wanted to accuse Ramsay of protesting too much, but he thought better of pushing him so far. "Excuse me, sir, but I did not say I thought you had committed murder. I merely asked if you might, in some ways, see it as an act of justice."

"What kind of policeman are you, that you think murder could be an act of justice?"

This was perfect. The man was getting completely emotional, a state in which he would reveal much more than he intended. "Please, Dr. Ramsay. You misinterpret what I have said. But let me ask this: Is there someone else, not you, certainly, but someone who might have wanted to take that woman's life because of what she did to those girls?"

"You can only mean Miss Van Slyck. Which is ridiculous. Clarence McIntosh has told me what a fine fellow he thinks you are, the most moral policeman in the Protectorate. Well, he might be right, but that speaks more ill of the police force than

it does good of you. Your true stripes are showing, Mr. Tolliver."
The man's typical taut posture had stiffened to stone. One hand
gripped the pen he had been holding as if it wanted to break it.
The other gripped the edge of the table. "Miss Van Slyck has
spent the day in the chapel praying for the girls who are now
in agony over what was done to them this morning. I remind
you, sir, that the native woman was killed *after* she performed
her mutilations." His voice had risen as if he were addressing
the Houses of Parliament. "If Miss Van Slyck and I were the
fanatics you make us out to be, we would have killed her *before*
she did her horrific business." The man was breathless by the
time he left off his tirade.

Tolliver allowed a moment to pass before he answered.
He then told Ramsay a lie and a truth. "I am sorry that you
found my questions so upsetting, Dr. Ramsay. It is very often
the case that understanding why a murder was committed is
the key to finding the person who did it." He closed his notebook and stood.

Like many of the people Tolliver had interrogated over
the years, rather than being relieved when it was over, Ramsay
seemed more frightened. He was too intelligent not to worry that
he had revealed things he had not intended to. Tolliver was sure
that the personal attack in that outburst would haunt Ramsay
every bit as much as it had troubled Justin to hear it. Guilty or
not, Ramsay must feel on the wrong side of the law now that he
had insulted a policeman.

Tolliver was halfway back to the village before he realized
that he had not had anything to eat.

Gian Lorenzo di Savoia walked along the dirt road and
planned how he would broach with Justin Tolliver the subject of
marriage to his sister. He didn't need Tolliver's permission, but
he wanted him on his side, hopefully to smooth the way with
Constance's father.

He found it hard to believe he was contemplating such an engagement. His friends in Italy would tell him that he was letting himself be overwhelmed by the romance of meeting Constance in such a setting.

They had already teased him for his *mal d'Africa*—his African disease—the way his countrymen described the sort of infatuation he felt for this land. But his feelings for Constance were not mere infatuation. He was not a man of trifling emotions. He had always been a serious person. He was only thirty-two, but he had already led an expedition to the Arctic, and set a world altitude record trying to climb one of the highest mountains on earth. He had not accomplished these feats by being impetuous. He had planned very carefully and followed the steps he had laid out. This was the secret of his achievements. If anything, he was pedestrian rather than starry-eyed.

True, he had not reached the North Pole as he had planned. Neither had he reached the summit of Chogolisa. Walking along now, he looked down at his left hand. He had lost the top of his third finger to frostbite in the Arctic. When Constance noticed it, unlike other women he had known, she had not looked away or demanded to know what had happened. She merely looked up into his eyes with sympathy in hers. He told her about the failed expedition and how—because of the frostbite—he had had to send the others on, to try to reach the pole without him. She had not grimaced.

"How sad for you," she had said.

"They did not make it to the pole."

"Perhaps," she had said, "if you had been with them, they might have." She put her hand to her mouth then and took in her breath. "Oh, I am sorry. I do not want to make you feel worse about it."

He had all he could do not to try to kiss her at that moment. He nearly told her that he loved her.

Instead he confessed that he had once been engaged to another woman.

"That's—that's—" She wasn't able to say whatever she was thinking.

"I want you to know this about me. We did not marry because my king would not give his permission for me to marry a commoner."

The glint of doubt this produced in her eyes was only momentary, then she blurted out, "I was raised an Anglican," and then blushed more profoundly than he had ever seen a woman do. That was the moment he knew for certain that she wanted him as he wanted her. She was everything that was right for him. Religion would be the sticking point for both sides. Since she was Christian, the Archbishop of Torino might accept a promise that the children would be brought up Catholic, but his prickly cousin the king would not. The king would...

As he approached the door of the guesthouse, his mind had fixated on children. More than anything, he wanted Constance to be the mother of his children.

As he reached for the knocker, Denys called out to him from behind. "I saw you coming toward me in a world of your own, with the expression of one of those saints in pictures in the Uffizi."

"Please do not tease me in front of the others. I am in earnest."

Denys put a hand on his shoulder. "Be careful, man. This could be the end of your mountain climbing."

"I have new adventures I want to try," Gian Lorenzo said, and rapped on the door.

In a plain navy European dress, the woman Simu looked to be middle-aged, but she said she had twenty-five years. She told the askari interpreter that she could not speak English, so he put her words into Swahili. It was the best Tolliver could do, since there was no one about who spoke both Maasai and English. He was not comfortable with this testimony being dragged through two languages before he understood it, but he had no choice. After a year in Mombasa, his command of Swahili had greatly improved, but it was not good enough to see clearly the connection between the woman's words and her emotions. How many times today had he wished for Kwai Libazo?

Her answers to his questions seemed hesitant, especially after he started to write down what she was saying.

Tolliver asked the interpreter to characterize what he heard. The askari believed Simu was afraid because she was alone with two men who were not her husband or her sons, something

Maasai women almost never were. In Tolliver's experience, this was not a cultural problem. Most people, even sophisticated Europeans, were unnerved by a police interrogation.

In the end, all Tolliver learned in the interview was that Simu had gone into the hut where the dead woman was because she heard a moan coming from inside. She arrived just as the old woman expired. She protested that she had touched nothing and saw no one in the place, but she admitted that she had been too frightened to look around. She thought she might have screamed. She could only remember running away. She made straight for the Mission and Miss Van Slyck. She seemed to view the missionary woman as a sort of protector. On her way, running along the path, she saw Ruth Van Slyck ahead of her. When she told her what she had found, Miss Van Slyck had urged her to go straight to the police *boma* and report it to A.D.S. Lovett.

"Did she remember seeing anyone else near the hut when she went in or when she came out?"

Tolliver watched her smiling mouth and terrified eyes as she answered. The smile seemed just another expression of her fear.

"She does not remember, Bwana," the askari said.

"Was Miss Van Slyck walking toward or away from the Maasai village when Simu came upon her on the path?"

The woman's smile vanished. Her eyes darted from the askari to Tolliver and back. She spoke then to the interpreter.

"She could not tell," he reported. "The Mission lady was not facing away and was not facing toward her."

Tolliver made a note of this, and while he wrote it he realized that Ruth Van Slyck's stance clearly indicated that she must have been walking away from the village. Then she must have partially turned when she heard Simu coming behind her. If she had been walking toward the Maasai village, she would have been facing in Simu's direction and would have seen her coming before they met. It was time to take his investigation to Miss Van Slyck.

"Thank her very much for her report," Tolliver told the askari.

The woman stood up and turned away. Then she said something more. It could have been good-bye for all Tolliver could tell, but it turned out to be a sudden recollection. She *had* seen another woman near the hut before she went in. A woman named Tigisi.

At luncheon that day, Madame Gillet served a delicious *coq au vin*, except that it was made with guinea fowl instead of chicken. Vera felt a bit guilty enjoying it so much when she knew that Justin would have nothing nearly so lovely.

Denys increased Vera's anxiety by asking if she had heard anything about the land officer.

Vera admitted to herself that until now she had harbored a prejudice in favor of the land possibilities closer to her father. She had imagined that Nakuru would be too much of a backwater to satisfy Justin and that it offered no social life to speak of, not even the paltry distractions of club dances and ladies' teas that she found in Nairobi. But if the land here turned out to be irresistibly better than what they had seen down in Ngong, she knew she could at least count on truly delicious meals at Madame Gillet's table.

Also, Nakuru would be growing very soon as the latest influx of settlers came into the area. That flutter of anxiety in her stomach asserted itself. All those immigrants. The white population of the Protectorate was mushrooming, and where was the land officer who was supposed to help them make their final choice before…

Vera saw that she was being overly anxious. She could not help it. She even knew that the reason behind her impatience made no sense. Somehow she needed her own piece of Africa so that she could finally belong here. She needed to become truly part of this country where she had been born, although her parents called another place home. The Mission where she grew up belonged to the Church of Scotland—not to her father, who had built it. In a way, she had never had a place she could call home. That was why.

Denys and the duke had arrived in time to share a *crème caramel* that would have won a prize in London. Conversation around the table waned as they finished their coffee, and Vera immediately proposed that they walk to the station to see if there was any word for her from the Land Office.

As the four of them left the guesthouse, they found the road between them and the Mission lined with Maasai warriors—at least thirty men, some of whom had been dancing early that morning, clustered in small groups. They were standing with their spears in the shade of the trees along the red road. There was nothing especially menacing in their demeanor or their expressions, but it was quite odd that they were here, and in such numbers.

Finch Hatton signaled Kinuthia, who as always stood like a guard on duty facing any door behind which Denys had disappeared. Denys went to him and spoke for a moment. They walked over to the nearest group of Maasai men and spoke to them.

"They seem quite calm," Gian Lorenzo said. "They do not appear at all angry."

Their calm attitude was just what made Vera's blood run cold. "The Maasai never seem agitated. But that does not mean they are feeling peaceful," she said.

Constance took in a quick breath.

Vera took her hand. "Don't fret, dearest. I didn't mean that they will do us harm. I have never known that to happen." She prayed this would not be the first time.

On his way back to them, Denys took his hat off, ran his hand through his hair, and replaced the hat on his head. Vera had learned from the time they first met that he did that when he needed to calm his nerves. "They say they are waiting for the Secretary of Native Affairs and the Nairobi City Magistrate, Bonham-Carter. They expect news about that lawsuit of theirs—the one that's been in the newspapers. Kinuthia says he thinks there is a lot they are not saying."

Vera looked toward Gian Lorenzo and Constance, who were in conversation, *sotto voce*. She pulled Denys aside. "Are they saying anything about the stabbing of that Maasai woman? What does Kinuthia think is going on?"

"They are not saying. And you know how the natives are about hazarding guesses. Kinuthia will never do that."

Vera bit her bottom lip. "If they were just waiting for the administrators, they would wait at the train station, wouldn't they? But they are on this road, near the Mission."

The duke and Constance moved closer to her. "Excuse us a moment, ladies," the duke said. He put an arm over Denys's shoulder and drew him away to the end of the front walk. They conferred in whispers and then Denys went into the guesthouse.

"What is happening?" Constance asked. She had been calm enough until now, but her blue eyes darted from Gian Lorenzo's face to the Maasai under the tree and back.

The duke's pleasant expression did not change. "We are merely taking precautions," he said. "Nothing to be upset about. What is the expression you used, Mrs. Tolliver? Better safe—"

"Than sorry," three of them said in unison.

After just a few minutes, Denys returned. "I'll instruct Kinuthia." He walked off to confer with his tracker.

"What is happening?" The level of alarm in Constance's voice was up an octave.

"We have asked Monsieur Gillet if we can move our camp onto his property. Denys is arranging to have the boys break camp and move our tents to the field behind the house."

"All sorted," Denys announced. "Shall we walk down to the station? That is where we will find our best sources of information."

Ordinarily, their group had walked in twos or threes. This time the men kept them four abreast, with her and Consty between them.

As they passed, Vera glanced over her shoulder at all those Maasai men between her and Justin. Over the past year and a half, when he was on duty, she had spent many hours waiting for him, not knowing if he was in danger. She had taught herself to hold a pretty picture in her mind against her fears—of him walking to her, as she had seen him emerge from the sea after bathing, when they were staying in that lovely beach cottage in Mombasa. Tall, trim, and sturdy. His broad shoulders, his rosy complexion that would be the envy of many girls. His thick golden-brown hair. The depth, the strength of their connection to each other. She imagined their love circling around them, spinning and binding them together. He would be all right. He would.

Unaware of the delicious lunch that had been served at the guesthouse, Justin was quite satisfied with the snack that Marcal had managed to find for him at around two that afternoon. It was a dish the natives called *ugali*, a white paste of boiled corn-meal that, like them, he ate with his fingers. The stuff itself, made without salt, had little taste, but when he dipped a sticky nugget of it into a sauce made with fish fresh from the lake, it was quite satisfying. Hungry as he was, he might have found a child's pap delicious.

He considered his next step. Lovett seemed to have abdicated any responsibility for the investigation and had gone off, claiming he needed to be on hand when some district bigwigs came for an announcement about relocating the Maasai. At least he had agreed to send for Kwai.

Tolliver decided that Ruth Van Slyck's testimony should come next. He would ask the missionary woman for background on both Simu and Tigisi. Then he would see what would emerge from Ruth Van Slyck's testimony about what she had seen and done at the time of the murder. He would also have to find the woman Tigisi—the one Simu had seen near the dead woman's hut.

When he reached the road, the sight of Maasai *ilmurran* grouped under every tree put him on edge. Walking deliberately, without haste and not looking at them, he made a quick detour back to the guesthouse. Vera? His sister? He had to be sure they were safe.

Monsieur Gillet told him that they had walked to the station in the company of Denys and the duke—to find news of the land officer, he thought.

"The duke and Mr. Finch Hatton have asked if they can move their camp to the field behind my house. I like this idea. It will bring their men here to protect the ladies, but also it will protect my house, just in case."

Justin was also glad of this news. Having the duke so devoted to Constance was beginning to feel more like a blessing than a curse. "When my wife and my friends return, please tell them to stay here in the house. I will send a few askaris to guard the place as well."

"Do you expect such terrible trouble, Monsieur?" The Belgian looked more doubtful than concerned. "Madame Gillet and I have been here for nearly seven years. We have never had any worries with the Maasai. I think people fear them because of things they have done in the past to the other natives. But they never made us worry about being near them. They like to keep to themselves. To live in their own way. I think that is all they want."

Justin saw no need to further alarm the man by reminding him that the British administration was about to force his otherwise peaceable neighbors off the land they had occupied for centuries. "I am a policeman," he said instead. "I am very likely being overcautious. The things I have seen in my work make me err in the direction of overprotection. Would you do me the favor of sending for me when my wife returns? I will be either at the

Mission or in the Maasai village. Send one of my askaris. Anyone will be able to find me."

The gracious Monsieur Gillet agreed, and Justin, walking apace, made his way past an increasing number of Maasai men lounging along the road to the Mission.

The Mission office was empty. At Miss Van Slyck's house, a houseboy who was cleaning the kitchen and spoke excellent English directed Tolliver to the chapel, recognizable by the cross over its entrance.

Tolliver passed a boy lethargically sweeping the open ground between the empty school and a storage shed. All the Mission buildings were of grass and wattle, and all but the shed had exterior walls that went only halfway from the ground to the roof.

He passed through the chapel entrance and found Ruth Van Slyck on her knees at the foot of a tall plain wooden cross, her head bowed over her clasped hands. The cross and a sturdy pulpit were the only indications that this was a house of worship.

Tolliver stood at the entrance a moment to see if the noise of his boots on the gravel had warned her of his approach. When she did not look up, he spoke softly: "Forgive me, Miss Van Slyck."

She started and turned to him with an accusing stare.

He bowed his head. "I apologize for disturbing you, Miss Van Slyck, but I have been recruited to look into the death of the Maasai woman who was stabbed this morning. I need your help with my investigation."

"Her name was Naeku," she said in a chilly tone, as if he had insulted the dead woman by not knowing her name.

"I wonder if you would step outside with me for a moment so I might ask you some questions."

She rose and dusted off her skirt. He followed her to a bench in the shade of a tree.

Justin took out his notebook. "Thank you for telling me her name. Neither A.D.S. Lovett nor Dr. Ramsay seemed to know it. Would you spell it for me?"

"Naeku. Nah-eh-coo. N-A-E-K-U."

He wrote it down. "Thank you."

She looked askance at the notebook. "Why are you investigating?"

"I have been a policeman of the Protectorate for two and a half years now."

She looked him up and down. "A policeman? I thought you were the son of an earl or something. That's what the other missionaries said when you were married, that Clarence McIntosh's daughter had married a Yorkshire nobleman. I distinctly remember that Robert Morley, the Wesleyan from Mombasa, teased your father-in-law that his daughter's life had been 'made glorious summer by this son of York.'"

Justin could not help but smile at the reference, but Ruth Van Slyck was not in a joking mood. He decided to tell her the truth, which might very well encourage her to take a more sympathetic attitude toward him. She was American after all and likely held an excessively democratic attitude when it came to the British nobility. "Yes, my father is the earl of Bilbrough, one of those massively impecunious British aristocrats who could not afford to stake his second son to farm in this wilderness. I became a policeman because I wanted to stay in Africa, and I needed to earn my own way."

She did not exactly warm to him, but at least the disdain left her expression. She looked at the notebook. He took that as an invitation.

"I need to get some background information to understand what happened this morning. What can you tell me about the atmosphere of the village? How the people relate to one another."

"Not very much. My work here is mostly administrative. I do not have much close contact with the majority of the tribal people. I teach the girls at the Mission school, the few that we get. It is very difficult to reach out to the Maasai with the promises of Our Lord. They are exceedingly tenacious when it comes to their culture. Other white people seem to think that they will surrender their way of life to the new ideas that have immigrated here with the Missions, the British government, and the settlers. Other tribes have been more amenable, the Kikuyu and the Kavirondo, but the Maasai are tenacious. They will not yield easily, perhaps not at all." She closed her mouth and then opened it again as if she wanted to say more, but she did not.

He made a quick notation.

"What about the woman Simu who found the body—what can you tell me about her?"

"She is a convert, a very devout one." She looked expectant, as if she had answered the question and he would now ask about something else.

"You really know nothing more about Simu?" He found this strange, since Simu seemed to be so focused on Ruth Van Slyck as some sort of mentor or protector. Otherwise, when she was in shock from finding a dead body, why would Miss Van Slyck be the first person she ran to for help?

Ruth Van Slyck's expression carried an accusation that he was prying into something that was none of his business. It was his least favorite response to an inquiry; it reminded him too much of his mother's warning looks when he was being ungentlemanly. He forced himself not to blow out his breath but to wait patiently for her to answer his question.

She sighed, in that very way his mother always did when she found him impossible. "Very well," she said. "Ramsay has a concern about her. I don't know if I share it, but he says that Simu takes everything a Christian says as something she must believe. As if our objection to that operation is a tenet of the Christian faith. He says that converts often have this overly devout response, thinking any opinion a Christian offers is divine revelation."

Tolliver paused. This was a circumstance that bore thinking about. It called to mind conflicts he had seen among the Muslims in Mombasa, people saying their religion required them to do things, when others of the same faith vehemently disagreed.

"Simu looks up to you. What can you tell me about the facts of her existence?"

That sigh again. "I know only what everyone else knows. That she was rejected by her husband."

"Why would he do that?"

"It seems to me that the Maasai men do whatever they want with the women. She does not have any children. That may be the reason. I daresay she would be better off without a husband to slave for, if it were not for the stigma of having been rejected. And now she has no means to feed herself except the charity of others."

"Tell me more about that," Justin said, though he was not at all sure this line of questioning would yield anything useful.

She looked down at where her wedding ring would have been, had she had one, and then up into his glance. "A woman who has failed to attract a man is a second-class citizen here, just as she is in London or Paris or Boston, or your native York, I imagine. If I were a missionary's wife, instead of a spinster, I would have an established role to play. But I am not. Like all other men, my Mission hierarchy looks down on an unmarried woman like me. It does not matter to them what my capabilities are. I am marginalized, kept in a junior role. The status of a woman like Simu is similar. She was married, as all Maasai girls are, but her husband has sent her away. She has no position. She is shunned and friendless."

It occurred to Justin that a woman in such a position might crave revenge. In which case she might want to kill her husband, but there was no way to connect her with the dead woman. Ruth Van Slyck, on the other hand, was obviously bitter and angry and had a motive to commit the murder that had taken place. "Well, let us focus on the dead woman. Na—Nae—Please pronounce it again for me."

She harrumphed. "Naeku. Nah-eh-coo."

"Thank you. What can you tell me about Naeku's relationships with the others here in the village?"

"Naeku was not from this village," Ruth Van Slyck said. "The *enkamuratani*, the person who performs that disgusting operation, is usually from another settlement."

"Ah, yes. Dr. Ramsay did say that to me this morning." He had her spell the long Maasai word for the dead woman's title and wrote it in his notes so he would put it in his report correctly. 'There is another woman I need to investigate. Her name is Tigisi."

Miss Van Slyck was suddenly disdainful. "That vain little vixen. What is your business with her?"

"Simu told me that she saw Tigisi near the hut where the murder took place. Since the victim was dying when Simu went in—"

"Wait," she said. "Naeku was not dead when Simu found her?"

"She told me that she heard a noise like a moan coming from inside the hut. That was what drew her inside."

"Simu may be somewhere on the grounds right now. She has built herself a little house behind the office." Miss Van Slyck stood up and made for the door.

Tolliver hurried after her, but before she had crossed the compound, Marcal came shouting onto the Mission grounds. Another askari was following him. "Sir. Sir," Marcal called. "This man has come from the railway station. You are urgently wanted there."

Justin's first thought was of Vera. Neither of the askaris showed any alarm, but that did not mean anything. "Is this about my wife?"

Marcal looked at the other askari, who shook his head. "The men have come from Nairobi," the askari said in Swahili. "They want you, Bwana. Immediately, they said."

Ruth Van Slyck had come to his side.

Tolliver took three breaths and tried to force his heart to stop racing. "The men from Nairobi? Magistrate Bonham-Carter? Secretary Hollis? That lot?"

The man looked at him blankly. "Two men that came on the train," he said. "They are with A.D.S. Lovett in the station."

Tolliver turned to Miss Van Slyck. "I am afraid I will have to postpone the rest of our conversation. I will come back when I can."

She smirked. "What is the death of a Maasai woman compared to the official business of the British government?"

He followed the askari, who began to jog along the red dirt road, and he jogged along too, turning over in his mind the paltry information he had so far. The two Maasai women who had been near the hut might have had reasons to kill Naeku, but he could not imagine what they might be. Maasai women evidently approved of the procedure that the *enkamura*—whatever she was—performed. And it was a leap for him to believe that a person who came to Africa to preach the word of God would actually take a life over a tradition. What they were doing to their girls was certainly heinous to any European, but it was not actually against any commandment. Besides, killing that woman would not stop the practice. From what Ramsay had told him, it was prevalent not only among the Kikuyu and the Maasai, but in other areas of Africa, including Somalia. It was barbaric. He saw the need to wipe it out, if they were truly here to bring civilization, but no one in his right mind would choose to fight the practice by killing the women who did it.

He was so lost in his thoughts that at first he did not see the others coming along the road toward him when he was about halfway to the station.

Constance waved. "Justin," she called out, and came near.

"Hold up," he shouted to the askari.

"You've missed the excitement," she said. "A group of officials arrived. There was a band on the platform to welcome them. I imagined them to be very important people, but Finch Hatton says they are not."

Denys had come up behind her. "Except in their own minds," he said with a mocking smile.

Justin shared his opinion of the puffed-up officials of the Empire but did not think it right to say so with the duke and the askari looking on. "They have summoned me. I know not why."

Vera took his arm and drew him away. "What have you found out about the murder?"

He shook his head and smiled ruefully. "I knew you would ask that. Precious little. I was called away before I learned very much at all."

"Will you be long with the district mucky-mucks?"

"I have no idea."

"I received some bad news from the stationmaster."

His skin froze. "Not from your father?"

The slightest flicker of alarm passed in her eyes but then she smiled. "No. No. Papa reports that all is calm. It was from the land officer. He says he is not coming."

"What? Not at all?"

She shrugged. "Not this week. Secretary Hollis gave me the message. When I tried to ask why, he offered no more information, except to say that he had told me all he could."

The askari, standing a few feet away, was waiting for him. "I am afraid I must go," Justin said to Vera. "You have your tea. I'll send a message by seven if I can't return by dinnertime."

"Oh, I hope you won't be that long."

He caressed her cheek. "I hope not." He hurried off.

Vera watched him go and looked up at the sun. It must have been a full hour before teatime.

She caught the others up. "You go ahead," she told them. "I am going to make sure the missionaries are all right."

Gian Lorenzo gave her a look half way between shock and disbelief. "You are not going to go alone past all those sulking Maasai men?"

She tried to laugh off his show of concern. "I was born here. I have spent half my life alone with native people."

Denys took her arm and drew it into the crook of his elbow. His eyes were gleeful. "I have an idea what you are going to do," he said. "We will accompany you and try to make ourselves useful." He started to walk with her toward the Mission, past the still-lounging men in red and blue.

Constance and the duke hurried to walk with them. "What is Vera going to do?" Constance asked. "And how do you know?"

Denys chuckled. "I was there," he said, "two years ago when she struck off into the bush with only a ragtag bunch of her Kikuyu in pursuit of a killer."

"This is a story I must hear," the duke said.

Vera grimaced. "I will let him tell it, but only if Constance promises faithfully never to tell her parents what I did."

Constance made a cross over her heart. "I promise."

Vera went up on tiptoe and whispered in Denys's ear: "Please don't tell them about my brother."

When Justin reached the railway, he was surprised to find the askari leading him not into the station but to a siding just south of it, where two railway cars were left. The first one turned out to be a parlor car where the men who had summoned him were meeting. Before entering, he turned to the askari. "Please tell Sergeant Marcal to send a contingent to keep guard at the Belgian guesthouse."

The boy saluted and ran off, and Tolliver mounted the steps and entered the car. Lovett and the two bigwigs were sitting on wingback leather chairs and sipping gin and tonics as if they were in a club in London or Bombay.

Lovett took his pith helmet off the chair to his right and, with a gesture, invited Tolliver to sit down.

Before doing so, he went around and shook the hands of the other two. He knew Magistrate Bonham-Carter very well from having prosecuted cases before him.

"Mr. Hollis?" he said to the other.

Hollis nodded, but showed no sign of warmth.

Tolliver had seen him only once, a few years ago at the reception to welcome the American president Theodore Roosevelt. Then the man who was now the secretary of Native Affairs had had a very full dark beard and mustache, typical of the end of the last century. Now his facial hair was trimmed and, at the chin, peppered with silver. What made him recognizable were his piercing light brown eyes and his unusually intense air. He was a scholar as well as an official.

"I heard from my wife, sir, what you told her—that the land officer will not be keeping his appointment with us. Do you know why?"

Bonham-Carter interrupted. "Please sit down, Mr. Tolliver. We have important information that affects the events that are about to take place here. Once you hear what we have to say, the reason for postponing any assignments of land in this area will become clear."

Tolliver took the seat next to Lovett, who was staring at the unlit hurricane lamp that hung from the ceiling.

"We want you here," Bonham-Carter continued, "because you are the senior police officer on the scene and because of your reputation for fairness to the natives."

"I do not think that reputation extends to the natives themselves," Tolliver said, thinking with shame about how very wrong things had gone in some of his investigations.

"I was the one who wanted you here," Hollis said. "I was very pleased to know you were in the area. There has been a development in the case before the High Court in Mombasa. The one brought against the Protectorate by the Maasai."

Tolliver looked around at them. Why did they all seem to be focused on him? "I know only what has been in the newspapers, sir. I don't understand any of the technicalities, really. Or what the Maasai expect at this point."

Hollis raised his hand and turned to Bonham-Carter. "Magistrate, would you, as simply as possible, summarize the issues on which the court has pronounced judgment? I am sure we can all use a review, complex as it is."

Lovett stifled a yawn. Tolliver wasn't sure if he was purposely being rude.

Tolliver leaned forward and concentrated on Bonham-Carter, a handsome, slender man with brilliant blue eyes and blond hair so curly it entirely resisted the pomade attempting to keep it in its place. None of his physical characteristics gave the slightest hint of how serious and thorough a man Tolliver knew him to be.

"I will do my best." He reached down into a brown leather satchel that sat on the floor beside his chair. "I have brought along a copy of Mr. Hamilton's judgment."

"When was the judgment delivered?" Lovett surprised Tolliver by asking.

Bonham-Carter flipped to the last page of the sheaf of papers he was holding. "It was 26 May 1913," he said.

Lovett clasped his hands together in front of his chest and leaned back in his chair. "Less than a week ago."

"Yes," the magistrate said. "I, as you know, was not involved in any way in this case, but I have followed it carefully. The Maasai brought the case as a challenge to the Protectorate's decision to move them off this, their northern reserve. The salient issues are these." He held up the thumb of his right hand and began to enumerate them. "In 1904, the administration agreed with the *lybon*—the chief of all the Maasai—that they would move away from the Rift Valley. At that point, they split into—"

Lovett interrupted. "This *lybon*, how did he achieve his position?"

Tolliver didn't know what Lovett was aiming at with his remarks. His attitude was in complete opposition to how he had behaved for the last two days.

Hollis gave Lovett an annoyed look. Bonham-Carter, true to form, answered factually. "The Crown chose the representative of the Maasai tribe."

Lovett sneered. "So our side appointed people we liked and then negotiated with them."

"It would appear so," Bonham-Carter said.

Tolliver was beginning to see that Lovett was taking a position he himself shared, though he would not have expressed it in such an argumentative way. Having done that sort of the thing in the past, he had learned from bitter experience that challenging high officials like these often got one the opposite of what one wanted.

"Please go on," Hollis said.

Bonham-Carter did. "As I was saying, after that first agreement in 1904, the Maasai tribe split into two groups. The agreement gave them the right to an open road between their two reserves and access to certain lands." He looked down and read from the document: "'Whereat we can carry out our circumcision rites and ceremonies in accordance with the customs of our ancestors.' That agreement stayed in place until two years ago, when the administration of the Protectorate decided that it wanted to reunite the Maasai by moving them off this northern reserve and putting them together on lands that are all south of the railway." He held up the sheaf of papers. "It was then they opened this case to stop that happening."

"The decision has been a long time coming," Hollis said, "but the matter was resolved with Mr. Hamilton's judgment last week."

Bonham-Carter went on. "The claims of the Maasai and the administration's defense were both based on technicalities. In the end, Hamilton's decision came down to a fine point of jurisdiction. He quoted a famous case in India." He read again: "'There are considerations into which this court cannot enter. It is sufficient to say that even if a wrong had been done, it is a wrong for which no municipal court of justice can afford a remedy." He looked up at them. "The action was dismissed."

Justin saw immediately how announcing this decision could stir up enormous trouble. "So we are about to tell the Maasai that their grievance has been dismissed on a technicality, which I can barely understand and could never explain to them even in English. God only knows what it would sound like put into a language that has no legal jargon."

Lovett sat up straight. "It is obvious to me," he said in a tone that ignored his inferior position in this group, "that the administration must have known what the verdict would be months before Hamilton's announcement in court. In fact, I guessed this was going to happen because of the position I have been put in here."

Hollis's ears turned red. "I beg your pardon, sir. What can you mean by making such a statement?"

Lovett remained completely impervious to the apparent rage of a man three levels above him in the chain of command. "Sir," he said without a hint of deference, "the decision the magistrate read was signed five days ago. Yet I received orders to prepare my askaris to handle the move more than two months ago. Six weeks ago, thirty men were moved here from Naivasha to reinforce our numbers. At the same time, a company of the King's African Rifles was moved to be within striking distance. All this was done *before* the judgment was made in court. Yet we are to believe this matter was later decided and fairly. If Hamilton had found in favor of the Maasai, none of the preparations would have been at all necessary. It smacks of a kangaroo court, if you ask me."

"No one has asked you, Mr. Lovett," Hollis said. "I suggest you listen to what we have to say and not get so far above yourself."

One might have thought Lovett was risking his position, but Tolliver had known for some time that as insistent as the higher-ups in the administration might be about the deference they deserved, when it came to the police force, they were so hard up for English officers that they might bluster, but they would never force a man out unless he committed an actual crime. He doubted Lovett had had time to learn this. He was challenging them because he had stopped caring if he lost his position. Tolliver did not blame him.

He now understood exactly why the land officer was not coming. The administration would want to complete the evacuation of the Maasai before they started moving settlers into their former territory.

"Given the steps we must next take, Mr. Tolliver," Hollis was now saying, "we will want you to join me and Mr. Lovett in directing matters once the move is under way."

"Begging your pardon, sir," Tolliver said, "District Commissioner Cranford told me that I might have to attend what he called a powwow, but he assured me that I would not be involved in any real trouble. I am traveling with my wife and my sister. To be honest, I am already concerned about them, considering the alarming thing that has happened."

"What alarming thing is that?" Hollis asked.

As delicately as he could, Tolliver described for them the murder of the Maasai woman that morning and its connection to the ritual for the girls. "I was interviewing witnesses when I was called here."

Hollis looked shocked. Evidently Lovett had told them nothing. "Whom do you suspect?" He directed the question to Tolliver.

"It is too early for that, sir," he answered. "Mr. Bonham-Carter has read from the 1904 agreement a statement about the importance the Maasai attach to the land where they perform their rituals, and they were about to be driven from this place. Evidently they expected to have to leave because, as I understand it, they advanced the day of the rite so that it might take place before the move."

Tolliver was becoming more and more certain that there was a relationship between the move of the Maasai, the ritual, and the death of Naeku.

Though in the past Vera had involved herself in Justin's investigations, and to good effect, she felt a bit guilty about poking into this one now. He was being so lovely—taking it upon himself to defend the missionaries and still sensitive to her anxiety about the land selection. He hadn't even scolded her for siding with Constance about the Italian. She wanted to keep him sweet. If he caught her pushing in on his work, he would turn all cross.

She had thought to characterize her visit to the mission as a social call on her father's colleagues, but she had failed to get that fiction past Finch Hatton. Justin would never fall for it. She had none of the typical British woman's aptitude for subtlety and beguilement. Everyone seemed to be able to read her mind.

The Maasai men along the sunbaked road, handsome and chic, but as ever emotionless in their aspect, did not seem to take any notice of them. But Vera was certain they watched every single movement.

When she and her little group arrived at the Mission compound, she asked the others to wait for her outside, to which they readily agreed once they saw that there was a bench under a flame tree with a gorgeous view of the lake.

She found Arthur Ramsay where her father would have been on the last day of the month, poring over the ledgers in the Mission office. He looked behind her when she entered, and seeing she was alone, visibly relaxed. "Can I offer you a cup of tea?"

"No, thank you. We will be taking tea at the guesthouse shortly."

"We?"

"Constance, Finch Hatton, and the duke are out gazing at the wondrous panorama." She indicated the accounts open before him. "While you, I see, are slaving away on this gorgeous afternoon."

"I am pitching in for these people until they get a replacement. It doesn't take much. Miss Van Slyck's work is always perfect."

"Couldn't she pay the accounts, if she is capable?"

"I am sure you are right, but her superiors in Nairobi felt it might be best to have a man oversee what she was doing."

Vera might have argued the point. Until her death her mother had always been the better of her parents with figures. But just now Vera had other fish to fry. "My husband has been called to a meeting at the railway station. It seems there is a pretty high-level committee here to oversee the move that is to take place."

"I suppose word has come from the court." Disgust had entered his glance. She knew very well the dicey relationship between the Crown's administration and the missionaries. The former said they were here to "protect" the natives—protect them from interfering with Britain's goals in the area, more like. The latter sought to bring the local people to Christ, but they talked almost exclusively about combating slavery by making the natives "fellow Christians."

"It surprises me that you have not voiced any opposition to the move. Knowing your views on preserving tribal rights, I would have expected you to be vehemently against this land grab."

He shook his head and began to parry her thought in a tone more appropriate to a sermon than to a friendly conversation. On some level he seemed to be defending his point of view to her, as he would have to her father. "I am not entirely against this move," he said. "One can argue that the Maasai will have an easier time preserving their way of life if they are all together on one continuous reserve. Shortly before I arrived in the Protectorate they were moved and split into two groups, which is how they have remained for nearly ten years. Wouldn't it be better for them to consolidate themselves?"

"But isn't it the Maasai themselves who appealed to the court to keep to the old agreement and remain split into two?" She could not resist parroting a phrase she had heard him say many times in conversations with her parents. "After all, if we are here to protect them, we must protect their right to continue to live where they have for centuries." She shooed away a fleeting thought that she and Justin were about to choose land to take as their own.

A wry smile crossed his features. "Unity has always been my preference. Miss Van Slyck, who after all works directly with the Maasai, convinced me that this move is for their benefit."

It was time to lead him into talking about the dead woman. "I wanted to ask—"

The door behind her swung open.

"It *would* be better if they moved," Miss Van Slyck said as she entered.

"Oh," Vera said, a bit shocked by her sudden entrance. She wondered how long the woman had been behind the door listening. Obviously, Ruth had heard their last exchange.

"Pardon me for barging in," she said without a hint of regret. "I saw your friends out under the tree and they told me you were here."

"Yes," Vera said with more warmth than she felt. "My husband is engaged this afternoon, and I thought I would stop by for a visit. I have known Dr. Ramsay since I was a child."

"She says that to make me feel old," Ramsay said.

Miss Van Slyck pulled up a chair. "To get back to what you were discussing," she said, all business, "the Maasai have an ulterior motive for wanting to keep to these lands."

"What could that be?" Vera had always thought the Maasai were completely straightforward.

"They have always practiced that revolting ceremony on this land. Therefore they say this land has special significance. I saw in the newspaper that the Maasai claimed in their lawsuit that this is sacred land to them. It seems they will fight anything that in the least way weakens that tradition, if you can call it such."

Vera could think of several things wrong with this line of thought. "Surely you don't you think that, if they are moved from here, they will simply give up the practice?"

"Of course not," she replied. "But it might weaken the pull of the past if the place were removed from their control."

That circumstance seemed a shot in the dark to Vera. She turned back to Dr. Ramsay. "You have always been one to defend the Africans' right to live in their traditional ways."

"Don't tell me you approve of their horrific practice." Ruth Van Slyck's voice was filled with outrage.

"No, of course not," Vera said. "I grew up among the Kikuyu. I knew they had a ceremony for girls. For all I knew, it involved dressing them up and fêting them. My friends disappeared for a while afterward. My mother and my Kikuyu nanny told me they were preparing to become good wives. I imagined they were getting cooking lessons and learning where babies come from. Which they already knew."

They continued to look at her as if she had to prove to them that she was on their side.

"I think it's horrible. I truly do." Her voice was becoming shrill. She did her best to lower it. "I also know that if it has been their custom for such a long time, and if not doing it makes a girl a complete outcast, it will be extremely difficult to make them stop. Belonging is everything to them." She had more than an inkling of what being an outcast would mean to a Kikuyu girl. She was one of sorts herself and it hurt her intensely, and she was supposed to be an independent-thinking Scot. She imagined being shunned would kill them. They would be homeless. They might starve to death.

Ramsay glowered at her. "Not doing it may make them outcasts, but doing it inflicts unspeakable pain, puts them at risk of infections. It can cause infertility, and in some cases even death. Many, many suffer their entire lives. Some, quite a few, suffer for years and ultimately die of the infections. I am a doctor. I cannot let such a thing happen to human beings right under my nose and do nothing about it."

"In my opinion," Ruth Van Slyck said, "tribal customs almost always give great advantages to the men and none to the women. Custom says that all the heavy work must be done by the women, that it is a slight to a man's honor to carry water or build his own house. Where is the justice in that?"

"I have to agree with you," Vera said. She thought to point out that European customs might be different, but they were also unkind to women, not in such a nasty physical infliction, but in many harmful ways. They would think such an opinion jejune.

Shadows were lengthening outside the window. She stood up. "I am sure my friends have had enough of gazing at the lake. I think I must go."

Ramsay rose. "I hope you will come back for more visits while you are here. How long do you expect to stay?"

"I am not sure," Vera said, which was precisely the truth.

Ruth Van Slyck looked up. "Your husband believes that I killed Naeku, doesn't he?"

Vera found the very notion shocking, but now that the woman had said it, she could not stop herself thinking it was true.

Having had no breakfast and little by way of luncheon, Tolliver was ravenously hungry when he sat down to tea. Everyone he had interacted with all day, except for the askaris, had already eaten before he got there. The askaris had been glad to share their rations with him, but he did not think it right to take too much of their food from them.

Madame Gillet's little cakes and sandwiches, served in her lovely front parlor, were miraculously sophisticated and delicious considering that she had prepared them in the midst of a vast wilderness, but they were elegantly delicate and understated. His hunger would not have been satisfied if he had eaten them all. As it was, his nanny would have been appalled at the speed with which he had consumed more than his share. When they were all eaten up, he stood up greedy for more.

Denys stood too. "I am going to take the ladies out on the veranda to watch the sunset," he announced.

The duke was looking at the ladies as if waiting for them to leave before he spoke.

Tolliver had planned to take the men aside to talk to them about the possibility of danger and what they should do next. Vera rose and looked at him as if she wanted him to come and be alone with her. She could make such a thought clear to him with nothing but her eyes. She was not after their typical afternoon lie-down. He could see that, too.

Denys, then, in his typical forthright fashion, suggested the thing they all might think improper, but the only one that made sense. "It's time for us to stay right here and talk over what we are going to do in light of what may happen over the next several days."

"Including the ladies?" the duke said with an expression just shy of aghast.

Vera nodded agreement and marched back to the chair she had vacated. "Yes," she said, "including the ladies. It was precisely what I wanted to suggest to Justin." She looked to the duke. "We are grown women, my dear Gian Lorenzo. We will not faint if we face the facts of our situation."

"No indeed," Constance said, but her glance at the duke sought his approval.

"Let us be modern then," he said with only a tinge of disapproval.

Denys went and asked Madame Gillet to bring more tea.

"You had better start things off, darling," Vera said to Justin, once they were settled. "You are the one with the latest information."

Tolliver looked to his sister. In the entire course of their lives, they had never discussed anything remotely this unpleasant. It was considered very bad form for a gentleman to say such things in front of a lady, and he had spent his whole life feeling protective toward her. He refilled his teacup in case he needed a graceful reason to pause, and then he began with the results of the trial in the High Court in Mombasa.

He took a sip and crept up gingerly on the subject of the Maasai ritual and what relationship it might have to the death of Naeku. After he had hemmed and hawed, his sister spoke up.

"You needn't be so discreet about what they do to their women," she said. Her voice was determined and strong, even if she was blushing near to purple. "It's perfectly horrid and must be stopped."

Tolliver looked from her to the duke, who was gazing at her in disbelief. It surprised Tolliver to realize that it would profoundly disappoint him if Gian Lorenzo gave up on Constance because of her ability to talk about such unpalatable matters. When the duke glanced at him, he looked on his sister and smiled with pride. He had meant it to send a message to her beau, but he realized that he was genuinely proud that she was not the shrinking violet she had been brought up to be.

"Well," Justin said, "I am not sure why, but I can't give up the idea that there might be a connection between the moving of the Maasai and the death of that woman."

Vera was nonplussed. Justin's instincts as a policeman were ordinarily quite accurate, a talent in which she knew he took great pride. He was frustrated by the compromised form of justice the administrators meted out, but all that mattered little at the moment. She put her doubts aside and reported what she had learned in her conversation with Dr. Ramsay and Miss Van Slyck.

He grunted his exasperation. "I might have known you would put your nose in."

Denys came to her defense. "We kept close to her, and I must say, this focus on the dead woman is all well and good, but what about the trouble that might explode when the court's decision is announced. Do we really want these ladies to be in the midst of that?"

"I don't want to be," Vera exclaimed. She would not have felt this way in the past, but she was someone's mother now—a thought that rekindled the longing that imposed itself on her every few hours.

Tolliver reported what he knew. "Bonham-Carter is going back to Nairobi. Hollis is meeting with the officers of the King's African Rifles and then will go on and bring the news to the *lybon*."

"The *lybon*?" Constance and the duke asked in unison.

"The chief," Vera and Justin responded, also in unison. They all grinned at the coincidence.

Justin went on. "Evidently the *lybon* and his tribal council were the plaintiffs in the court case, so they will not be happy, but they are very unlikely to launch into precipitous action. Such tribal decisions are taken very slowly."

"My father calls it moving on African time," Vera said. "I was born here and it still makes me impatient."

"It seems they are cautious," Gian Lorenzo said, "and in this case caution is called for on all sides, don't you agree?" He looked around the table, where all heads were nodding.

"My guess," Tolliver said, "is that it will take at least until day after tomorrow before the announcement of the move is made and at least several days after that until the first groups are made to move out."

The duke's brow knitted. "But what about those men who have been standing along the road under the trees?"

"They always do that," Vera said. "It is what all the tribal men do unless they are hunting or fighting one another—which they don't do all that much anymore."

"The famous *Pax Britannica*," Denys said with a smirk.

Vera pressed on. "The Kikuyu men now work for the settlers. The Maasai refuse to do any such thing. The young warriors, the *ilmurran*, go on cattle-raiding parties once in a while, but otherwise they do what their male ancestors have always done—just hang about."

"They look dangerous to me," the duke said.

"They want you to think that," Finch Hatton said. "I will ask Kinuthia to find out if they are actually up to something."

Justin put a stop to the chitchat. "At any rate, I've been told I will have to stay until the move begins. I think we should plan on getting the rest of you away sometime tomorrow."

"I don't want to leave you," Vera said, but she knew she must go.

"In what direction will the Maasai be going?" Denys asked.

"To land adjacent to the reserve on the other side of the railway. South and a bit west," Tolliver answered.

Denys opened his hands as if he meant to speak the obvious. "Gian Lorenzo and I can take the ladies east and back to the Scottish Mission. They can enjoy the sights along the way."

"No," Vera said, "if I must go, I want to take the train. Walking on safari is lovely, but I want to get home as quickly as possible."

Constance looked a bit crestfallen until Gian Lorenzo said, "In that case, you ladies still must not travel alone. Finch Hatton and I will escort you and Lady Constance on the train."

"What about the safari boys and all the equipment?" Constance asked.

"They can trek back," Denys said. "Kinuthia and Gian Lorenzo's tracker can oversee them."

"We can put them on the train as well," the duke said.

"But that would cost a fortune," Vera blurted out. And then groaned at her own faux pas.

Finch Hatton laughed merrily. "You must forgive her, Gian Lorenzo. She is Scottish, you see. Spending money is against their religion."

They all laughed, Vera as heartily as any of them, grateful as she was for Denys's covering her bungle.

In bed that night, Vera and Justin felt none of the passion that had consumed them the night before. They clung to each other and whispered about how they did not want to separate, although they must.

"The down-train will not leave until after midnight tomorrow," she said. "We will have all the day to be together."

"Yes," he said, though he knew his time would very likely be taken up with police duties.

It was just at dawn that Tolliver learned how very prescient that thought had been.

Having more napped than slept deeply, he had barely begun to dream when he was awakened by a banging on the front door just below his and Vera's room. He was up in a flash and saw out the window an askari's red fez. He opened the casement. Vera had come to his side.

"What is it?"

"A murder, sir. You are wanted at once."

Tolliver closed the window, went to the basin, and quickly washed his face.

"Who could it be?" Vera asked.

He was pulling on his underdrawers. "I have no idea, but two murders in as many days? This is very bad." He wished he had his uniform. It would make him feel more up to the challenge. He needed his pistol. And Kwai Libazo at his side. Why was Lovett taking so long to bring Kwai up from Naivasha? He tucked in his shirt and buttoned his trousers. "Yesterday I asked Lovett to send for Kwai. I hope he arrived on last night's train."

"Oh, I would feel so much better if—" Vera stopped. She would not express her fears for Justin's safety. She knew he would hate that. She started to dress too.

"Would you do me a favor, dearest?" he asked.

"Anything," she said.

"Stay very close to the others. Keep Constance always with you. I will come back to check on you during the day, as many times as I can, but you must remain right here, preferably on the back veranda, where the safari boys can be at hand. And always near Denys and the duke."

She grinned at him. "There was a time when staying near Denys was the last thing you would have asked of me."

He did not smile. "Promise me."

She kissed him. "I promise. And you must promise to take every care of yourself."

"I will be fine."

She kissed him again. "You are fine. Very fine."

He went out into the corridor and found Denys and the duke halfway up the stairs. "Did I hear there has been another murder? Can I be helpful?" the duke asked.

Tolliver went past them and on down. "Yes. Guard my sister and Vera. Don't leave them for a minute."

"You can count on us," Denys said.

He found the askari still waiting outside the front door. Madame and Monsieur Gillet were nowhere in sight.

The askari started to move down the road as soon as Tolliver joined him. There were no Maasai men under the trees.

"Who was killed?" Tolliver demanded.

"The missionary lady."

Tolliver had to stop and take a breath to dispel his disbelief. "Truly? Are you sure?"

"Yes, sir. Her houseboy found her this morning in her bed."

Tolliver ran.

The door to Ruth Van Slyck's cottage was guarded by six askaris. Arthur Ramsay and Lovett stood just inside. Ramsay gave Tolliver an angry, accusatory look, as if the woman's death could somehow be chalked up to him.

"She is in there," was all Lovett managed to say. He looked as if he'd be running for the bushes any second.

Ruth Van Slyck's body lay across the bed. She was clad in a chaste white muslin nightdress. Her hair, which had always been pulled back in a tight chignon during the day, was loose, thick, a beautiful rich brown. Large bruises—black, blue, deep red—ringed her neck.

Ramsay entered the room behind Tolliver. He came in and drew up the gown. Her legs were also covered with bruises. "I examined her. I thought whatever monster did this might have—" He stopped.

"Might have what?"

"I thought she might have been executed for her opposition to female circumcision. I thought they might have cut her there."

Tolliver's stomach turned in revulsion. He now understood Lovett's repugnance. "And?" he asked, though he did not want to hear.

"She was not, but that does not mean they did not kill her for that reason."

"Was she molested?"

"Do you mean raped?" The man seemed to take a nasty pleasure in saying things in the most shocking way.

"That is what I am asking," Tolliver said as evenly as he could manage.

"No," Ramsay said, his voice less strident. "She died a virgin."

Tolliver did not know why, but it struck him as almost martyrdom that a woman who had never exercised her own sexuality might have died trying to preserve the sexual integrity of young girls.

"Do you know when this might have happened?"

"No. She was cold when I arrived, so some time before midnight."

"What time did you come to her this morning?"

Ramsay stared at Tolliver, as ever his sense of affront on a hair trigger.

Tolliver waited.

"At about six, I imagine," Ramsay answered after a moment and a scowl. "The sky was barely light."

"Do you know when anyone might last have seen her?"

"I last saw her at dinner. She gives me dinners whenever I am here. Afterwards, I went to my room, just there." He pointed out the window to a small cottage about fifty yards away, behind the Mission office. "I read until about eleven."

"Did you hear anything strange in the night?"

"No. Only the usual insect sounds and small animals rustling in the bushes. I soon dozed off."

Tolliver remembered how—out in the bush—Ramsay had often reported hearing hippos prowling or cats growling in the night. The duke had remarked on what a light sleeper Ramsay was.

"She did not die easily," Ramsay said. He indicated the bruises on her legs and neck. "She was beaten *before* she died. And whoever killed her tried to choke her. The bruises on her neck were made when her heart was still beating. As were the ones on her legs."

The brutal pictures this brought to mind were too disturbing. "Surely if she were being beaten, she would have screamed, moaned, called out."

"I would have thought so."

"Unless the assailant had her by the throat," Tolliver said, thinking out loud.

"She would not have been able to make more than a soft grunting noise while being choked like that."

Tolliver pictured it. "But," he said, "no one could have been beating her on the legs and holding her by the throat at the same time. He looked to Ramsay. "But you heard nothing?"

Ramsay held out his palms and raised his shoulders. "Nothing. Or I would have come running."

Tolliver reached out and lightly touched the white sheet that hung to the floor. "That...mm...that can only mean there was more than one assailant. One who had her by the throat and one who was beating her on the legs."

"I see what you mean."

"It is the only circumstance that explains the facts." Tolliver's eyes went to the bright sunshine coming in through the window. There had been enough moonlight to make things in this room visible in the night. "It was the houseboy who found her, not you?"

"He came shouting for me," Ramsay said. "Ruth had very regular habits. She rose at five thirty, went directly to the chapel to pray. Raila—that is her houseboy's name—would then come in to fix her breakfast while she was at prayer. She never departed from that daily routine. This morning he watched for her to leave so he could go in, but she did not come out. When too much time went by, he came in and called for her. Then he found her."

Tolliver took out his handkerchief, unfolded it, and placed it over Ruth Van Slyck's face.

"God rest her soul," Ramsay whispered.

Tolliver knew that his own soul would not rest until he had found the persons who had done this heinous thing. Given the lack of noise and the condition of the body—the bruises on her neck and her legs—he was convinced that there had been at least two assailants. He also knew that, if it had been some of those Maasai men who had been lounging about under the trees all the day before, it would be next to impossible to identify exactly which ones they were.

He went out. The sun was up and reflected on the surface of the shimmering lake. Africa did this—showed itself to be glorious and terribly, terribly dangerous at the very same moment.

"Did Sergeant Kwai Libazo arrive from Naivasha?" he asked the askari next to the cottage door. If anyone here was going to be truly helpful in investigating this murder and the one of yesterday, it would be Kwai.

"No, Bwana. No one has come from Naivasha."

Tolliver was annoyed. "Where is Marcal?"

The askari stood at attention and looked straight ahead. "The big men went to talk to the *lybon*. Marcal has gone with them, Bwana."

"Call me sir."

"Yes, sir."

"A.D.S. Lovett?"

"He is in his bungalow, Bw—sir."

Tolliver turned to Ramsay. "You are the only doctor hereabouts. I will need you to write a statement about the condition of the body. After that, I can release it for burial. How will you take care of it?"

"Simu, the Maasai woman who has helped Ruth here at the Mission, will help me."

"The Maasai are not like the Kikuyu? They will handle a dead body?"

"I am not sure, but I trust that Simu, who is a convert here, will help me."

"Very well. Please write that description for me, be as specific as possible."

"I am a doctor," Ramsay said.

"Yes, I know. I am going to find Lovett." Tolliver marched off. The askaris had come for him, not for Lovett, when Ruth Van Slyck's body was discovered. Every reason Tolliver could imagine for that led him to conclude that Lovett had won very little respect among his men. His drinking would certainly not put him in good stead with them. Yet yesterday, at the meeting with the Nairobi contingent, he had shown a much more upstanding side of himself and the courage to speak his mind to those with the power to punish him. Perhaps there was more mettle in the man than he showed to his underlings.

Tolliver had seen that sort of dichotomy in the army when he served in South Africa—how men could be very different looking up the chain of command than when they were looking down it. Some men there had shown an obsequious side of themselves to their superiors and turned autocratic and bullying to their men. Lovett was looking like the exact opposite: weak in leadership and overbearing with the brass.

Tolliver found him in his bungalow, shaving.

"Come in," he said. He wiped his razor on a towel and continued to scrape the blade along the left side of his jaw. He showed no sign of dismay over what had happened on his watch.

"Have you heard about Miss Van Slyck?" Tolliver asked.

"Yes. Ramsay came for me just as dawn was breaking. I sent him to you."

Tolliver could not hide his resentment. "This is your territory!" he fairly shouted.

Lovett's reflection in the mirror gave him an accusing stare. "Listen, my friend," he said with all the warmth of the ice cap of Kilimanjaro, "two years ago you went off trekking through the bush on a wild-goose chase, supposedly after a killer, and left me to hold the fort in Nairobi when I was as green as grass, and with no one but bloody Cranford to help me. I made a shambles of everything I touched. For punishment they have stuck me here with no one to help me. I've had to amputate a man's leg. I have had to deliver a settler woman's baby after her husband was killed by a hippo. You are the one everyone says is the African Sherlock Holmes. So now I am sticking you with these murders. It's your turn to clean up *my* mess."

Tolliver's brain was boiling with outrage and excuses to counter what Lovett had said. His mouth opened and closed, trying to let fly his defense at such accusations. But an insistent voice drowned out any words that came to mind. His memories of what he had done were too vivid to ignore. Jodrell had been away. District Superintendent Cranford had tried to prevent Tolliver from following the person he was sure was a killer. When Cranford claimed that Tolliver could not be spared from Nairobi, he had vouched that the newly arrived Lovett was up to the job. It had never occurred to Tolliver what pain he might be inflicting on Lovett in the process.

Tolliver watched him rinsing his razor and washing his face of the remains of the shaving soap. "You are right," Tolliver said.

"I owe it to you to do what I can here and now." He was relieved that Vera could not hear him betraying his promise to her.

Lovett dried his face and hung his towel on his shaving stand. He offered no forgiveness, but his expression had calmed.

"I need another man to work with me," Tolliver said. "Have you called for Kwai Libazo as I asked? He was my sergeant for over two years. He would be very useful here at this time."

"I sent for him and they told me he was off duty at the moment. You were lucky to have him. Except for Marcal, my lot here are ignoramuses." Lovett had finished buttoning up his shirt and buckling his belt. "Since Sergeant Marcal is the only one worth his salt, I had to send him with Hollis. There is no one else."

Tolliver bit his lip against giving voice to his conviction: it was up to Lovett to find askaris with the potential and to train them. He was not capable of leading his own men, and now Tolliver needed to lead him, so he said something conciliatory instead. "My first choice, of course, would be to work with you on this. Between the two of us, we ought to be able to gather enough information to get to the bottom of it." In reality, Tolliver sincerely doubted they would get anywhere, even if they had Sherlock Holmes himself on the case. But saying that would make this situation worse.

Lovett had donned and was buttoning his uniform jacket. "I have never solved a murder in my life," he said.

Tolliver picked up his hat and stood. "Wait until you see how mundane most of what we will have to do is. The way to go about it is not at all as glamorous as the general public think."

Lovett placed his pith helmet under his arm. "My houseboy will have a proper breakfast ready. Will you join me? I am sure you had no time for food when you were called this morning."

Much as Tolliver had been enjoying Madame Gillet's delicious pastries for the past couple of mornings, he relished the eggs and sausage and, though tinned, quite passable beans at the table on the patio behind Lovett's bungalow.

While they ate they made a plan. Lovett would begin by finding out what he could from the natives about movements around the Mission in the night, taking with him the one askari left there who spoke both Maasai and English. Tolliver would go to the Mission and take up where he had left off yesterday when he was called to the station. At that point, he had been on his way to investigate the murder of the *enkamuratani* Naeku. Now he needed to find out what Simu knew about the movements around Ruth Van Slyck's house since sundown last evening. He and Lovett agreed to compare notes in an hour and a half and then to collect Ramsay's report. After that they would together interrogate Raila, Van Slyck's houseboy.

Vera's heart was pounding as she sped along the road between the guesthouse and the Mission. Denys and Kinuthia were keeping up with her. The duke and Constance had stayed behind to organize the rest of the porters while they broke camp and packed up to take the down-train at two thirty in the morning.

Vera's insides were seething. When Justin had left her less than two hours ago, he had not told her anything about the second victim. She had imagined another death in the Maasai village although it had seemed unlikely. When it came to tribal life, animals killed people. People almost never did.

Then an African woman had come to the Gillets' back door and told Madame that Ruth Van Slyck had been killed. *Shocking* was the only word to describe such an event. One awful theory chased another through Vera's mind: the person who had killed Naeku had also killed Ruth. But why? Ruth had killed herself. But that seemed absurd. She was such a prayerful woman. She would never succumb to despair. Besides, the messenger had said murder. Murder it likely was. Ruth was not a likeable woman. She was prickly and judgmental. Vera felt a twinge of guilt having found her so sour and annoying. But no one would murder a person for being annoying.

Dr. Ramsay was the only person who had openly disagreed with Ruth Van Slyck. She had heard them shouting at each other about what was the best way to put a stop to the practice they both abhorred. Arthur could have lost his temper with Ruth. But Arthur Ramsay was a good man. She had known him since she was a child. He had come many times to visit her father. At fourteen, the budding woman in her had seen in him the picture of a dashing hero, a soldier of God. She could not believe he would do violence to another person, much less to a close ally in the fields of the Lord.

As she approached the Mission compound, she heard Justin call out to her from her left, across a field. He was approaching from a path that led to the police lines, where members of the force were billeted. Oliver Lovett was with him.

Denys came to her side. Kinuthia stood off, as was his wont. Justin jogged to them. As he neared, he threw Denys a reproachful look. "Has something happened? What are you doing here?"

Vera answered, "Just as we finished breakfast and were going out to organize the safari boys, a woman named Simu came to tell Madame Gillet what had happened to Miss Van Slyck. It is appalling. I felt I had to come."

"Nothing has been established but that she was attacked in the night. Mr. Lovett and I are here to begin our investigation in earnest. I was about to look for that woman Simu and find out what she knows."

"I spoke to her only briefly," Vera said. "She is still at the guesthouse. She helps Madame Gillet with the housecleaning. She seemed reluctant to talk, but the Maasai are often reticent."

"I will walk with you and speak to her there." Justin held out his hand, indicating the way back to the guesthouse.

Vera took a step in the other direction. "I want to express my condolences to Dr. Ramsay."

Justin gripped her arm. "No, darling. He is writing a report on the condition of—" He paused. He did not want to get into the details with her, much less utter the word *corpse*. He might discuss the case superficially with her in private, but he was not going to treat his wife as less than a proper lady in front of Finch

Hatton. "Ramsay's report is essential. It is best for such a thing to be written before the witness has too much time to think about it."

"Witness!" Vera's dark eyes widened in shock. "Was he there when it happened?"

He took a few steps up the road. "No. No. He is writing a doctor's report. Please, darling. When I have spoken to Simu, I myself will bring you back so that you can speak to Ramsay."

She relented.

Finch Hatton did not say a word as they walked back, which was entirely unlike him.

Tolliver asked Madame Gillet's permission to interview her maid in the house, but then suddenly he remembered that Simu spoke only Maasai.

"What is it?" Madame Gillet asked. "You look vexed."

He toyed with the idea of asking her to translate, but it was certainly not a proper request to make of one's landlady, and her interpretations might very well be tainted by sympathy for Simu. Or antipathy to her, for that matter. "I have to bring in a translator."

"Oh, no, Monsieur. She speaks English."

"Really?" The word came out a question, but there was no reason to doubt Madame. It prickled his suspicions that Simu had lied to him. He would get to the bottom of that.

They found Simu in a back room, ironing bed linens. He took her into the small parlor. She was used to the house, having cleaned it for he knew not how long. He wanted her in a place where his authority would put her out of feeling comfortable. After being married to Vera for nearly two years, he had learned from her not to lord his white authority over anyone, but it was absolutely necessary at this moment. Without his uniform as his badge of authority, he needed another way to intimidate her. He sat her on one of Madame Gillet's upholstered chairs, the likes of which he was sure she had never occupied in her life. He stood and looked down at her.

"You speak English, I hear," he said without preamble.

She nodded but did not utter a response.

"Yet you denied that the first time I questioned you. Do you know," he demanded, "that it is a crime to lie to a policeman?"

She looked shocked and as if she might be sick, but remained silent.

"Why did you lead me to believe you spoke no English?" He made it sound as if she had committed a major felony.

"My English badly," she said. "Fright me."

Very well, he thought. It was possible that she feared saying the wrong thing in a foreign tongue. He certainly knew how that felt. He fished Lovett's notebook out of his pocket. It occurred to him that he had it and Lovett did not. "I will speak simply," he said in a more moderated tone. "I want to ask you questions about both of the killings that have taken place here in these past two days." He paused. "Do you understand what I am saying?"

"Yes."

"Do you understand why I am asking you these questions?"

"No."

"You were the one who found Naeku's body?"

"Yes."

"You're a witness—a person who saw a crime. This is why you must answer my questions."

She nodded.

"Can you tell me why you went into the hut where Naeku was?"

"Saw Tigisi go way. With cloth in hands. Heard Naeku—" She made a moaning sound.

"Tell me about what Tigisi was carrying. What kind of cloth?"

"*Enkamuratani* get prize. Uh, present. For work." She swallowed and grimaced as if she did not want to speak of the operation. Surely she must have had the same done to her when she was a girl. "Naeku get many present by girl fathers."

"And they were wrapped in that cloth?"

"Cloth was big present."

"What were the others?"

"Many jewelry. Many for the here, the here, the here." She touched her earlobes, her wrists, her neck, her ankle. "Some nickel. Some were"—she wrinkled her brow, trying to think of the word—"*shaba*." She used the Swahili word for "brass," and in a tone an Englishwoman would have reserved for pearls or gold.

"Inside, presents not there. Naeku dying. Die while I see."

'Tell me exactly what you saw."

"Naeku on bed, bleeding." She moved her upper body like a person writhing. She gestured a knife to her chest. "Bleeding."

"And you watched her. You did not try to get help."

"She made noise." She raised her chin and made a gurgling sound. "She was—" She let her arms and her upper body go limp. "I run to Miss Ruth. To bring. For Ramsay Bwana."

"Why not for the other women in the village?"

"Ramsay Bwana is doctor. From England. England doctor are better."

He had to agree with her there. He made some notes.

"Did you think that Dr. Ramsay could help Naeku? Make her better?"

She was silent for a moment. Then she said, "Ruth Memsaab pray. I pray."

And shouted and screamed as Tolliver recalled both Ramsay and Lovett saying.

He made a note. "Let us talk about Ruth Memsaab. Were you in her cottage last evening?"

"No."

"Where were you?"

"In hut." She tapped her fingers on her chest to indicate the hut was hers. "Behind chapel of Mission."

"Do you live on the Mission grounds then?"

"Yes."

"Why do you not live in the Maasai village with your people?"

"I am Christian now. I live with Christian."

Tolliver could not recall seeing other converts around the Mission grounds. And Ramsay or Miss Van Slyck, one of them had said this woman had been rejected by her husband. "Are there many Christians living there?"

"Only me and Ruth Memsaab. And Ramsay Bwana when he here." She looked a bit crestfallen for a moment. "Warner Bwana went away. Warner Memsaab have died in cold place she not like. Boston." She pronounced it Bosstone. "Warner Memsaab very kind to me." Tears glinted in her eyes. "Her one child die. My one child die." She closed her eyes and was silent.

He waited a moment. His next logical question would be hurtful. He put it off. "Did you hear anything or see anything in the night? Anything that might have been someone going to harm Miss Van Slyck?"

"My hut in back, near trees. Hear birds, monkeys, little animals. Not like silence."

"So you did not hear any strange sounds?"

"Bad men always silent," she said in a tone that condemned them.

"Why did your husband reject you?" He said it as if it was just another question, which of course it was not. And she took it as the intrusion it was, biting her lower lip and clenching her jaw.

He waited a moment and then forced the point. "You must answer me." He kept his gaze on her eyes.

She stiffened her neck and gave her head a prideful tilt. "I have tell you. One child. She die. Good wife give children."

Constance made for her brother as soon as he stepped out onto the guesthouse veranda. Gian Lorenzo was at the rear of the encampment behind the property. He and Finch Hatton were seeing to securing the guns and ammunition. This was her chance to speak with her brother alone.

"Hello, Consty. Where is Vera?" he asked.

"She is upstairs, reading I think. You were with that woman for a long time. Did she have anything useful to say?"

"I don't discuss my cases while I am working on them," he said, as if he were putting off a journalist from *The Leader*. "I am sorry," he said. "I am distracted. There is too much happening."

"I am about to distract you even further. She watched his expression, certain he would anticipate her subject. He did. But instead of the disapproval she feared, he gave her a warm smile.

"I love him," she said. "I am certain of it."

"There will be a lot of hurdles for you both to jump. I am sorry you have to suffer them, and I don't want a row with Father and John, as there certainly will be."

"Gian Lorenzo and I know that. We are prepared to do whatever is necessary. I want you, I need you to be on my side, Justin." Her eyes glistened.

He put a hand on her forearm. "Religion is going to come into it. Father will object without really thinking about why, and John will have apoplexy, to appease the archbishop's daughter."

"I fear John's response more than Papa's." John had always been stricter and more disapproving of her than her parents. It was the worst possible trait in an older brother—taking everything his sister did as either a boost to or a smear on his own reputation.

"The only thing he cares about more than staying on Eleanor's good side is money and social position," Justin said, and then grinned, just as he had when, as children, they put one over on John. "Well, Gian Lorenzo is a duke and a royal one at that."

"And quite rich." She laughed.

"That too," Justin said. "I hope in this case John will run true to form and prefer money to all else." He was not at all sure John would succumb to the title or the wealth, since both were unimpressively Italian, but Justin could not help consoling his sister.

"I thought that about money making the difference, but I was not sure. That you agree gives me greater hope." She pecked him on the check. "You will help us convince John and Father then?"

"Yes, I will, not that my weighing in on your side will actually help when it comes to John."

"It helps me that you will try. You seemed so against it at first."

"I was when I first saw the way his eyes lit up every time he saw you, but I have seen how he is with you. I have watched the kind of man he is. How do you expect to handle the question of religion?"

"I will convert. To tell you the truth, it does not make any difference at all to me. None of our family has ever been all that devout until John married Eleanor, and he only does it to please his mightiness the Archbishop of Gloucester."

"I think with Father and John even religion has more to do with social standing than anything else. Let's hope Mother will have an influence." His opinion would help when it came to Mama. She didn't always approve of him to his face, but she was his greatest source of support when it came to Papa and John. Still, he hoped he was not giving Consty false hopes, but he could not bring himself to wipe away her smile.

She hugged him. Over her shoulder he saw Gian Lorenzo watching them from a distance.

"I want to have the kind of love you and Vera have," she said. "That is more important to me than any other consideration."

"That is what I want for you too. How could I oppose you? I needed no family approval to marry Vera. If a son needed that, they would not have given it me. Well, they might have once she became an heiress, but I had decided to marry her well before she learned her grandfather's fortune would come to her."

"Whenever you were not present, John and Eleanor were so rude to Vera when you were at home on your honeymoon."

His skin prickled. "What did they say?"

She colored. "I thought she must have told you or I would not have said."

The dislike he carried for his prig of a brother chilled into icy anger. "She told me nothing of it."

Constance's lashes fluttered. "Oh, just a lot of nonsense. Eleanor gave her one of her backhanded compliments one afternoon about how she had heard that Vera's father came from a good family even though he was now a missionary."

Justin's breath stopped. "John made a few such remarks to me. I had no idea they had the audacity to say such things to Vera's face. I tried to put John in his place." He had not tried hard enough. "I should have punched his toffee nose."

Constance put a hand on his arm. "Your revenge is that he will spend his life married to Eleanor, while you have Vera. She is wonderful," she said.

"Yes, she is," Justin said.

Constance laughed. "I want to see that look in Gian Lorenzo's eyes when he talks about me after we have been married for two years."

"And I want to go and kiss my wife before I go back to the Mission. I will return for dinner and to see you all off to the station. Gian Lorenzo has been trying to talk to me. I will find a few private minutes for him before you leave."

"I'll tell him that. Denys has gone to the station to arrange for space on the train for all that great lot of paraphernalia." She fairly danced across the grass toward the duke, who as soon as she started in his direction, sped toward her.

Justin found Vera in their room, with the property maps spread out before her on the bed. As soon as she saw him, she turned over on her back and when he leaned to kiss her, pulled him on top of her. As ever, no matter what his mind told him, his body responded to her.

He kissed her for a full minute before he came up for air. "I have no time for this," he said.

"That's fine. I just wanted to prime the pump."

He kissed her again. "You are too naughty."

"We are married. It's allowed."

She held on to his neck, and as he got up, he pulled her back into a sitting position.

"I have been thinking about the land," she said. "This piece." She put her finger on the parcel that they had chosen of the two in Ngong. "It is lovely. I think we should give up the idea of choosing a parcel up here. Let's just take this one."

"Without even a look at the other sites?"

"This one in Ngong is close to Father, closer to Nairobi's advantages, such as they are."

"True enough," he said, recalling the two narrow rivers, the flatland, which was right for orchards and horses, the rising section that would do for cows.

"To be perfectly frank," she said, "I don't think I want to live up here. It will always make me think of these terrible things that have happened in the past two days."

"I agree wholeheartedly," he said. "You should know, though, that Gian Lorenzo and Constance will always remember these days as the sun-filled ones when they fell in love."

She jumped up in that graceful way of hers that seemed close to flying. "Do you mean? ... Has he asked? ... And you?" She looked as if she would burst with happiness.

"Yes," he said. "I will help them convince the earls, present and future. Not that they will listen to anything I have to say, but I will support her. They deserve to be as happy as we are."

"True. True."

"I will send a cable to the land office in Nairobi telling Mr. Evans of our choice. Yes?"

"Yes! Oh, I am so happy that it is settled!" She threw her arms around his neck and kissed him again.

He peeled her off him. "I have to go back to work," he said.

"Very well," she said, "but I shall make you pay double later."

All thoughts of such delights left him as soon as he exited the guesthouse. The Maasai warriors were back under the trees, and though he told himself their presence was not necessarily meant to be a threat, he could not help seeing it as one.

At the Mission, Justin met up with Lovett, and they went over Ramsay's report together and signed off on it. Afterward, Lovett sent for the woman Tigisi. They drank tea with Ramsay while they waited for her.

"Simu came back from the guesthouse in a terrible state," Ramsay said. "What did you do to her?"

"I?" Justin resented the accusation. "I questioned her about what she knew about the murders."

"Well, I think you should know that she says it is your fault that Ruth was killed." The way Ramsay reported it, he seemed to be saying he believed it too.

Lovett bunched his fists as if he meant to leap up and break the missionary's nose.

"Just how does she think I did that?"

"Evidently, the natives learned that you had questioned Ruth. They concluded that you believed she had murdered Naeku. They are saying you knew Ruth had done it because Ruth wanted to stop their girls being—um, cut. The local men then took it upon themselves to revenge Naeku's death by killing Ruth." He said it all calmly and straightforwardly, as if he were reporting facts to some committee on Mission finances.

"Now look here," Lovett said. "That is a deal of rubbish."

"You and I may not believe it," Ramsay said, "but if the natives do, there is nothing to stop them acting on it."

Tolliver's mind would not deal with these ideas. They were too preposterous.

Lovett, fists still clenched, looked as if he was going to thrash Ramsay, but he walked to the door. "You stay here, Tolliver, and question Tigisi. I will talk to the villagers. I want to see if they believe any of this insanity."

"If they do," Tolliver said, "please try to disabuse them of it." In reality he held out no hope that Lovett could change their minds.

He and Ramsay sat in an uneasy silence for the time it took the girl to arrive.

She was beautiful, with a smooth, rich brown complexion. Her head was shaved, of course. Her face was lovely, with high cheekbones, a small nose, and even, white teeth, perfect except for a small space at the front. By and large the Maasai were an extraordinarily handsome people, but this woman stood out even from that crowd. She was draped in bright cloth and wore multiple pieces of jewelry.

Her beauty seemed to bring out gallantry uncharacteristic of Ramsay. He stood when she came into the room and sat only when she did. He seemed to have forgotten that this woman might be a murderer.

Then, suddenly, Ramsay stood up again and moved toward the door. "I'll leave you to it," he said, and marched off.

Tolliver put aside his puzzlement at Ramsay's behavior and launched in. "I understand that you were near Naeku's hut yesterday about the time she died," he said in English.

She looked at him in complete confusion. He tried Swahili, but still she did not understand. Ramsay must have known that she and Tolliver did not have a language in common, and he had left Tolliver to find it out for himself. The man was a missionary, but he was a bastard nonetheless.

Tolliver went out of the Mission office to find an askari to translate. The man who had brought Tigisi had gone and another had taken his place, one who spoke only Swahili, English, and his own tribal language—Turkana. Tolliver wondered if he would ever be able to name all the tribal languages in the Protectorate, much less say even as much as hello in all of them.

"Do you know where Dr. Ramsay went?"

"To the chapel, Bwana."

"Call me sir. Go and ask him to come here. I need him to interpret for me." Fuming, Justin wished he could arrest Ramsay for obstructing justice—not that he was actually guilty. He was just insufferable, and there was no law against that—more's the pity.

"What do you want me to say?" Ramsay asked in a rather testy tone once they returned to the office. It occurred to Tolliver that he had no idea if this man was married. In his experience, most missionaries were. Or they were widowers, like Vera's father. Or had a sister in tow, like Robert Morley and his sister Katharine, who had left Mombasa to go south to German East Africa last year. He pitied Ramsay's wife. If he had one.

"Tell her I want to know what she was doing near Naeku's hut yesterday just at the time the old woman was dying."

"Was she there?" Ramsay asked.

"Please, Arthur," Tolliver said. "I will answer your questions later. For now let's get this woman to answer mine."

Ramsay spoke to her for a full minute. She answered in what sounded like four words. "She wants to know who told you she was there."

"She must answer. If she evades my questions, I will have no choice but to put her in Mr. Lovett's lockup."

"Is that true?"

"It is what you are going to tell her every time she does not give you a direct answer."

"I will not lie for you."

Tolliver was wishing he had stayed with Vera. He felt like threatening the missionary with the lockup. "Dr. Ramsay, you are not saying anything. You are merely translating for me. I am saying what I must say to do my work. Kindly carry on before we are both old and gray."

"I was looking for someone," was the girl's answer, when it came.

"You had in your hands a cloth that had been given to the *enkamuratani* as a gift for her services."

Tolliver watched her as Ramsay spoke the words in Maasai. She looked at him in fear. "No one could have seen me."

"Someone did."

She started to tremble. "It was a ghost. It could only have been a ghost who told him. I want to go away. I want to go away from this man who talks to ghosts."

"Get her to explain to you why she thinks only a ghost would know what she did."

"What I did, no one was there. I did not take away the cloth."

"And the other things, the jewelry that is missing from the dead woman."

Her voice shook. "I never took it away. I did not. I will never go back."

"Don't say anything to comfort her," Tolliver told Ramsay. He went to the door and asked the askari to bring the girl a glass of water. He stood watching her until it came.

When she had taken a drink, he asked if she was married.

"My parents are going to betroth me to a man who has many cattle, but he already has two wives. I want to be a first wife."

Tolliver saw no use in continuing. There was something in this testimony, he was sure. He needed to let it soak into his brain for a while. "Tell her that she must stay here on the Mission grounds."

"That will cause trouble," Ramsay said.

"She already has trouble. When Lovett returns and I have had a chance to talk to him, I will come back to her. In the meanwhile, she must not leave. I will interrogate Ruth Van Slyck's houseboy."

He brought in the askari guard. "Take her to the school-room and stay with her," he told the constable. "Do not let her go until I come for her. Ramsay, you may leave now, but I may need you to translate again later."

Ramsay prickled. "Ruth's body is in the chapel. I wanted to bury her tomorrow morning. I thought perhaps you and your friends would come, so I won't have to lay her to rest all by myself."

"Yes, certainly," Tolliver said, knowing that Vera would want to. "My wife and the others are taking the down-train at two thirty in the morning. If they are to attend, the funeral will have to be this afternoon."

Ramsay's expression turned to pain. "It is highly irregular. These things are usually done in the morning." He looked as if he might have the audacity to ask four people to miss their train to please him.

Tolliver held his temper. "The next train is not until Monday."

Ramsay relented. "Come at four."

"Very well. I will get a message to them." He motioned to another askari guard. "As soon as A.D.S. Lovett returns, ask him to come to me. I will be in Miss Van Slyck's cottage."

He marched across the open sward between the Mission buildings, glancing out at the magnificent view of the lake, thinking it would soothe his troubled heart. Its beauty did him no good at all.

He found Raila cleaning the room where Ruth had died. Tolliver reminded him they had met briefly that morning.

"Yes, sir, we did," the man said in perfectly pronounced English. He was medium height, very dark skinned, and dressed in a short-sleeved white shirt and khaki shorts. His shoulders were broad and his arms powerful. He looked as if he could have easily fought off an intruder. Or caused those terrible bruises.

"You are not Maasai."

"No, sir. I am Luo, from the slopes of Mount Kenya."

"How is it that you come to be here?"

"I was a porter for the railway builders. I worked for them until the line reached here. Then I came one day to look at the lake. Mr. Augustus Warner spoke to me. He told me he needed someone to work here. The Maasai will not work. Do you know that, sir?"

"Yes, I do. Is that boiled water in that jug?" He pointed to a green pottery pitcher on the table.

Raila turned to the stove. "Yes, sir. But there is also tea. Would you like tea?"

While Raila put on the kettle, Tolliver continued to question him. "When did you last see Miss Van Slyck alive?"

"Last night I served her at dinner with Dr. Ramsay, cleared, and cleaned the dishes. When I was nearly done, I saw her go across to the chapel." He pointed in its direction. "This was how it always was. I finished my work and went away."

"Where did you go when you left this cottage?"

Raila looked at the floor. After a moment, he spoke. "I love this Mission and the people here, but I am not a Christian."

The kettle's lid rattled, and he busied himself with serving the tea. Tolliver was not sure which he wanted more—the drink or the information. He took a seat at the kitchen table and accepted a cup. "Again, you must tell me where you went when you left here last night."

Raila stood with his head hung down like a boy before the headmaster. "I keep a woman in the town, near the Indian market, next to the railway station. She has my baby."

"You went to her then?"

"I go there every night."

"Did you see anything unusual when you left here?"

"No, sir."

"And when you left, Miss Van Slyck was still in the chapel?"

"Yes, I think so, sir. I saw her go that way, but I did not walk there and look at her. I never do that."

"What time was it when you left here?"

"I do not keep a watch, sir, but the clock there"—he pointed to the wall behind Tolliver's head—"it said almost ten past ten."

Tolliver looked up. It was a quarter to one now. He drained his cup and stood up. Nothing anyone was telling him brought him even an inch closer to knowing what had happened here. "I may need to talk to your—your woman about this."

The man looked alarmed, but he did not object.

The duke found Denys reading—stretched out in the shade of a sausage tree in the garden at the side of the guesthouse. He put his finger between the pages of his book and sat up. "You look entirely too happy for a man who has been robbed of a hunting expedition by two murders."

Gian Lorenzo was bursting to tell Finch Hatton the good news Constance had delivered to him, but it would be improper to talk of it to anyone but her family before they were formally engaged. First and foremost, he had to secure permission from his king. Once his regal cousin had approved, he would be able to go to York and meet with her father face-to-face. Until then, whatever Denys might surmise must remain a supposition.

"The aromas from Madame Gillet's kitchen are enough to put a smile on my face," he said instead of the private truth.

Denys picked a blade of grass and used it to mark his place. "You Italians and your food," he said with a chuckle. "It's a wonder you aren't all fat as hippos."

Gian Lorenzo laughed. "We use up our nourishment making love."

"Not today, you will not." Oh, no! It was Tolliver's voice behind him!

"*O Dio!*" The duke hit the heel of his hand against his forehead.

Denys was holding his stomach in paroxysms of glee.

Tolliver's face remained severe.

"I—I—"

"Aye-aye-aye!" Denys said.

Gian Lorenzo recovered himself. He had not been raised to be intimidated. "I have been waiting for an opportunity to speak privately with you, Justin."

"Time for me to enjoy the aromas of the kitchen," Denys said, picking up his book and loping across to the house.

Tolliver moved into the shade of the tree and took off his pith helmet. He was smiling now. "Fire away," he said.

Gian Lorenzo removed his hat too. "I love your sister," he said. "And she tells me that she loves me. I want to marry her." He looked directly into Justin's eyes.

"I can't give you permission," Tolliver said.

"I know that," Gian Lorenzo said. "I can't make her a proposal just yet. In families like mine in Italy, it is often the case that a person must marry for other reasons—of politics, to make alliances, to make an enemy into a friend. I must secure my cousin the king's permission before I can make a formal offer."

"The same happens among the royals in Britain," Tolliver said.

Gian Lorenzo saw that Tolliver was trying to make it easy for him, which gave him confidence. Constance had already reassured him that, despite his frowns at first, her brother would take kindly to their courtship. He squared his shoulders. Giovanni Lorenzo di Savoia was a man who led expeditions into dangerous places. He would not be intimidated by these circumstances to give up the woman who was perfect for him. Winning Constance's hand meant more to him than reaching the summit of any mountain he had ever attempted.

"I am far enough removed from the Italian throne that it should not make a difference whom I marry. However, my king is a stickler for form in such matters. As soon as I know I have your support in this, I will write to my king. Then I will go to your father."

"Go? Not write?"

"I want to do this properly. I do not want anything to spoil my chances."

Tolliver gave him a bolstering squeeze on his shoulder. "I was unhappy about this prospect when I first saw the light in your eyes when you looked at her."

"I saw your disapproval."

"But as she probably told you, I have thought better of it. My wife has a way of softening my viewpoints on many things. She has on this."

"Vera is a wonderful woman."

"You will have no argument from me on that score."

"Lady Constance loves her very much. And she has found your and Vera's love for each other an inspiration for herself. I am grateful to you both for that."

"Religion may be a stumbling point for my father," Tolliver said. "I imagine it will also make things difficult with your king."

"Constance has told me that she will become a Catholic."

"I want it to go well for you," Tolliver said, though with a trifle too much doubt in his tone to comfort Gian Lorenzo. "Where will you live? Where is Sulmona?"

Gian Lorenzo could not help but smile. "It is in a forest. Except for the Alps, I think it is the closest thing Italy has to this." He swept his arm to take in the hills that surrounded them. "But my title has more to do with the land than with a residence. I have a palazzo in Turin and a villa with a vineyard in a place called Le Langhe. Do you know its wines? They are the best in Italy."

Tolliver laughed. "Don't tell Denys or his friend Berkeley Cole that, or they will be proposing marriage to your sisters."

Gian Lorenzo pretended to pout. "I have three sisters, but alas all are married."

Tolliver's expression turned serious. "Pleasant as all this is, my dear duke, I do have some serious things to tell you."

"About Constance and me?"

"No, about what is likely to happen in the next few days. I will need your help."

"Whatever you need."

"This afternoon, we will all attend the funeral of Ruth Van Slyck. Vera's family is part of the missionary circle here in the Protectorate. I think it only right that we pay our respects."

"Certainly."

"And you already know that, since I have to stay behind on duty, you will be taking Constance and Vera back to Athi River in the small hours of this coming morning."

"Yes. Please be assured that I will take every care of them."

"If things heat up here, I may have to stay for some while. Do you know my situation with the police force?"

"Constance has told me something of it. She also told me that you have been assured there is little chance of real danger here."

Tolliver could not suppress a scowl. Bloody Cranford was a liar as well as a pompous fool. "That is what I was told, but now there have been two murders, and the local man up here isn't up to coping with it all. I am forced to take charge."

"What can I do to help?"

"It is already a great relief to me that you will accompany them home."

Gian Lorenzo grinned. "You are thanking me for doing the most pleasant thing I can imagine, staying near Lady Constance. If there is the slightest chance she might be in danger, I will not leave her for a moment. It is how I will love her for the rest of my life."

Tolliver returned his smile. "I am very glad of that, Gian Lorenzo. I truly am. And, for my sake, try to amuse Vera or she will worry unnecessarily. Music will distract her."

"And the *bambino*."

"Yes. So will the *bambino*."

Vera looked out the side window of their room and saw Justin. Her first instinct was to run down to tell what she had learned about Ruth Van Slyck's murder and ask him if it was really true. Then she saw Denys leave him alone with the duke. Given what they were likely to be talking about, she waited, checking often to see if their tête-à-tête had ended.

When they continued to talk for such a long while, she began to worry. Why was it taking so long? Overly polite as Justin was, it always took him far longer to say no than yes. From the position they were in, she could not see their faces. Then all of a sudden Justin turned and looked up at her as if he knew she had been watching.

He shook a playfully scolding finger at her and waved for her to come down. When she did, they met in the lower hall. His demeanor matched hers exactly. "You and Gian Lorenzo have had your talk," she said.

"We have, and it is agreed. I will support his suit."

"But you don't look entirely happy about it."

"We ended by talking about his escorting you home. I don't want to be separated from you."

"Nor I, you."

"I wish I could come, but—"

"I know." She nodded and then looked around as if to see who might hear them. "I have something I must ask you." She hesitated.

He drew her into the parlor and closed the door. "What is it?"

"Madame Gillet described what happened to Ruth Van Slyck. I am sick about it."

He was puzzled. "She was murdered, but you knew that."

"Yes, but I did not know about the mutilation. It is horrific."

"Mutilation?" His blood chilled.

"Like what happens to the girls." She shuddered.

He scowled. "Do you mean of her ..."

"That is what Madame said."

"I cannot believe it. I heard nothing of this."

She could not bring herself to ask him if he had checked on her condition for himself. He had frequently had to do things as part of his work that he absolutely refused to speak about with her.

"I had better ask Madame," he said, and went into the hall. "Whoever started this rumor knows something I must learn."

She followed him to the kitchen where the landlady was overseeing her Goan cook in the final preparations for luncheon. The aroma of baking bread made his mouth water. He swallowed and told Madame what he wanted to ask. She put a finger to her lips, pointed to the cook, and waved them into the dining parlor.

"Yes," she said once they were alone. "I had heard it already from Sumi. And my cook said the news was all over the market by midmorning. I told him he should not repeat such gossip. I would have thought you already knew, Monsieur Tolliver."

"I do not believe it is true," he said.

"But everyone is saying it."

"Please don't repeat it to any of the others here," Justin said.

Vera saw the wisdom in that.

Grateful as he had been for a chance at the luncheon that smelled so appealing, Tolliver lost his appetite at Madame Gillet's revelation. His sister and Gian Lorenzo sat across the table from him, imagining that no one saw they were often holding hands beneath the cloth. Constance was glowing. Denys was charming them all into good cheer, regaling everyone with vivid descriptions of the game they would see from the train once dawn broke and with hilarious character sketches of doltish White Hunters he had accompanied into the wild.

Vera was subdued. Tolliver could think of nothing but that monstrous rumor and whether it was true. And what he would have to say and do to prove or disprove it.

He picked at his meal and excused himself before pudding was served. "Thank you all for agreeing to come to the funeral." He pulled out his watch. "I will see you there in an hour." He kissed Vera, wishing he could say something to comfort her, but he could not imagine what that would be.

Once outside, he sped down to the Mission compound, passing the Maasai warriors gathered under the trees in their irksome silence and their daunting patience.

He found Ramsay seated on the ground under a tree, eating a sandwich, while Raila, off near the chapel, dug a grave. The patch of ground that served as a graveyard contained one cross. Ramsay pointed to it. "It's for Augustus Warner's only child. A daughter. She lived to only five years old."

Tolliver sat down beside him. There was no delicate way to bring up what he had to say. He sank the vestiges of his gentlemanly upbringing, as he had so often to do in his role as policeman, took a deep breath, and forced out his words. "There is a nasty rumor circulating like wildfire, that Miss Van Slyck's...

that her private parts were mutilated. Like the, um—like the operation that Naeku performed."

Ramsay looked at him aghast. "It is not true. I know it is not true."

"You told me you had...you had examined her...there."

"I am a doctor!" He sounded like a man defending himself from an accusation of perverted behavior.

"I know that, Arthur." Justin used his Christian name in an attempt to calm him. It did not. Ramsay leapt to his feet. "It is standard procedure for a doctor to check, in such a situation, to see if the woman had been violated."

Justin rose too. He knew what he had to do, repulsive as it was. "Every fiber in my being is revolted at the thought, but I think...I must corroborate your...observation." At the thought of it he was afraid he would lose what little lunch he had consumed.

"That is outrageous!"

"I can understand your feelings, but—believe me, if I could avoid this, I would. But you are not an official of the realm. You know as well as I that once a rumor gets started in this country, it is next to impossible to quash it. If the truth of her condition is ever going to win out, an official of the Protectorate will have to be a witness. I am in the unenviable position of being the official on the scene. I cannot imagine Lovett doing it."

"She is in her coffin in the chapel. Do you propose doing it in there?" There was no way to interpret his tone but as an intimation of blasphemy and desecration.

"If you and Raila will help me, we can carry her into the office." It took all he could do to make his voice neutral and official.

Ramsay looked at him for a long time.

Tolliver offered a rationale that was just short of a threat. "It will be best for you if you have me to back up what your report states." Unable to utter another word, he walked off to fetch Raila.

Ramsay followed them into the chapel. A plain wooden coffin had been placed on two trestles at the front of the simple house of worship. They lifted it, Tolliver and Ramsay on one side, the powerful Raila on the other. It was surprisingly light, reminding Tolliver that, despite the strength of her convictions, Ruth Van Slyck had been a small, almost frail woman.

"You may go finish the digging," he said to Raila when they had placed the box on the office desk.

Ramsay went off and returned with a crowbar and a hammer.

Justin reached out to take them, but Ramsay began to open the coffin himself.

They lifted the lid and stood it against the wall.

Ruth Van Slyck lay seemingly at peace, dressed in what she had worn in life, a sensible navy skirt and a white shirtwaist. Her arms were folded across her chest over a plain wooden cross that reached from her chin to her waist. Her hair had been pulled back in a braid. "Simu dressed her," Ramsay said, answering the question that Tolliver could not bring himself to ask.

He stood at attention, fists clenched, breathing only shallowly, while Ramsay rolled back the front of her skirt and pulled down the front of her underdrawers. Tolliver wished he would go faster. This was excruciating.

"You see, the pubic area is normal. And her legs here are normal." He pulled aside the flesh of her thighs. Tolliver could not bear the thought of how cold they must feel. "You see. There is no mutilation."

"None," Tolliver said, choking out the word.

"I can show you the intact hymen if you need to look at it."

Tolliver felt his face burning. "That won't be necessary. It is the rumor of mutilation that we seek to disprove."

"We are done then?" Ramsay asked, though he was already replacing the disarrayed clothing. His voice was icy.

They remained silent while Tolliver re-nailed the coffin lid and, without Raila's help, they carried Ruth Van Slyck's remains back to the chapel to await the funeral service.

When Lovett arrived, half an hour later, Tolliver sat him down with Ramsay, and they altered the report to include the testimony that Van Slyck's corpse showed no sign of mutilation. Ramsay and Tolliver both signed the addendum. Lovett wrote: *Signed in my presence, this 29th day of May 1913*, and signed his name. "It won't stop them talking," he said.

"Nothing will stop them talking," Tolliver said glumly, "but at least we have set the record straight."

The funeral of Ruth Van Slyck was the saddest such occasion any of them had ever attended, all the more so since there was no blood relative of the deceased with fond memories or deep regrets.

Justin looked on his sweet wife with pride. She had thought to beg a garden bouquet from Madame Gillet. Before the service began, she went to Ruth Van Slyck's bungalow, took down the American flag, placed it over the coffin and laid the flowers on it. But for her gracious gesture, the ceremony would have seemed perfunctory at best.

Constance sat close to Gian Lorenzo, embarrassed that she was not dressed in appropriate black and resenting her childhood training that emphasized the form of things so much more than the matter of them. If she had attended a Yorkshire funeral dressed in khaki and a pith helmet, people would remember the event more for Lady Constance Tolliver's strange getup than for who had died and how.

She was in love with the man next to her, so much so that her heart swelled every time she thought about it. But by marrying him and becoming part of the Italian court, she would let herself in for a great deal more of that same protocol-bound way of life. And she would be dealing with expectations she had not learned of from birth. She would be out of her element, just as much as Vera was at Tilbury Grange, making trivial mistakes, like wearing too much jewelry for an occasion, or not enough. Such gaffes were insignificant but deadly in that sort of closed atmosphere. When Constance Tolliver went to live among the Italian royals, she would have all the wrong instincts and constantly put herself in the way of other people's whispered ridicule.

She imagined what they would say. *Did you see that she reached for cutlery to serve herself, instead of waiting to be served? She came in linen instead of silk. Can you imagine?*

If such imaginings were not daunting enough, as Arthur Ramsay began to intone the prayers for the dead it occurred to Constance that it was a very bad omen that the first public ceremony she and Gian Lorenzo were attending together was a funeral. A pall fell over what until a few minutes ago had been her happy heart.

Denys Finch Hatton took the book *Nason's Hymnary* from the slot in the back of the chair in front of him. There was a chalkboard at the front of the chapel on which was posted the number 59. Just as Arthur Ramsay said "Amen," to his last prayer, Denys opened the hymnal, stood up, and began to sing: *"Holy, holy, holy! Lord God Almighty!"* in a beautiful baritone voice. Soon they were all standing and all but Gian Lorenzo singing. Not caring what anyone would think of her for it, Constance held his hand until they had sung all three verses.

Vera took the bouquet. Oliver Lovett removed the flag, folded it, and for want of an American in the group, handed it to Constance. The four men shouldered the coffin and led their sad little procession of three: Vera, Constance, and the Maasai convert Simu.

Raila stood looking downcast beside the open grave. After they lowered the box onto ropes laid out on the ground, Vera handed each of them a flower. When the men had lowered the casket, they each let fall a flower and a handful of the rich brown-red soil of East Africa.

As Justin let a red rose drop onto the coffin, he suddenly remembered the Maasai woman he had left guarded and waiting in the schoolroom. He bid a quick good-bye to Vera and the others, promising to join them for dinner before they left for the station.

As he and Lovett crossed the compound, Tolliver sketched in for Lovett what he had learned earlier that day. "Did you find anything in the village about the movements of the people there?" he then asked.

"Precious little," Lovett said.

"As I expected. Do you still have the guard on Naeku's hut?"

"Yes, but I don't see the point." Lovett was back to his disinterested self.

"Neither did I until I questioned Tigisi." He did not tell Lovett what he had surmised.

When they entered the office, the askari, who had been sitting on the floor with his back against the wall, jumped up. His eyes were heavy with sleep. Tigisi slumbered in an armchair in the corner.

"Wait outside," Tolliver ordered the constable in a voice loud enough to wake the girl. Fear filled her face the moment she laid eyes on him and Lovett. "Tell her she must come with us," he asked of Lovett.

Lovett complied. His command of Maasai seemed quite good.

The girl began to weep. She moaned and cried and protested the entire way along the path to the Maasai village.

"She is going on about a ghost," Lovett said. "Why is she so afraid of a ghost?"

"I will tell you later. For now, it is entirely a good thing that she is so frightened. Do not tell her there is no such thing as a ghost."

When they entered the village, it was deserted except for a few old women snoozing in the shade. Two askaris armed with rifles stood on either side of Naeku's hut. "Most of the women are indoors comforting the girls," Lovett said.

Tolliver winced. "I imagine they need it."

As they neared the entrance to the hut, Tigisi stopped in her tracks. At first Tolliver thought he would have to drag her inside, but in the end, Lovett managed to convince her. She stayed close to him and eyed Tolliver with distrust.

The interior was as gloomy as a forest on a moonless night. Tolliver took a torch from his jacket pocket and shone it around the main room and then into the girl's lovely but terrified face. He switched off the light. "Take her outside for a minute," he said to Lovett. "When you come back inside go directly into the room where the dead Naeku was found. Do not carry a light."

When they had gone out, Tolliver took off his khaki jacket, leaving only his trousers and shirt, both dark brown. And his brown hat. He rolled up the jacket and left it in the gloom near the entrance doorway.

He went into the tiny, windowless bedroom and waited— his head bowed behind the brim of his hat, his hands behind his back, still and barely breathing—in the darkest corner, away from the sleeping platform.

In a moment, Lovett entered with the loudly protesting Tigisi. They walked directly into the room where Tolliver waited. The girl left off talking and merely whimpered. Tolliver counted to ten, pointed the torch at his own face, and lit it.

Lovett gasped. The girl screamed and collapsed to the floor, moaning. "What the devil!" Lovett exclaimed.

"Pick her up and tell her that I will not bother her again, if she tells me where she hid the gifts she stole from Naeku."

It took Lovett several minutes to calm the shaking girl enough so that she could follow orders. She knelt down next to the sleeping platform, pulled a bunch of sticks out from under it, and then, from farther underneath, a rolled-up length of cloth.

Tolliver took it from her and picked up his jacket on his way out of the hut. When Lovett and the girl joined him outside, he pointed to the path from the village back to the mission grounds. "Tigisi may go. You and I will return to the Mission. I need to find and arrest Simu."

"Oughtn't we be concentrating on finding whoever killed Ruth Van Slyck?" Lovett asked.

"Yes," Tolliver said, "but that is a much more complicated question, and I am not at all sure it's possible. I thought there might be a connection between the two murders, but I now doubt that the same person killed both women."

"I agree," Lovett said. "The most honest thing I heard from any of the natives this morning was said by another old woman— that Ruth deserved to die because she had killed Naeku to stop her cutting the girls."

"That is not true."

"Evidently not. I hated to think so, but it did seem a plausible conclusion from their point of view, given how vehement Miss Van Slyck has been about the need to stop it."

They started along the path. After a few moments, Lovett spoke again. "They also told me that they thought Ramsay had killed the *enkamuratani*. They say he wants to stop the practice so he can have sex with Maasai girls. I told them I thought that was ridiculous, but they wouldn't give up the idea."

"We have just proved it wasn't Ramsay," Tolliver said, "but I have no idea how we might displace the rumor with the truth."

"Do you think Ramsay killed Miss Van Slyck?"

"Don't be absurd. He killed no one."

Vera did not like Simu. Nor did she like to think that her feelings stemmed from the age-old animosity between the Kikuyu and the Maasai. All the children she had grown up with had hated the Maasai and called them names. When she was about age seven she had brought those epithets home to the family dinner table, and her father had become incensed. One of the few times he had threatened her: if she ever uttered such hateful words again she would be banned from the Kikuyu village and from any and all contact with her former playmates. If they were going to teach her to hate, they could not be her friends.

Vera had grown up trying to do as her father did—to find good in everyone. She found it impossible.

Whatever her father might think, she disliked Simu's sour disposition. On top of which the woman cleaned the guesthouse with very little fervor and at the same time bragged about how hard she worked. If she were to share this criticism with her father, he would point out that a tribal woman's sense of neat and tidy was very different from a European's. Simu had grown up in a hut with a dirt floor. "Cleanliness is next to godliness in Scotland," her father used to say, "but not in Africa."

Simu also repeated the phrase, "I am a Christian," far, far too often. But again, Papa would not object. He said that converts often felt so full of grace that they spoke of it incessantly.

What troubled Vera most about Simu was how quickly her expression turned from grim to a beaming smile when she found someone looking at her. Her smile was lovely, but her eyes said it was false.

After the funeral, Vera and Simu had walked side by side back to the guesthouse. Vera had tried to engage Simu in a conversation about Ruth Van Slyck, and though the woman spoke many words, they did not add up to any clear sort of picture.

Vera was frustrated. She had hoped to find something, anything that might help Justin to discover who had killed Ruth. She detested having to go back to the Athi River without him. The sooner he finished his investigation the sooner they would be back together again, and when they had secured their land, they could plan and work in earnest to get themselves and their baby boy settled.

After tea, Denys and the duke went off to oversee the porters carrying the safari gear to the railway station. She and Constance found nothing to do but sit on the veranda and read. They had chatted much of the morning about Constance's future with the duke, which was all very exciting, but since the funeral service, her sister-in-law had become subdued. Now she was reading one of Madame Gillet's French novels, something called *L'immoraliste* by André Gide. Vera was quite certain that neither Justin nor the duke would approve of Constance reading a story with such a title. Vera herself, not being able to read French, was reduced to reading Monsieur Gillet's five-day-old copy of *The Leader*. Vera ordinarily detested newspapers. This one was like them all, full of trivialities about life here in the Protectorate that everyone already knew, and a great deal of detail about the conflicts between the nations of Europe, none of which could have any possible effect on her life. She threw it aside, and went to take one more try at getting information out of Simu.

She found her in the kitchen, not quite scrubbing a pot. The cook was not there. "Looking for Cook? He gone to hotel at train. Cook for travelers come from lake."

"No actually," Vera said, "I came to talk with you. My father is a missionary, you know."

"Everyone know that." She rinsed the pot, picked up a knife, and began to cut up a very large pumpkin that had been sitting on the table.

"Oh, do you eat pumpkin?" Vera asked. As far as she knew, the Maasai diet consisted entirely of milk, beef, and cow's blood.

"I am Christian," she said, and kept on cutting. But she did not do it deftly, the way the Kikuyu women did. She managed to get the knife embedded in the pumpkin and was having trouble getting it out.

"Here, let me help you with that," Vera said. She reached for the knife, intending to pick it up, pumpkin and all, and slam it down on the chopping block to complete the cut and free the knife. But Simu grabbed her hand and pushed her away at the same time. The pumpkin fell from the knife. Vera lost her balance and slipped on the greasy floor and fell.

At that second, Justin burst through the door from the kitchen yard. "Stop!!"

He knocked Simu away from Vera. Rolling away, she heard Simu scream and Justin grunt.

"Good God," Justin moaned.

Vera sat up. Simu lay on the floor immobile.

Justin felt her pulse. "Either I knocked her unconscious or she fainted."

It was half an hour before Tolliver's heart settled into its normal rhythm. It had not mattered how many times Vera protested that Simu had not been attacking her with a knife. He could not dismiss what he had seen. He had been on his way to arrest a woman he knew had stabbed another woman to death, and he had found her standing over Vera with a knife in her hand. Had he had his pistol in his hand he would have shot Simu dead. As it was, he had hit a woman, something he had never done or expected to do in his life.

He stood behind the divan in Madame Gillet's small back parlor, holding Vera's hand, while Arthur Ramsay examined the still groggy Simu who was slumped in an armchair.

Ramsay shined a light in her eyes and declared her not seriously hurt. He took the cloth from her head, dipped it into a basin of water on the floor next to her chair, and replaced it on her forehead. She moaned and closed her eyes.

Ramsay turned to Tolliver. "Explain to me now how you concluded that it was Simu who killed Naeku."

Vera looked at him as if she wanted to hear it too.

"When I questioned Simu, she told me that she had seen Tigisi walking away from Naeku's hut carrying a cloth. She was accusing Tigisi of stealing the cloth and the ornaments that Naeku received for her services. She also said that Naeku had moaned and that was why she went into the hut."

"But that all makes sense," Ramsay said.

"It did to me too," Tolliver agreed. "It threw suspicion on Tigisi, but it was hard to imagine that the girl had killed such an important person in the village merely to get her jewels, such as they are. Would they not have been recognized if she wore them?"

"I think not," Ramsay said. "Their jewels all look alike to me. Half of them these days are made from stolen telegraph wire taken from along the railway."

"They are distinguishable to them," Vera said, but without that annoyance she reserved for Europeans who underestimated the natives.

"At any rate," Tolliver said, "when I questioned Tigisi and told her that someone had seen her taking the cloth she started to scream about ghosts."

"I was there," Ramsay said. "That is exactly what she did. She seemed truly terrified to me."

"To me too," Tolliver said. "Tigisi said she called out before she entered the hut, but there was no answer. Naeku was dead when she went in. Her terror came from my knowing she had tried to steal the cloth and ornaments. She insisted that only a ghost could have told me about her theft. As I thought about it, I realized that the person who saw her with the cloth had to have been inside the hut, but hidden, when she arrived. It is very dark inside there. A person could have hidden in the gloom. Simu had told me that she saw Tigisi walking away with the jewels and the cloth. If she knew about the theft, and Tigisi had never left the hut with the cloth, Simu had to have been the one who was hiding inside when Tigisi went in."

"So that is why you hid yourself inside the hut. So that you could test to find out if a person standing where you stood would have been invisible."

"Yes," Tolliver said. "I wore dark clothing, as Simu always does. With her dark skin and her dark clothing there was nothing about her that would catch light, whatever light there might be. And when Lovett and I took Tigisi back into the hut, she showed us where the stolen items were hidden—inside, under the sleeping platform. So Simu was lying. She could not have seen Tigisi outside with the cloth and jewels, because Tigisi had never taken them from the hut. The only way Simu could have known Tigisi touched them was to have seen her in the room with the dead woman."

"But why would Simu have wanted to kill Naeku?" Vera asked.

Ramsay groaned. "Because Ruth and I were so vehement about stopping the—the procedure. She must have done it because we gave her the wrong..." His voice trailed off. "It is what has always troubled me. We teach the converts the tenets of Christianity. But then they often pick up other thoughts, other behaviors of ours and take them to be also tenets of the religion. Things they must believe or do. She must have thought she was doing a Christian thing by murdering that old woman." He hung his head. His sigh turned into a sob.

"You wrong." Simu's voice was loud and vehement, though she had not opened her eyes.

They all turned to her. "Sit up," Tolliver commanded.

She did not. She did not even raise her head.

"Are you denying what I have said?" he asked.

She did not respond.

"You are the only one who could have killed Naeku," Ramsay said. "A.D.S. Tolliver has explained that quite logically."

She finally rose to a sitting position. She stared at the floor between her feet. "Mr. Tolliver right. I kill her. Dr. Ramsay wrong. Not kill to stop from cutting girls. Killed because she cut me, when was my turn, in a bad way. To ruin me. She hate me. I sick for long time. Her *ilmurran* went to her after her married. Came also to me when girl. Want to marry me. Not go to her anymore. Marry me. My husband."

She looked at Ramsay. "You and Miss Ruth say cutting bad. Maasai man think cut girl not want man. Not true. Cut girl still want man." She looked Tolliver in the eye. "I still want man. Not have man."

Ramsay lifted his head and seemed about to speak but then he slumped back in his chair and clenched his jaw.

Simu returned to her tale. "Miss Ruth say sickness come on me after Naeku cut me. Made me…mother one child. No more. She cut my daughter, made her sick too. Naeku hate me. Kill my daughter with sickness. Stole my child. My husband sent me. Never have another children."

Vera came forward and took a chair next to Simu. "But why? Why did you let her—let her—cut your daughter? If you knew what it had done to you, why did you let her do that to your daughter?"

"It done to everyone. To men. To women."

"But the boys are not really harmed by it, painful as it might be," Ramsay said.

"Daughter not cut, no husband. No man marry girl not cut. No bride price for father. She want it. She want be woman. Have husband. Now dead. No husband. No children."

The room fell silent. None of them looked at one another. They stared away, at the lace curtains, at the Turkey carpet, at the photograph of a square in Brussels on the wall.

Simu broke the silence. "I not care what happen to me." There was a profound sadness in her face, tinged with defiance. "Mrs. Augustus Warner gone forever. Only Miss Ruth speak to me. I hate Naeku. Miss Ruth hate cut of girls. I stop Naeku. Now Miss Ruth, she gone too." She looked away.

No one spoke.

Tolliver went to Vera, taking her hands into his. "I have to go and settle this with Lovett."

She smiled wanly at him. "Go ahead. I'll tell the others what we have just learned."

"Very well." He turned to Ramsay. "Please keep Simu where she is. A.D.S. Lovett and I will confer and decide what to do with her next."

He stepped into the narrow hall that separated the parlor from the dining room. It smelled of roasting beef.

Lovett was waiting for him just outside the front door. "A crime of one native against another will not be within the Protectorate's jurisdiction," Tolliver said, knowing full well that Lovett already understood that.

"We are supposed to turn the matter over to the *lybon* and the tribal council to deal with her in their own way. Fat lot of good that will do." Lovett's tone spoke profound disgust.

Tolliver grimaced. "I could not agree more. They will have no time for this, considering that the move must take place."

Lovett's eyes looked pained. "The last news from Hollis is that they will start moving the Maasai in the next few days. Their *lybon* agreed to get them going before there is time for trouble to brew."

Tolliver was relieved and guilty to be so glad.

"Do you think Simu could have had anything to do with Miss Van Slyck's death?" Lovett asked.

"No. Except for the fact that she killed Naeku, and then the rumor was circulated that Miss Van Slyck had done it. Not that

Simu could have anticipated that. I cannot say for sure that the Maasai tribesmen killed Ruth, but it seems quite clear that they are going to brook no interference with their way of life."

"What troubles me now," Lovett said, "is how they are likely to react to the news that their lawsuit has been denied." He gave Tolliver an enquiring, almost pleading look. "You are going to stay here for a few more days until they are prepared to go off?"

"Yes, I told Hollis I would."

Lovett breathed a sigh of relief. "I am glad of that. I never thought I would say that of you."

"I do want to dig around a bit more to see if there is any chance of discovering who killed Miss Van Slyck."

"I have grave doubts as to the usefulness of that," Lovett said.

"As do I." Tolliver put on his helmet. "What about my sergeant? Where is he? What is holding up his arrival?"

"That's a good question. I will find out."

In the end, Arthur Ramsay agreed to stay one or two more days to deal with Ruth Van Slyck's belongings and await a response from the American Congregational Ministry in Nairobi about their plans to send a replacement.

From time to time during that day, Vera and Justin had both fantasized that they would make love before dinner. But what with the funeral and dreadful revelations of Simu's accusation and confession, neither one of them was much in the mood. They went to their room, where Vera packed her few things in her rucksack. Then they lay on their bed holding hands and saying very little.

"How long do you think it will be before you can come home?"' she asked.

"I can't imagine it will be as much as a week. I believe it was some native or other, or perhaps even a group of them, that murdered Ruth. But you know as well as I that it will be impossible to get anyone to give evidence."

She turned on her side and put her head on his shoulder. "I know it has been difficult for you to give up policing. I can imagine that you want to stay on until you find her killers."

"I would have thought so myself, but I think I have totally lost my taste for it. Suppose I actually found the murderers and suppose they were Maasai *ilmurran*. The administration would care more about keeping the move peaceful than they would about getting justice for some American spinster."

She put her hand on his chest, over his heart. Once they took their land, he would be at home, seeing to the work of the farm, being always nearby, being safe from the dangers he so often faced in his work. But she also wanted him happy, and his work used to give him the kinds of challenges that he seemed to crave. What would give him such satisfaction in the future?

Without her having to ask, he responded to her thought. "I have tried to serve justice, but we both know how precious little of it I have been able to deliver."

She thought of the important cases he had faced, how he had been profoundly angered when the wrong person was punished. Last year in Mombasa, he—well, they together—had discovered who had killed the ivory trader, but neither one of them had been satisfied at what had happened in the end.

After a few moments, he went on. "I cannot think what would be best to do when it comes to accusing Simu before the *lybon*. The tribal tempers are up because of the move. Telling them that it was not Ruth Van Slyck who murdered Naeku will set the record straight on Simu, but it will not bring Ruth back. And punishing Simu seems...She has spent her whole life suffering."

"I wonder," Vera said, "if Ruth really was killed as revenge because they thought she had murdered Naeku. Could it be that they so resented her opposition to their practice that they might have killed her to warn off meddlers with their customs? We may be risking a great deal by becoming involved."

He sat up. "Surely you don't think they should be allowed to go on doing that to girls. They are still children."

The Blasphemers

"To you and me they are children, but in tribal terms, they are becoming women." She sat up too and looked him in the face. "Oh stop looking so disapproving. I do agree that what they do is abominable. I am just saying that they will not give it up easily. We must try, but we must expect it to take a long time."

"You have always defended the natives' rights to carry on with the life they have always led."

"And I still do. We call our being here a Protectorate. That is supposed to mean we are here to protect them. It seems to me we are protecting them out of their land, their freedom, their whole way of life. I agree that this part of the way they live is horrifying. It must change. I agree. It must. All I am saying is that they will see it as interference and that they will not distinguish between our telling them to stop it and our telling them they can no longer live on this land."

"It is hideous," he said.

"How many times do I have to say it? I agree entirely. I am just being realistic about how they will respond. I am looking at what we say from their point of view."

He took her hand. "It astonishes me that the women themselves embrace the idea."

"They don't want their daughters to be outcasts. They have nowhere else to go. No other way to live." She pulled his hand to her lips and kissed the backs of his fingers. "It isn't at all the same, but British women accept many things that are unfair, and inflict them on their daughters. Wherever I look, I see that we are protected by men from deciding for ourselves. When you and I made love before we were married, it was I whose reputation would have been ruined if the word got out. And women would be every bit as disapproving as men. Perhaps more so. Whether among the Africans or among the Europeans, women are given rules that are supposed to be for their own good. But if you ask me, they are made for the benefit of men, not of women."

They were sitting cross-legged on the bed, facing each other. "I love you, Justin," she said. She realized when she said it that she almost never called him by name. Always "darling" or "dearest."

She took his hands in hers. "I have been thinking so much about our lives—Constance falling in love with the duke, those horrid tribal practices, the death of poor Miss Van Slyck—these have set me to wondering. I—I—I am so happy to be your wife. Not just someone's wife. But yours. You are the best man I know."

"And you are—" he started to say, but she interrupted.

"Hear me out. Please. I understand about your attachment to your work. I know that there are things about it that you have not wanted to leave behind."

He dropped her hands and took her gently by the shoulders. "Vera, dearest, I have come to the end of this policing. Its frustrations far outweigh its satisfactions at this point. I feel as if I want to bury my uniform when we are home. It has become a symbol of all the injustices that are done here."

"You love this land the way I do," she said. "You are the only person I have ever known who does."

"And when a part of it belongs to us, we will belong to it."

She pulled his arms around her. "And always to each other."

"Yes," he said.

The light was fading fast. There was practically no dusk here at the equator.

"The parcel we have chosen," she said. "Are you happy with it? Truly happy?"

He brushed her hair out of her eyes. "Until we learn its flaws." He chuckled. "But by then we will love it despite its flaws."

The room was dark now. He got up and lit a hurricane lamp. "I will come with you to the station and stay with you until you board the train. I promise I will extricate myself from all this as soon as ever possible."

In the hour before dinner, she napped and he wrote as detailed a report as he could to send off to District Superintendent Jodrell in the pouch that would go on the train. In it, he asked to be relieved of any more responsibility for what was going on here. He did not know what Jodrell thought of Lovett's capabilities, but unreliable as he had seemed when Tolliver arrived, he was trying to do his duty now.

The Blasphemers

The likelihood of apprehending whoever murdered Ruth Van Slyck was practically nil. He did not want to waste his time on a wild-goose chase. His report reiterated the truth about the condition of Ruth's body and the need to quash any rumors that she had been mutilated. Such a falsehood would only create an outcry over the incident: spawning urgent demands from the public for someone to blame. People who did not give a fig about Ruth Van Slyck while she was alive would suddenly be demanding justice about her death. They would find a scapegoat. There was nothing Tolliver loathed more than the administration's propensity to punish somebody, anybody to appease the white population.

He ended his report by saying he preferred to take the down-train that would arrive in Nairobi on Wednesday at noon, but he would keep his word to Hollis unless Jodrell could arrange things differently. Writing that sentence made him feel how very much he wanted to be seated on Clarence McIntosh's veranda thinking about something other than perverted justice and savage African practices.

Having been awake until four in the morning seeing Vera and the others off, Tolliver slept until nine the next day. When he came down to the dining room, he was delighted to find that Madame Gillet was ready to lay on a proper English breakfast. He was slathering some of her excellent orange marmalade on a fourth piece of toast when Lovett entered. He told Tolliver that the officials had returned from their palaver with the *lybon* and that there was no threat of an uproar over the move. This was to be expected since the Protectorate of British East Africa had hand-picked the man who represented the Maasai tribe. He wondered if the *ilmurran* who had spent the past two days lounging under the nearby trees would so easily abide by the decision.

Lovett offered the reassurance so often mouthed on such occasions. "We have the King's African Rifles, and they do not."

It was true enough. The whites had firearms that the Maasai were denied.

Tolliver dropped his last piece of toast and pushed his plate aside. Nothing like the possibility of violence to set a man off his feed.

He followed Lovett back to the town proper to meet once again with Hollis in his parlor car. The two assistant district superintendents of police made a verbal report to Hollis about the deaths of the past two days, telling what they did and did not know about who had committed the crimes.

When they were finished reporting, Hollis asked them the question they had hoped to ask of him: "What do you plan to do about this woman Simu?"

Lovett began to sputter. Tolliver intervened. "We thought to seek your advice on the matter, Mr. Hollis, as Superintendent of Native Affairs, knowing what a delicate situation we are in right now."

Hollis scratched his short beard. "When it comes to native-on-native violence, we have no responsibility. Are you absolutely sure this Simu woman did not also murder Miss Van Slyck?"

Lovett found his voice. "Yes, sir. As A.D.S. Tolliver has said, she had a personal vendetta against the *enkamuratani*. She was devoted to Miss Van Slyck as one of the few people who was kind to her."

"Besides which," Tolliver said, "from the condition of the corpse and the facts of the scene of the crime, it was clear that two quite strong people were involved. Miss Van Slyck was a small woman, but it would have taken at least three hands to stifle her cries and beat her legs. We have absolutely no evidence to aid us in identifying who those people might have been, but there is, as Mr. Lovett pointed out, no reason whatsoever to suspect Simu."

Hollis raised his unruly salt-and-pepper eyebrows. "You both agree on this?"

"Yes, sir. Most definitely." They spoke in unison.

"The missionaries cause more trouble than they do good," Hollis said.

Tolliver's temper prickled at this slight. Surely Hollis knew that his wife was a missionary's daughter—the gossip mill in Nairobi had talked of little else when he and Vera were married—but he did not defend the missionaries. "As I said, sir, Simu had been rejected by her husband and then ostracized by the tribe even before she took baptism."

"And where is she now?"

"With Dr. Ramsay. He agreed to watch over her, but he is leaving tomorrow, trekking back to Kikuyu."

"And the natives hereabouts have not been told she killed their *enka*—whatever you call her?"

"No, sir."

Hollis nodded. "What I had heard about you is correct, Tolliver. You are more capable than many who serve in your capacity. I will ask Dr. Ramsay to take the woman with him and get her away from here. We need her to disappear, to make this hubbub about killings go away as quickly as possible. I will ask the Mission Society in Nairobi to give her work as a maid."

Lovett looked shocked. "Will they want to take a murderess into their midst?"

"They will not know that about her, will they?" Hollis said, clearly giving an order rather than asking a question.

Tolliver was so surprised by the suggestion that he could not think what to say. Nor did he have the right to object to any decision Hollis might make.

Hollis read his expression. "Sometimes, Mr. Tolliver, an expedient is the only choice we have. I know you are well aware of this from your past experiences on the police force."

"That is certainly true, sir."

Hollis turned to Lovett. "We won't have any difficulty, will we, Assistant District Superintendent?"

Lovett gave the only possible answer. "No, sir."

Hollis then sank Tolliver's heart by insisting on knowing exactly to what extent Ruth Van Slyck's body had been mutilated.

Tolliver tried and failed to keep his face from turning scarlet. He liked to think he had outgrown blushing, but this subject overwhelmed whatever control he had. "There was no mutilation, sir. I assure you. Dr. Ramsay did the examination and found none. When I became aware of the rapidity with which that rumor was spreading, I made it my business to confirm Dr. Ramsay's conclusion."

Hollis looked as shocked as if Tolliver had reported this news at a formal dinner party. "You looked at—"

Lovett looked away in disgust.

Tolliver answered quickly in the hopes of putting them all out of their misery. "It is in the report that Dr. Ramsay wrote, signed also by me, and witnessed by A.D.S. Lovett."

Everything Tolliver had done to quash the ugly gossip had evidently failed. It baffled him why people wanted to pass around such an unspeakable story.

"The business of this native practice on their women is not our affair," Hollis said. "We are here in the form of a Protectorate. In my position, I must do what I can to keep the peace between the natives and the needs of His Majesty's government. However strange and horrid we may think their customs, we are not here to change them. I have it on the authority of several eminent professors that it would be arrogant in the extreme to tell the natives how they must live. The missionaries will have to abide by the government's decisions on such matters."

Tolliver said nothing. Arrogant in the extreme? In his mind, Justin heard Vera's and her father's opinions as loudly as if they were shouting them in his ear, but he would not chance saying anything of them to Hollis. From his work on the police force, he knew that, even if Hollis sincerely wanted to oppose the practice, powers above him would not hesitate to override his decisions. They did whatever was best for the Empire and offered whatever available rationale supported it. Tolliver forced his nose not to react to the rat it smelled.

Hollis looked at him for several seconds. "Let that be that then."

To keep his expression neutral, Tolliver refilled his teacup and fussed with the cream pitcher and sugar bowl.

Hollis then gave them an actual order. "We are going ahead as quickly as possible. While we ready the Maasai to move, I want the two of you to put on a show of power over the next twenty-four hours. Post your askaris about the town. March them on parade in a changing of the guard a few times a day. Show everyone in the town—Maasai or otherwise—that we are completely in charge. According to the local district commissioner, the non-Maasai people here are quite in accord with us when it comes to this move. It will mean great freedom and prosperity for all hereabouts. As long as the first four days go off without a hitch, you will be free to leave the area, A.D.S. Tolliver."

Tolliver could not help asking a policeman's question. "What about the investigation into the murder of Ruth Van Slyck?"

Hollis stood. He was several inches shorter than Tolliver. He looked up at him askance. "I am sure you know better than I how unlikely it is that we will ever discover exactly what happened there."

"That is true, sir. I have experienced such disappointments before, as I think you must have heard."

Hollis said good-bye, and that was an end to it.

Tolliver parted company from Lovett and went to the railway station to send a cable to Clarence McIntosh. He wanted Vera to know as soon as she arrived home that he would likely be joining her in but a few days.

He spent the next few hours working with Lovett to organize the askaris, just to give himself something to do. As time for the midday meal approached, he sent a runner to the guesthouse to tell Madame that he would not be returning for luncheon. Then he invited Lovett to dine with him at the Midland Hotel.

The interior of the hotel—the sturdiest structure in the town—lived up to the exterior's promise. The lobby was done up quite nicely with carpets and draperies and that sort of mahogany furniture one found in upper-class men's clubs in Nairobi and Mombasa, and in smaller market towns in England for that matter.

The clock over the reception desk said twelve twenty-five. If there had been no delays, Vera and the others should be arriving at the Athi River railway station just about now. Justin resented being kept here, given the paltry little he was allowed to do. He pictured them descending, unloading all their gear. Clarence McIntosh would have sent the buggy to fetch Vera and Constance. Justin so wanted to be there and not in this damned hotel.

He and Lovett stopped in the bar for a gin and quinine while they waited for the dining room to open at one o'clock. They did not discuss what had happened that morning. There was no point in expressing their frustration to one another.

They took club chairs near a window. When the drinks came, Lovett raised his. "Here's to my hopes that my next posting will be in Mombasa. Mosquitoes or no mosquitoes, I think I am ready to be in a place that is at least somewhat civilized."

Tolliver raised his glass too. "Vera and I liked it there very much."

Lovett shrugged. "With my luck they will put me at the lake." He did not have to say which lake. Victoria Nyanza was notorious in the police service for being the worst posting—the most remote from any of the nicer amusements of life in the Protectorate, and a horrid sink of malaria to boot. Tolliver could only think how truly dangerous it would be for Lovett, with his propensity to overdo the alcohol. Men less tempted than he had succumbed to drunkenness, there being so few other amusements available there.

Tolliver nearly spoke his gratitude that he was leaving the service without having to go there, but he thought better of it. By the time they ordered their third round of gin and quinine, drinking on an empty stomach, Tolliver was not exactly sober when Sergeant Marcal approached the door and signaled them. They waved him over.

"Sirs," Marcal said. "Word has come from Naivasha. Sergeant Libazo has gone absent without leave." He handed Lovett a note.

Tolliver's scalp turned to ice. "What does it say?"

Lovett looked up and shrugged. "Nothing more."

Tolliver could not take this in. "I don't believe it. Libazo is the last man on earth I would have expected to do such a thing."

Lovett made a noise that might have been a laugh. "Native boys do that all the time. You must know that."

"Not Libazo." Tolliver's voice was emphatic and loud enough to turn heads around the room.

Marcal took a step closer. "May I speak, sirs?"

Lovett said, "No."

Tolliver overrode him. "If you know something, tell me now."

"Sir," Marcal said. "The boys have been talking. They say Sergeant Libazo has a woman somewhere—a Somali woman that he dotes on. They say she is with child. The sergeant did not say this to me, but the others—who served with him in Mombasa. They know of it."

Tolliver divined at once why Kwai had run off. Profound disappointment seeped into his heart. Aurala was giving birth, and Kwai—who had never been an impetuous man—had lost his control and run away to be with her. If Tolliver had not heard it with his own ears, he would not have believed it. Libazo would be off the force. Good God! Did he realize he might be shot for desertion?

Tolliver rose to his feet. His head swam.

Lovett came to his side. "You've become flushed. What is it?"

"I have to send a cable." He ran toward the telegraph office at the station. His first thought was that Vera should tell Kwai he must immediately report back to duty, but by the time he was halfway across the road, he realized that they would arrest Kwai as soon as he arrived. Vera must hide him. Whatever was going on with Aurala, if they were looking for Kwai at the Mission, they must not find him. The boys in Nairobi might know he had Aurala there…No. No. Kwai had told him over and over that he had trusted no one with any knowledge of Aurala or where she was.

The sound of a Klaxon from an approaching motorcar woke Tolliver from his reverie in the middle of the street. He stiffened. Good God! He was tipsier than he thought three drinks would make him.

He sped to the stationmaster, a Sikh with a somber look about him that matched Tolliver's mood. "The down-train that left here early this morning, I must know where it is? Was it delayed before it arrived in Nairobi?"

"You are speaking with great authority, sir," the Sikh said.

"And who are you to remark on that?" He was barking, and he knew it. "Tell me what I want to know at once."

At that point, Lovett came up behind Tolliver. "This is A.D.S. Tolliver of the Protectorate's police force. Tell him what he needs to know immediately."

Tolliver looked down at himself and realized that without his uniform the man had no way of knowing that he should be obeyed. "Yes. Please," he said.

The Sikh pointed to the map behind him. "The blue pin is for the up-train. The yellow for the down. The telegraphers at each station send a message to all of us once the train has arrived. This way we know whenever there is trouble and help might be needed." A yellow pin was stuck in the map at the Nairobi Station.

Tolliver shook his head trying to think clearly. The clock on the station wall said five past one. The train must have been delayed, or it would have passed through Nairobi and arrived at the Athi Station half an hour ago. The normal layover in Nairobi was forty-five minutes. Tolliver blew out his breath. "What time did the train arrive in Nairobi?"

The man riffled through some papers on the counter before him. "It arrived in Nairobi nearly half hour ago. I imagine it will be leaving in fifteen or twenty minutes."

Tolliver shouted, "Thank you," over his shoulder as he ran to the telegraph office, where he wrote out his first message for the Athi Station, to Clarence McIntosh: *Aurala's husband must not be seen. Under no circumstances should he be discovered.*

He handed it to the telegrapher. "I am A.D.S. Justin Tolliver. Please send this immediately."

The Blasphemers

The man went right to his key and began tapping.

Tolliver wrote out a second for delivery to the Nairobi Station, for Mrs. Vera Tolliver on the down-train: *Aurala's baby's father wants to be present at the birth. Vital he keeps it secret.*

He handed the message over. He blinked. His head was clearing. He had tried to communicate the urgency of the situation without revealing too much. Telegraphers were never supposed to reveal the information they gleaned from their work, but who knew how faithful they actually were to their oath.

20

In the dining room of the railway hotel just across the road from Nairobi Station, Vera took a few desultory bites of the chicken curry on the plate in front of her. She did not want this food. She wanted to take her child in her arms. The layover in Nairobi was an expected part of the journey. Like their fellow passengers, after almost ten hours confined to a small compartment on the train, her companions had been glad of the opportunity for a good meal and a chance to stretch their legs. They were treating the entire ride as a lovely social event. Happy Constance, the bride to be, enthralled with the sightings of animals from the train, had been delighted to have Denys identifying the many species of antelope and hawks circling in the azure skies. She had held hands with the duke and even dozed with her head on his shoulder in the gloom of the night, when she thought no one would notice.

But for Vera, an hour's delay at the beginning of the trip, for reasons no one ever explained, had made her anxious in the extreme. For a while she had become more or less accustomed to being away from Will, being out hunting and selecting their farm site that would one day be his, but her time confined to the train had brought with it terrible thoughts that the baby might be in danger. She had no reason for the fear, but it haunted her.

She was doing her best not to be a spoilsport about this luncheon, telling herself that it was less than an hour to Athi River once they were under way, but Denys kept looking at her as if he expected her to burst into tears at any moment, which made it more difficult for her not to.

Then something quite strange occurred. They were crossing back to the station and getting ready to re-board the train when a boy approached them. He wore the navy shorts and khaki shirt of the railway telegraph messengers. He asked if one of the ladies was Mrs. A.D.S. Tolliver and then handed a telegram to Vera.

Her blood froze and her stomach churned. The baby? No. Justin. Something awful had happened to Justin. She stared at the envelope.

The duke thought to hand the messenger a coin. The boy took it and ran off.

"You are as white as a sheet," Constance declared.

Denys gently slipped the cable from her hands. "Let me help you with that," he said quietly.

She gladly let it go. It felt as if he had removed a deadly snake from her hands.

Denys turned aside. She moved to stay near him. He opened the envelope, read its contents, and smiled at her. "It's from Tolliver and it makes no sense at all," he said.

She took it and read it and puzzled over it for several seconds. Denys was right. Was Justin drunk when he wrote— wait. She understood. He had not used Kwai's name because Kwai was in some sort of trouble or danger.

She read and reread the words. Good lord! Kwai had left Naivasha and was headed to Aurala. She had to hide him because he was in trouble. For running away!

Her blood had run cold at the sight of the telegram. Now her breath stopped. Aurala was in danger from those brothers of hers. Justin had not mentioned them in his message, but she was sure of it. They had killed their other sister for dishonoring the family. Aurala had always said that they would come looking for her, that they would not rest until they killed her too. Kwai had somehow learned that they were here. She could not imagine how he could have found it out. But somehow he must have.

The conductor blew his whistle and shouted, "All aboard."

The duke gave Constance and then Vera a hand up the steps to their compartment. When they were all inside, Denys locked the door just as the train started to move.

"What was that about?" Gian Lorenzo whispered to Denys.

"It could be something dreadful," Vera said. She could hear the shrill tone of her own voice. Her heart was fluttering.

Denys gave Gian Lorenzo a warning look.

She looked Denys in the eye. They had been friends from his earliest days in the Protectorate. She did not want to speak her fear to him. It would make it too close, too real.

"Tell me," Constance insisted. "Is my brother in some sort of mortal danger?" Her neck stiffened. "I insist on knowing it now!" Vera had never heard her speak with such authority.

"No," Denys said. "The message is from him and concerns the constable who was his sergeant."

Constance looked from him to Vera. "Then why are you so frightened? You are. Don't deny it."

Vera took a breath and spoke her fear, beginning with a palliative for Constance. "I don't know exactly what is going on, but Justin is trying to protect Kwai Libazo—his sergeant who is father to Aurala Sagal's baby." Then she went on to explain that the previous year, Aurala's Somali brothers had discovered that their runaway sisters were in Mombasa. To avenge their family's honor, they had found and beheaded Aurala's older sister.

Constance gasped.

Gian Lorenzo glared at Vera. "Really? Must we—"

Denys held up an open hand to the duke. "Lady Constance is not a child. All of us knowing what is afoot will make the situation safer for everyone."

Vera went on. "From what Justin's message said, I surmise that the brothers have somehow located Aurala. Justin's plea to me was to make sure that Kwai is not discovered. I don't know why he said that."

"Mmm," Gian Lorenzo said. "If this Kwai is part of a military unit and went off without permission, he will have put his life on the line."

"The B.E.A. police force is comprised of officers seconded from the military," Denys offered.

"Then they may view Kwai Libazo as a deserter."

"He wouldn't desert his post for any other reason," Vera said. "But if Aurala is in danger, nothing would stop him."

"We will do whatever we can to help," Gian Lorenzo said.

"Absolutely," Denys echoed.

Vera suddenly realized that the murderous brothers would be heading for her father's Mission. And baby Will. Her breath quickened.

She could not reveal that. She was sure it would start Constance screaming. She was about to start screaming herself. She held it in and stared unseeing out at the vast plain that had been her home since birth. They had thought that the mere size of it would conceal Aurala. Now all that size meant only that it would take another hour before this train would arrive at the station. An eternity. All she wanted at this moment was to hold her baby in her arms and know that he was safe. How would she bear the wait?

She ought to pray. "Oh, please, dear God," she silently began. But that was as far as her prayer would go. She just kept repeating it. "Oh, please, dear God. Oh, please, dear God," to the rhythm of the wheels on the rails.

Kwai Libazo, making his way along the forest road between Nairobi to the Scottish Mission, would not have called what he was doing praying, but his thoughts were very like a prayer. He had descended from a third-class railway car on that same train that Vera and her companions had taken from Nakuru. Kwai knew that, during the train's layover, he would make better time going to the Mission on foot. Besides, he could blend in with the crowds at Nairobi Station. If he waited to descend at Athi River, he would be noticed by whomever was at the station. Something he knew he must not allow.

Without his uniform, dressed in the ubiquitous dark orange *shuka* of a Kikuyu tribesman and carrying a Kikuyu spear, Kwai felt safely invisible to anyone looking for a runaway constable. Before he left Naivasha, he had done everything he could to make sure that it would be a good long while, if ever, before he was missed. A.D.S. Lovett, the lackadaisical man in charge of his unit, was far away in Nakuru and seeing to a potentially explosive relocation of the Maasai. He would not be asking for Sergeant Libazo. Kwai was not sure that Lovett even knew who he was.

The path Kwai followed went through a wilderness area where wild animals might lurk. He knew how to defend himself with the spear. Out on the open plain he had passed harmless creatures, like impala and kudu. As he entered the forest, he had to be on the lookout for their predators—lions, hyenas.

Kwai's deepest fears had nothing to do with creatures with claws and teeth that might be watching him from behind that rain tree. His concerns were not at all for his own life. No. Only for Aurala Sagal and their unborn child. He would give up his own life without a thought to protect them.

A devout Muslim would say it was only through Allah that Kwai had discovered the danger to Aurala and the baby. He had been meeting the imam at the mosque in Naivasha, thinking he would surprise Aurala by converting to Islam. She had not asked him to do this, but he had nothing else to give her. He did not own one cow or even one goat. He could give her respect by becoming what she was.

The imam's son had told him that two Somali men from the coast had asked in the town where they might find a British policeman named Bilazo. The boy rightly imagined that they must have meant Kwai.

Kwai knew at once that they could only be the Sagal brothers, looking for him so they could find their sister. Last year, when he had taken her from Mombasa to the Scottish Mission, he thought he had saved her from them forever.

He feared what they would do to her. And he hated them. He would never understand why they wanted to take their sisters' lives because of what those poor girls had been forced to do.

Before Aurala met Kwai, her sister Leylo was the only person who had loved and cared for her. When Leylo was newly married, thieves had grabbed her on the street and dragged her away. Just thirteen, Aurala had donned a burka and followed far enough to find out where they had taken Leylo. Then she ran away to Mombasa to find her sister, her only friend. When she did find Leylo, in a brothel in the souk, Aurala herself had become a captive and been forced to work there.

Eventually their brothers discovered where they were and had come to Mombasa to kill them, to defend the honor of their family, they said. They caught Leylo. But not Aurala. Not yet. Never. He would strangle them with his bare hands.

As fast as he had been running, Kwai picked up his pace. He had been foolish to think Aurala was safe. It would have been easy for her brothers to find him if they learned their sister had taken up with a policeman. All they would have to do to find Kwai was ask casual questions of the policemen in Mombasa. They could pretend to know him, to owe him money, for instance. That was what Kwai himself would have said if he were trying to find a particular askari.

They could easily have learned that he had been posted to Naivasha, and so they had found him. He tried to convince himself that they still might have no idea where Aurala was. No one up in Naivasha knew anything about her. He had told no one, not even the imam.

But if they had found him, they might be clever enough to find her. If they learned he had worked with A.D.S. Tolliver, they would easily connect him with the Scottish Mission.

Wasn't that extremely unlikely? Wasn't he being overly cautious?

That did not matter.

He ran faster.

When he got to Aurala, he would never leave her side. Even if that meant he would never again be able to call himself Sergeant Kwai Libazo. Never again have the pleasure of thinking the way a policeman thought. It was the working out of things— what questions to ask, who to ask them of, what did not fit with the stories he was told—until he saw the answer. These were the things that pleased him so much about being a policeman. He loved the idea of justice, even if it was not always possible in the world of the British overlords.

He hated Aurala's brothers all the more because they had robbed him of his work. They were clever, but he was more clever. He would not rest until they were dead.

As he neared the Mission, his pace slowed by the rise in the land, he needed to watch the undergrowth for predators. Though the sun had passed its zenith, the cats would likely still be sleeping, but one did not rely on the predictability of cats.

As he emerged into the clearing above the Mission, he saw the Reverend McIntosh leaving by the road to the Athi River Station. Kwai thought to hide—not to be seen by him until he could speak with him and explain his presence.

But the missionary saw Kwai and stood in the buggy to hail him. Kwai had no choice. He waved his open palms and went to speak to the reverend.

At two that afternoon, waiting at the Athi River Railway Station for a train an hour and a half behind schedule, the Reverend Clarence McIntosh did nothing but pray. He was a prayerful man. One who held in his soul the hope that the Almighty would grant solace if asked. Not always, certainly. But God would. Prayers were answered. Besides which, there was naught else he could do at the moment.

As a Scot he had been raised to believe that his fate in the afterlife had been predetermined at his birth. Not the sort of belief to make a man optimistic. But Clarence had studied at Magee College in Ulster in Ireland with ministers of the New Light. Their liberal approach to their religion matched more closely to his natural inclination to be a joyful Christian.

Joyful was not what he would call himself at the moment. Just as he was leaving his Mission to meet Vera's train, he had encountered Kwai Libazo—dressed not in his constable's uniform, but in the orange *shuka* of a Kikuyu tribesman. Kwai had told him the most horrifying news—that the lovely Aurala, heavy with child, was being hunted by her vengeful brothers.

More than the heat of the African sun, the terror of the situation weighed on Clarence. Then, halfway to the station, a messenger boy had found him and put into his hands an indecipherable telegram from Justin. It said only that Libazo was in trouble and had to be hidden. Nothing about the reason for such a request. Surely if Justin knew that Libazo was coming home, he knew why.

Justin was being cryptic in the extreme. He, who teased Clarence unmercifully about being too thrifty to pay for extra words in a cable. Clarence might have been brief, but his messages were clear. Justin was being terse—creating confusion by not saying enough.

He looked down at the orange envelope, took out Justin's message, and reread it. There was no doubt that Justin was asking him to protect Kwai. At the Mission, not half an hour ago, Kwai had spoken only about protecting the girl. Why was Justin expressing no concern about her? The poor child was in dire straits.

Clarence's prayers were only for her. Mark 13:17 kept running through his mind: "But woe to them that are with child and to them that give suck in those days!"

When the train finally pulled into view, he prepared himself to reveal the dangerous news to his beloved daughter. There would be no hiding from her that something was amiss. She would see it in a glance. From infancy, she had always matched his moods, even the sorry ones that he tried to hide from her. Especially the sorry ones he tried to hide from her.

When the train came to a stop and the compartment doors opened, that nice Italian leapt out and helped Vera descend. And as soon as Clarence saw her, he knew she had already been told. He could not imagine by whom.

Porters unloaded half a car of safari gear with astonishing alacrity. The Italian count or prince, whatever he was, conferred with his gun bearer. Denys Finch Hatton went to speak with his man Kinuthia.

More than twenty people had been waiting on the platform to take this train to Mombasa. The numbers traveling to and from this station had been increasing rapidly, but this crowd was surprisingly large.

The new down passengers pushed forward and climbed on, and soon the great iron beast was chugging east on its way to the coast.

Clarence went and embraced Vera. "You know then, my lass?" he whispered in her ear, not sure which of the others knew or should know.

Vera embraced him. "Yes, Papa. Will is...?"

"The wee one is just fine," he said.

She sighed with relief. "As to the other matter," she said, and smiled rather wanly, "we have brought reinforcements."

Clarence could see she meant it in a cheering, joking way, but it fell flat for both of them. "We will be safe," he said. "I have the buggy here, but it will take only four. Do they all know about the brothers?"

"Yes," she said, and went to speak to Finch Hatton, who talked to the Italian. Constance seemed focused only on her beau. She turned and saw Clarence watching her. She blushed. "I am sorry, Reverend McIntosh," she said. "I was distracted by all the activity. Thank you for coming to meet us."

"Of course," he said. The lass was so well trained to say the polite thing that it seemed to fall from her lips regardless of the circumstances.

The Italian came to them. He was carrying a rifle. "Denys will walk with the porters. I will come with you."

"Just a minute," Vera said. She went to Denys, who took off his hat and ran his hand through his hair in a gesture McIntosh had seen him make many times.

They took two more rifles. Vera returned carrying hers, and Finch Hatton handed one to Lady Constance. He held up his hand to the Italian. "In England," he said, "it's a sign of breeding for a lady to know how to shoot. Here it's—well, you never know when you might meet a lion."

"Too true," Clarence said. He led them to where the buggy waited in the shade of a thorn tree. His own rifle was lying across the driver's bench.

Vera tried her best not to show her anxiety to her father. He looked as if he was doing the same.

"The boy is extremely well," he said, his voice strained despite the good news he was imparting.

Gian Lorenzo had taken the reins with Constance beside him, leaving Vera and her papa in the rear seat.

She took his hand and sat very close to him as they bumped along the rutted road. "How did Aurala take the news? Does she even know?"

"I dunna know. I was in the buggy on my way to meet your train when I saw Kwai Libazo coming into the compound on foot from the high road from Nairobi."

She started. "He's already here?" Her mind scrambled to imagine the events that might be taking place at the Mission. How had Kwai found out the brothers were coming? She had imagined that Kwai, leaving Naivasha, told Justin who then telegraphed her. If that were the case, how could Kwai have gotten here so soon? She knew too much and not enough about what was happening. She wanted to spirit her baby away. And Aurala too.

She felt as if she wanted to leap down and run faster than the horse could draw the buggy.

"I know that we must keep Kwai from being discovered," her father said. "At least I think that's what Justin's cable meant."

"Justin wrote to you?"

"Yes." Her father reached into his inside breast pocket. "His message wasn't very clear."

She snatched the message from him. Then, scanning it, she drew Justin's message to her from her own pocket and gave it to her father. "Justin doesn't know about the brothers," she said.

"Oh, he must." Her father pointed to the message in her hand. "Otherwise, why would he have sent that to me?"

"It says only that Kwai wants to attend the birth. If Justin knew those monsters were on their way to you, he would have warned you. I believe that he knows only that Kwai has left his post to be with Aurala when the baby is born."

"But a man in Kwai's position takes a grave step by leaving his post," her father said. "Justin must have known Kwai would not run off helter-skelter like that."

"I wonder about that too," Vera said. "I can only think that Justin has too much on his mind. There have been two murders in Nakuru." She sketched out those events to her father's increasing horror.

"Oh, my lass. Oh, my lass," was all he seemed to be capable of saying, while squeezing her hand when she spoke of the circumcision of the girls. "I never wanted you to know about that."

"I know, Father," she said. "You were protecting me."

They fell silent.

After a moment, Vera spoke. "At any rate, whatever is going on up there must have Justin so distracted that he isn't thinking clearly about this business of Kwai running away."

During the rest of the ride to the Mission grounds no one spoke at all.

As they entered the compound she saw native boys in their dark orange *shuka*s already posted in twos and threes under the trees in the open area between the buildings, at the side door of the hospital, and at the back and side doors of the house. Nothing like this had ever been necessary in her entire life.

Fearsome wild animals surrounded them here. Lionesses that would go for the throat. Hippos that could kill with one snap of their powerful jaws. The threat her father feared most: snakes. Mambas that would strike and kill instantly. Yes, there were ways to protect themselves from these creatures. But men bent on murder? Justin had always said that the most dangerous animals in Africa were the people.

As soon as Gian Lorenzo brought the buggy to a stop next to the hospital, she leapt from it. As she expected, Wangari was there, in the shade of the building, waiting with Will in her arms. Vera took her baby and clasped him to her. He looked at her. "Hello, my darling," she said. She was sure he recognized her. He put his little hand on her mouth and gripped her lip, the way he had begun to do before she left. Wangari had said it was because he wanted to learn how to speak, was touching her to find out how she did it.

"You feel how much he has grown," Wangari declared. "It is a child's work, and he does it very well."

It was a statement Vera would have loved to hear, except that Wangari did not smile. "Where is Kwai?" Vera whispered though there was no one near enough to hear.

Wangari spoke her worry. "Aurala is in labor. It does not go well."

"Where is she?"

"In hospital with Nurse Freemantle. The village midwife is also with her. Kwai stands at the door of her room."

Vera wanted to run to them, but she did not want to give up her baby. "Is there fever in the hospital now?"

"No. No fever has come since you left."

Vera carried Will with her and went to them. Wangari followed.

The boy Haki, the waif Kwai and Aurala had rescued from the streets of Mombasa, stood at attention next to a Kikuyu guard on the hospital veranda. He looked gravely at Vera. "I am here helping to guard my mother," he said. At ten, he was cannier and braver than any British child Vera could imagine, and devoted to Kwai and Aurala as the only parents he had ever known.

Vera touched his head. "You are a good son," she said and entered the sturdy stone building.

The doors to the native side of the hospital were closed. It was quiet there. Wangari pointed to their left. "They put Aurala on the white side, in a room alone. Nurse Freemantle was the one who said to do that."

Vera nodded. Nurse Freemantle had changed a great deal in the years since she came to this Mission, especially since the death of Uncle Josiah. Her opinions about sickness were stauncher than ever, but she now seemed to judge people less by what color they were and more by who they were. Vera thought of her granny in Scotland. Could Africa do that for her grandmother too? She would never know. Granny would never come to Africa.

Kwai stood guard at Aurala's door. He bowed to Vera in that elegant way of his, but he did not give her one of his beautiful smiles. He was a sight most whites in the Protectorate had never seen and never wished to see: A man in native dress holding a rifle—one of her father's hunting rifles she imagined.

He nodded toward the door. "She moans," he said. His brow was knit with deep worry that must have been sitting there since he heard the news of the brothers.

"It is normal," she said to him. She might have added that she had screamed while giving birth. But she knew that men never wanted such details.

She gave Will to Wangari and asked her to wait. She tapped lightly on the door and opened it. She could not mistake the anxious look on Nurse Freemantle's face. The Scottish Mission volunteer had served in South Africa during the Boer War. Normally, she seemed impervious to ordinary human emotions.

The village midwife knelt next to the cot on which Aurala lay, holding the girl's hand. Aurala looked too young. She was sixteen, past the time when most African girls gave birth to their first babies, but her lovely, smooth tawny face had always made her seem younger, and the sweetness of her expression erased anything womanly about her. At this moment, fear and pain made that childlike face not mature, merely pathetic.

Nurse Freemantle motioned Vera into the corner. "The baby is in breech position," she whispered. "She ought to have a caesarian section, but the doctor has gone up to Kikuyu to deal with an outbreak of typhoid at the army barracks."

Vera's blood chilled. "What can we do?"

"Nothing but wait and hope. The child is quite large for her slender hips."

Vera's heart sank. She went to Aurala and touched her cheek. "You are in the best possible hands," she said, knowing that the girl would think she meant Nurse Freemantle and the midwife. But she really had God in mind, or in Aurala's case, Allah.

Before leaving the room, she did her best to put on a brave face for Kwai. "She will be fine," she said to him as she closed the door gently behind her. She saw disbelief in his eyes. He was too intelligent to swallow her lie. She touched his arm and then took the sleeping Will from Wangari's arms and hugged him to her. She felt again the weight he had gained in the past two weeks, and vowed never again to leave him.

She found Constance and the duke on the veranda with her father.

"I have just been explaining to these lovely people," Papa said, "that I don't think we can arrange proper meals—what with the boys all armed and standing guard." He gestured toward Njui, their houseboy, next to the hall door, dressed not in his usual white *kanzu* and red fez but in his Kikuyu garb and holding a spear. Vera had seen Gothua, the cook, standing guard near the road from the station. There was a rifle or a shotgun next to every chair on the veranda.

Her father's expression held an apology, as if he were somehow responsible. He was like that. He took personally anything he thought would distress her. "We'll have to make do with sandwiches, I'm afraid."

She put a hand on his shoulder. "For the past several days we have been overfed by our Belgian hostess in Nakuru. We had a hearty meal in Nairobi at midday. I am sure Gian Lorenzo and Constance will be very happy with whatever comes our way this afternoon and evening."

Both murmured their agreement.

"I'll go make sure today's tea is extra good," Vera said. "I'll tell Wangari she's being recruited as a cook. She'll make us muffins." She did her best to keep her tone light.

They spent the rest of the afternoon all doing the same—pretending not to be terrified by the danger from Aurala's brothers. Vera kept to herself her anxiety over Aurala's birth pangs. She went into the kitchen and talked to Wangari.

Just before tea was served, they heard the porters, led by Denys, arriving from the station. He went into the house to wash up and then joined them on the veranda.

"Nothing of note happening here at the moment, I take it," he said, reaching for a chicken sandwich.

"Not much," Vera said. "Aurala is in hospital. The baby will come soon." She blew out her breath. She could not keep up this ruse. "Listen," she said. "From what my father and I surmise, Justin does not know that Aurala's brothers have resurfaced. His separate messages to us seem to indicate only his fear of Kwai's having left his post without permission."

The thought that fell into Vera's heart spilled out of her mouth. "I wish Justin were here."

Gian Lorenzo sat forward. "Isn't he set to take the next train?"

Vera shook her head. "He said he hoped to. He didn't say he would for certain."

Denys looked at the sky. "There is time," he said. "I'll go to the station and send him a telegram."

Denys stood and, taking a buttered muffin with him, turned toward the stable. "Let's make sure Justin is fully informed. It'll take less than an hour for me to get there and back if I can borrow a horse."

"Take mine," Clarence McIntosh said. He called to Haki who sped over. "Saddle Pilgrim for Mr. Finch Hatton," he told the boy.

Vera watched Denys gallop off and struggled to quell her doubts. Certainly Denys was doing the right thing. All the others approved. But she could not dismiss an illogical, but terrible premonition—that something bad would come of this.

She hugged her baby to her and prayed she was wrong.

22

That afternoon Tolliver and Lovett retuned to the hotel bar after having said good-bye to Arthur Ramsay, set to leave at dawn the next day with Simu the murderess and his contingent of Kikuyu. Then they watched while the Maasai made ready to depart for their new lands. The endeavor seemed to be going peacefully enough.

The pastoral, more or less nomadic tribe did not amass possessions. They prized their animals and their jewelry, all easy enough to move away. Their dwellings were simple in the extreme. It would take them very little time and no real expense to construct new ones when they arrived at their new homeland. At least that was what Justin told himself. He could not but think how resentful and even violent a group of Englishmen would become if a number this large were forced off property they considered legally theirs. It seemed more than anyone could hope that these virile men would go without a fight. But going they seemed to be.

The womenfolk and children had begun to set out within hours of the announcement. All except for the girls who had been cut only a few days before. They were being kept behind and were being given a chance to heal before walking for miles. It gave Tolliver a jolt from his groin up his back to consider how painful it would be to walk any distance under such circumstances.

All Tolliver wanted to do was go home. A direct order from Jodrell would be the only thing that could possibly persuade Tolliver to stay beyond tomorrow. And such was unnecessary: Hollis had the army standing by. The Maasai were going quietly.

As to the murders, justice would, as usual, fail to apply, so what would be the use of his staying? The best thing he could do to help Lovett would be to convince Jodrell to make his next posting Mombasa. Lovett might find enough decent companionship there and perhaps not be so funked. At the very least his excessive drinking would be noticed and the force could take proper steps to deal with it.

As dusk fell, Tolliver walked Lovett back to his bungalow. Given his overindulgence earlier in the day, Tolliver had limited himself to one gin and quinine. Lovett had had four. What kind of shape would the man be in when Tolliver took the down-train at midnight tomorrow? Well, Tolliver would cross that bridge when he came to it.

Once Justin turned Lovett over to his batman, he headed to the Gillets', wishing for Vera. The light of the setting sun had turned the waters of the lake to a fiery orange.

Monsieur Gillet was waiting for Justin and handed him a telegram the minute he opened the front door. The message startled him. Good God! The Somali brothers! How could he not have surmised why Kwai had run off? He must have been drunker than he thought.

Monsieur Gillet stared at Justin standing in the doorway. "This news is awful," the Belgian said. "Please come in, Monsieur. Can I get you a brandy?"

"No. No," Justin said, backing out of the open door. "I must answer this immediately."

He hurried back to the station and the telegraph office, composing two messages in his head as went. The first to Vera: *Will arrive soonest without fail. Monday on noon train at AR Station.*

The other to Jodrell: *Must leave tomorrow midnight train without fail. Emergency at home. Needed urgently.*

Just over an hour later, when a runner from the station brought them Justin's cable, all the new arrivals at the Scottish Mission were yawning and rubbing their eyes before their dinner—such as it was—was laid out at eight p.m.

They had just started on Wangari's pumpkin soup when a clatter outside brought Denys, Clarence, and the duke to their feet. Vera watched from the veranda doorway while her father rushed across the lawn to greet a contingent of askaris in their signature khaki and red fezzes led by a Punjabi sergeant, descending from the hilltop road. The duke stopped halfway between her and her father. She could not hear what the sergeant was saying to her papa.

Gian Lorenzo came back to her. "The sergeant says D.S. Jodrell had a telegram from Justin that there was trouble here. Jodrell knew Libazo had run off and surmised he was causing the trouble. He sent the constables to deal with—"

Her father shouted and ran after the squad as it sped toward the hospital. Vera made to follow after them, but Gian Lorenzo held her back. "Please let me—"

She wriggled free and ran.

She was too late.

In the doorway of the hospital building, two askaris were struggling with Kwai Libazo. He was silent. The Punjabi sergeant was giving orders through clenched teeth. As Vera came to them, the sergeant was holding out a pair of handcuffs. "Hold him fast. Hold him fast," he was saying.

"What is the meaning of this? Stop it." She spoke too loudly. Aurala must not hear what was happening out here.

"This is a police matter," the sergeant said. "You must not interfere."

Gian Lorenzo came up behind her and a few steps behind him was Denys. "Stop that at once," Denys ordered the sergeant.

"This is none of your affair, Bwana," he said. "This man is a deserter from the police force. He went missing from his post in Naivasha. He was out of uniform and holding a rifle when I discovered him hiding here."

Vera's hands went to her hips. "You are not in charge on this Mission ground."

The sergeant stiffened. "I beg to differ with you, Memsahib. When it comes to police matters, I have been put in charge of the detail. I have found an armed former police sergeant hiding here. It is my duty to arrest him. What happens to him next is up to my superior officers. I beg you not to interfere with me."

Kwai had stopped struggling. He let the sergeant put the handcuffs on him. His eyes looked utterly defeated.

Denys put a hand on Vera's shoulder. "Let me take your father's horse again. I will ride back to the train station and send a wire to Jodrell. There must be a way we can stop this."

"In the night it will be dangerous," Clarence said. "The animals."

"I will go with you," Gian Lorenzo said.

"No," Clarence said. "You stay here with Vera and Constance. I will go with Finch Hatton."

"What is your name, Sergeant?" Denys demanded, his voice more imperious than Vera had ever heard it.

The man stiffened his jaw. 'I am Sergeant Kang."

"Thank you. I will make it a point to remember that."

Within the next few minutes, Sergeant Kang had commandeered the Mission office and had two armed men there standing guard over Kwai Libazo.

Haki ran to the stable to saddle the horses. When they were mounted, Denys gave Vera a sunny smile. "We will be back in forty minutes. Save me some of those delicious chicken sandwiches." And they galloped off.

When Vera went back to the veranda, Constance was fretting. "It is too wrong. I was happy when I saw them. I thought they were meant to be coming to help."

Gian Lorenzo took her hand. "I am sure Justin did not think, when he wrote to his D.S., that something like this would happen."

"No, indeed," Vera said. "Gian Lorenzo, I need your help. That smug, officious Sergeant Kang will never listen to a woman. It will be totally dark once the moon sets. Would you please tell him what the real danger is here. The Kikuyu boys must remain on guard, and they must light torches and bonfires."

"I will do that now." He stood and walked toward the office, looking every bit the commander of men that he was.

Vera hurried toward the hospital and, praying for better news about Aurala, went to speak to Nurse Freemantle.

She tapped gently on Aurala's door and opened it quietly. Nurse Freemantle came to her immediately, with her forefinger to her lips. She pushed into the hall and whispered, "She is between contractions. We want her to rest as much as possible."

"It's been so long. Will she come through? Will the baby?"

"I do not know."

"Is there anything at all I can do?"

"Nothing. What have they done with Kwai Libazo?"

"He is under arrest, being kept under guard."

"Who will protect her if those monstrous brothers of hers come?" Nurse Freemantle looked fierce, as if she would deal with them with her teeth if they came near her patient. "Without Libazo to lead them, I don't think the Kikuyu guards can do what might be called for."

Loyal as she was to her Kikuyu friends, Vera could not imagine the local boys taking personal risks to protect a Somali woman who consorted with a half-breed like Kwai Libazo.

"Denys Finch Hatton can command the respect of the native boys," Nurse Freemantle said.

"He has gone to the station with Papa to send a cable to Jodrell to try—"

A sharp cry from within the room called Nurse Freemantle away.

Vera could not bring herself to watch Aurala's agony.

Outside the moon shadows lengthened. Vera went back to the house and fetched her rifle and then took Kwai's place outside Aurala's door.

In the parlor, Constance paced the Turkish carpet.

"It's getting dark. I will post my men at the doors of the house," the duke said. He went out.

Constance stiffened her back. "It's better to be safe than sorry," she said aloud to herself. She wished there was a second story on the house, where it would be easier to guard baby Will. It troubled her that all the rooms had windows easily visible and accessible from the ground outside.

She went to the kitchen and found Wangari. "We need to stop anyone outside from seeing in. Is there anything we can use to cover the windows?"

Wangari put her fingertips to her cheeks. "Vera's mother used to teach the native girls to sew dresses for themselves." She took a hurricane lamp into a large workroom next to the kitchen. "Here," she said, touching a bolt of dark cotton.

"Perfect," Constance said.

They cut the fabric into lengths and hung it over the windows, starting with the room where baby Will now slumbered in his cot.

Gian Lorenzo soon returned and helped them. They had worked their way through the other bedrooms and were about halfway finished with the windows in the parlor when a hue and cry went up outside.

"Go to the child," Gian Lorenzo said. Constance had already dropped the fabric she was holding, grabbed her rifle, and was headed for the hall to the bedrooms. Wangari followed her.

She and Wangari went inside the nursery. Constance took a chair and sat in it with her rifle across her lap. Wangari sat on the floor beside the sleeping Will. Constance had no doubt that she would throw her own body across the baby before she let anyone harm him.

They sat in silence. The more time that passed the more anxious Constance became. Light flickered in at the edges of the black cloth over the window. The Kikuyu boys and the safari porters had lit bonfires out on the lawn. That would keep off the animals, and give them a chance at seeing anyone approaching.

Every once in a while a rustling sound came, which could be a person or just a small animal scrambling by. Not knowing which or who made Constance's skin crawl.

She tried to dismiss images of Gian Lorenzo attacked and bloodied. It remained too quiet. Why didn't someone come to give her news? She wanted to go out and see for herself, but she was sure that the second she did, Aurala's brothers would come storming in and—She could not even complete the thought. She bit her finger and fretted.

And then finally Gian Lorenzo came through the door, looking disheveled. "The sergeant had the audacity to tell Finch Hatton that he should have asked permission to leave the grounds. I had to physically restrain Denys from thrashing the man."

"The better if he had," Constance said.

23

When he and Denys returned to the Mission complex, Clarence McIntosh looked immediately for Vera and found her outside Aurala's hospital room. He kissed the top of her head. "The baby?" he asked, pointing to the door.

"Nothing yet," she said as she relinquished the chair.

"Go to the house, my lass," he said, "and stay with your child."

As she crossed the compound, she saw Kwai handcuffed and under guard, lying on the ground outside the Mission office. The arrogant Sergeant Kang was sitting at her father's desk.

Haki was standing near Kwai.

"Aurala is still waiting for your baby brother or sister," Vera called to Haki, loud enough for Kwai to hear. Kwai raised his head, nodded to her, and watched her cross to the house.

Kwai's heart trembled. He wanted the baby to come, to relieve its poor mother from her agony. He called upon his Maasai ancestry for the fortitude he needed. From time immemorial, Maasai warriors knew how to wait calmly, to pace themselves during arduous treks across burning hot territory that could go on for days. He had never before thought that the Maasai part of him was the good part.

The men of both his mother's tribe, the Kikuyu, and his father's, the Maasai, had rejected him. He was never allowed to go through the circumcision ceremony with the young men of either group. Sitting here, bound and guarded, he wondered if any of his ancestors—Kikuyu or Maasai—had ever felt the way he now did. Alone and desperate.

Denys Finch Hatton approached. Kwai knew him. Everyone in the Protectorate seemed to know him, but he also knew Kwai. They had gone together to rescue Vera McIntosh when she went off to save her brother. He was a settler, but one who loved Africa in the right way. As if to agree with Kwai's thoughts, the boy Haki went and took Finch Hatton's hand.

"I have just come back from the railway station," Finch Hatton said to the constable guards. "I did not see anything that looked dangerous on the way." He was taking small steps backward while he was talking. Both guards were looking at him and away from Kwai. They too moved almost imperceptibly, widening the space between themselves and Kwai. Finch Hatton was moving them away on purpose. Kwai became alert to what his intention might be.

His answer came as a tug on his foot. He looked up. Irungu, the biggest and strongest of the Mission Kikuyu boys squatted at his feet, his finger to his lips. He signaled to Kwai to move toward him. Kwai did, as silently as he could, holding his hands apart so the handcuffs would not clink. Irungu slipped into his place and lay down and faced the wall as if he were asleep, while Kwai disappeared around the corner.

Outside Aurala's room in the hospital, Clarence McIntosh was at once grateful that the chair he sat in was too hard to allow him to fall asleep, but also annoyed that it was so hard it made his back ache and sent pains shooting down his legs. Standing and flexing his feet from time to time helped, but not enough.

A baby's cry from inside the room sent away any thoughts of himself. "Thank you, dearest Lord," he whispered to the dim air around him. "Thank you."

He retook his seat and berated himself for worrying over his own ordinary pain while that poor threatened girl had been suffering such agonies. He expected that Nurse Freemantle would open the door at any moment and tell him the news of the child. When she did not come, he began to worry. From time to time he heard words being exchanged behind the door and little newborn noises, the likes of which he had heard from his own children. Memories of them flooded him. His lovely Vera, so tiny at birth, who grew, but never became even as tall as her mother. His Vera, small of stature, but so full of life that she seemed larger than most of the women he had ever known. His boy—he stopped there. There was no way to banish the pain of thinking about his boy.

He listened to the Mission grounds around the hospital. Any sound outside would be muffled by the stoutness of this building, which he had been so proud of. In a land where the local people's dwellings were flimsy and temporary, this great symbol of Christian charity was built to outlast anyone now alive. He still believed in his Mission, but he could not help but entertain doubts—not in his God, but that this work here was, in fact, God's work.

Nurse Freemantle's appearance at the door stopped his sigh. Her news brought a gasp from the depth of his being. "The baby is well," she said. "A girl. But we have lost Aurala."

His mind wanted to leap to prayer, but his heart was too vexed to speak to his Lord. God's will. He knew he was not meant to comprehend the mind of God.

"Take one of the boys at the door to go with you and bring the news to Kwai," he told the nurse.

"While he is under arrest? Do we have to tell him now?" Even in the shadowy hallway, lit only by a hurricane lamp, he could see the pain in her expression.

"You are right," he said, but the man had to know. "You go. Tell Vera. She is the one who is the closest thing he has to a friend here. She will know how to break the news to him."

Nurse Freemantle nodded curtly and walked silently off.

Clarence McIntosh thought now he might leave his post. He had taken Kwai Libazo's place in order to protect Aurala and her baby from her brothers' intention to murder their sister. The poor girl was dead now, killed by that which destroyed so many of the female sex—the act of bringing new life. The baby was alive, within this room, with its dead mother's body and the midwife who would find a young mother to feed the child and keep it alive. Would the newborn babe's uncles want to kill it for being the product of what they considered their shame? He had no idea of the workings of minds such as theirs.

Kwai Libazo stood, catching his breath, with his back against the dark rear wall of the Mission office, listening intently. He wanted to go directly to Aurala, but he knew he would be recognized and rearrested. He did not know what that stupid Sergeant Kang would do when they noticed that Irungu had taken his place.

Bwana Finch Hatton was still talking and distracting the askaris who were meant to be guarding him. Finch Hatton was telling them they must watch for intruders as well as keep an eye on Kwai. "He seems to have fallen asleep," he said. "Good. That will leave you to do what you were sent here to do—to protect the family from a threat. See that you do." His footsteps faded in the direction of the missionary's house.

Kwai waited. The guards did not come in his direction. They spoke among themselves, quietly. They seemed to be moving away from him, because soon Kwai could not make out what they were saying. He slowly moved away from the building. The light from the bonfire out on the lawn cast the shadow of the building ahead of him, toward the woods. Though he had only his bare, handcuffed fists to defend himself from whatever awaited him, in the calm, assured way of his Maasai ancestors, he strolled through the deepest part of the shadow toward the woods.

Vera stared at Denys Finch Hatton with a combination of shock and admiration. It was unheard of for a settler to aid a native who was flouting law enforcers. Yet here was Denys telling her, Constance, and Gian Lorenzo what he had just done. "One of the Mission boys said he would give him a spear. How he will use it while handcuffed, I can't imagine, but I think it is the best we can do."

"What news did you get in response to your cable to the district superintendent?" Constance asked.

"None," Denys answered. "We waited for an answer from Jodrell for several minutes, but it was getting darker. The Reverend McIntosh was anxious for us to return here." He pointed to the half-moon, setting behind the treetops. "There will be no light shortly."

Vera wanted to believe that Aurala's brothers would also be intimidated by the darkness, but it seemed, as determined as they were, that the darkness would spur them on.

She had come into the parlor from guarding little Will when she heard Denys at the front door. "I'll go back to the hospital," she said.

"Let me," Denys said.

She was about to object when Nurse Freemantle came to the front door, looking like the wrath of God.

Denys took Vera's rifle and trotted toward the bedrooms. "It's the last door on the left," she said automatically.

Nurse Freemantle entered and grasped Vera by the forearm. "Aurala is dead." Tears Vera had never thought possible glistened in the nurse's ordinarily hard eyes. Pain seared into Vera's heart. "Kwai?" she asked without thinking.

"Your father thought you should tell him."

Vera's chest heaved. She despised the thought of carrying such a message. Aurala's baby lived, but that dear girl was gone. She could hardly bear it herself. What could she say to Kwai?

"If you—" Nurse Freemantle started to say.

"No," Vera said. "Father is right. But I cannot bring that message just now. Mr. Finch Hatton has found a way to help Kwai escape."

Nurse Freemantle stared in disbelief down the hall where Denys had just disappeared.

"You look done in," Vera said to her. "Please, there are sandwiches and tea here." She indicated a table. "Have something."

"I would take a cup of tea," she said. She helped herself.

"The baby?" It was Constance who thought to ask.

"A girl," Nurse Freemantle said. "A lovely little thing. The midwife is with her. The Reverend McIntosh is still keeping watch. I had better go back."

Clarence McIntosh stayed in his hard chair, holding his rifle across his lap, and went back to contemplating the will and the intentions of the omnipotent Creator and the meaning of pain.

Soon Nurse Freemantle returned.

"What have you seen out there?" he asked her.

"Mr. Finch Hatton has helped Kwai get away. The guards think the man asleep at their feet is still Kwai. But it is not."

Clarence felt a modicum of relief. "Do we know where Kwai has gone?"

"Just off into the darkness," she said. "He will not have gone far as long as Aurala is here. He does not know…" She did not finish the sentence.

"Reverend, sir," she then said, holding her hands clenched at her waist in a characteristic gesture. "What are we to think of a religion that tells men they should behead their own sisters? What kind of god do those people worship?"

"I don't think their religion tells them any such thing," he said, feeling suddenly very weary. "I learned about Islam and the Koran in seminary as part of my doctoral studies. The Muslim religion does not tell them that they should kill their sister."

"They act as if it does," she said.

He sighed. "It is the same as when Catholics and Protestants kill one another in the name of religion. They say it is in the name of God. But God has nothing to do with it." He paused, at that moment convinced of the sin such murderers committed, using God's name in vain. "If you ask me, it is blasphemy for men to use the name of God as an excuse to perform such a deed."

Gian Lorenzo was just coming back into the parlor after taking Vera a cup of tea. She was with Denys now, guarding her baby. Gian Lorenzo was about to sit beside Constance, who sat gripping his handkerchief, having wept over the death of that lovely Somali girl.

A knock came at the door. When he opened it, Sergeant Kang stood on the veranda, sputtering with indignation. "My prisoner has escaped." He glared at them and scanned the room. "Where is Mr. Finch Hatton?"

The duke moved forward, close enough to emphasize his height and his precedence over the policeman. "I think you are overstepping your bounds," he said evenly. "You have no reason or right to speak to us in such a fashion. Please go back to your duties." He turned on his heel and strolled over to the tea table and picked up a cup.

The sergeant blinked and backed out the door, but he did not walk off. He stood for a while on the veranda, as if to pretend he was not finished. Or perhaps that he was standing guard there.

No one saw the two black-clad figures carrying curved daggers slide along the dark verge of the station road and speed past the hospital privies, across the narrow open space to the rear wall of the big stone hospital building.

Clarence had once converted a Catholic who wanted to leave his church and join the Protestants. During his preparation for acceptance into Clarence's congregation in Argyle, he had said Catholics believed that suffering in this world reduced one's punishment in the afterlife. Not even a marginal Calvinist like Clarence could subscribe to such a notion, but given the torture of his back at the moment, he wished it were true. He had begun this watch anxious, energized, and determined, but perhaps a man could not maintain such an alert level for long periods. He would be asleep if it weren't for the...

The hairs on his arms reacted to the sound before he did. It was soft, like the clink of metal one might expect from the gentle touch of a knife to a dinner plate. Four seconds later the midwife within the room groaned.

Clarence leapt from his chair and flung open the door, rifle at the ready. A tall, slender man garbed completely in black, his face covered—all but the eyes—was in the room. His knife at the midwife's throat, he held her in front of him, but her head came up only to his chin. Another man, identically garbed, was coming through the broken window. Without thinking, Clarence pulled the trigger and shot the first assailant in the head. "Move," he shouted to the midwife in Kikuyu, but she was frozen. The man at the window growled. He had one leg inside. The blood-spattered midwife fell to the floor.

Clarence pumped another cartridge into the chamber and aimed. But then two hands, cuffed together, reached the second assailant from behind and grasped him by the neck. He struggled, twisted, grunted out words that sounded like curses. Clarence kept his aim and breathed in. He was about to shoot when Kwai Libazo's face appeared behind the man, sweating despite the cool temperature. His hands gripped the intruder's neck; veins stuck out on his forearms.

The man in black slashed with a knife behind him, drew blood from Kwai's upper arm. Kwai did not loosen his grip. Clarence took three steps forward and smashed his rifle into the wrist of the hand that held the knife. He aimed the gun at the man's face.

"No," Kwai said. "He is mine." The hands tightened around the throat. The man's eyes widened. His mouth opened as if to gasp for air, but no sound came. His eyes closed. His body went limp. Kwai's powerful grip held him even as he slumped lifeless. He did not let go. He and Clarence looked into each other's eyes for many seconds.

The midwife stood up. She grabbed a cloth from the table in the corner and went to Kwai. He let go of the dead man, who fell into the room with a thud. Kwai climbed in the window. Still bleeding, he went to the bed where Aurala's body lay. He touched her face, put his head back, and howled a grief such as Clarence McIntosh had never heard—an anguished sound that went on and on and on.

Vera came into the room from the hall. The duke was just behind her. And Nurse Freemantle. "We heard a shot," Vera said, the words tumbling out though her eyes saw the situation.

The nurse took the cloth from the midwife and tried to use it to stanch the cut on Kwai's arm. He pulled away.

Vera reached out to put her hand on his bare shoulder, but she saw that there was no consolation for him. Her mouth moved as if she wanted to speak, but she did not. She picked up the sleeping infant from the table beside the bed. It stirred but did not awaken. She wanted to show the child to Kwai, but she thought better of it. That time was not now.

Thirty-six hours later, when Justin Tolliver descended from the down-train in Nairobi, he had expected to re-board and go on to Athi River. But he found Vera and Finch Hatton on the steamy platform waiting for him. He had gotten a cable before he left Nakuru saying Aurala's brothers were dead, but the looks on their faces told him that the story was not over.

Vera kissed him and put her head against his chest, not the sort of thing a chap would want to have happen when they were in public and in the company of another man. He patted her shoulder. She needed comforting after her ordeal, he imagined.

"Have you come to ride the last hour with me on the train?" he asked, as if he had no suspicions that something the opposite of lovely had brought them there.

"You'll want to stay in town for a while, I think," Finch Hatton said.

Vera looked up at Justin with sympathetic eyes. He saw that she had come to give him solace, not to get it. "I've brought your uniform. It's in Denys's room at the club. You will want to see Jodrell as soon as you've had a chance to have a wash and get something to eat."

They were walking toward the club along a road still of red dirt, but crowded with the usual people of all varieties and carts pulled by mules and horses, and rickshaws, but also at least four motorcars, making an awful racket and giving off a foul chemical smell. "What do you mean that I will want to see Jodrell?" The first thing that came to his mind was that the death of Aurala's brothers had somehow become a police matter. "How did those barbarians die?" he demanded to know.

Though he had directed his question to Vera, Finch Hatton responded. "Let's wait until we are indoors," he said quietly— words vague enough to be truly alarming.

Nothing that came to Tolliver's mind in the next ten minutes stayed his worry. Once they arrived at the club, with a woman along, they had no choice but to settle in the tearoom for luncheon, all the other rooms being reserved for men only. He made short work of cleaning up and changing in Denys's room. He put on his uniform, puzzled as to why Vera had insisted that he should. He had agreed rather than have a row with her in front of Denys.

He joined them at a table. As it turned out, the setting felt far too public given the nature of the news they imparted.

Vera spoke first, looking at the napkin on her lap the whole while. "Aurala is dead," she said quietly and evenly.

"How?" he said with as much control as he could muster. "Why did you not tell me before this? Those foul brothers—"

She put her hand over his, but did not look up. "No. In childbirth. The delivery was complicated. Nurse Freemantle and the midwife were not able to save her."

"But what has Jodrell got to do with that?"

She looked into his eyes at last. "Kwai Libazo is under arrest."

"For killing those assailants?" His voice was far too loud. Why had they chosen such a place to discuss this private subject?

"Perhaps it would be best to hear me out," she said gently. There was nothing but concern in her eyes, and nothing but shock and anger in his heart.

She went on telling him a tale that turned his anger on himself. Thanks to his terse cable to Jodrell, the D.S. had misunderstood the situation and had sent a squad of askaris. Kwai had been discovered—the very thing Justin had thought to avoid. Not only arrested, but that dolt Sergeant Kang had humiliated him, at the worst moment of his life. Tolliver's brain burned. "And he is now in jail?"

"Yes," Denys said, "charged with desertion and resisting. I am afraid Cranford has already begun to talk about making an example of him."

The first thought in Justin's head flared. He grabbed his glass of claret and drained it in one gulp. "They want to execute him?"

Denys signaled for more wine. "That is not officially the case yet, but you know the gossip mill. The story has already been distorted. This is why Vera and I came to meet you. We knew you were the only one who could talk sense into them."

Tolliver put down his knife and fork. What he had had of an appetite had fled him. In the quasi-military world of the Protectorate police, it was perfectly plausible that a native policeman, even a sergeant with an impeccable record, could be put up before a firing squad for desertion. His stomach quaked. He pushed the plate of lamb stew away and pulled out his watch. It would be another forty-five minutes before Jodrell returned from his own luncheon.

He stood up. "I am sorry. I must go to the jail and see Kwai and then I'll have to talk some sense into Jodrell. This is intolerable."

Vera put her hand on his forearm. "They would not let me see him," she said, her eyes apologizing, as if the failure had somehow been hers.

"You tried?" It was a question, but he knew the answer. This was his Vera, who would do what no proper wife would do and make him both appalled and proud of her at the same moment.

"Stay hereabouts," he said, looking more at Denys than at Vera. "I may need some time."

"Take all you need," Finch Hatton said. "I will keep Vera company while she waits."

Tolliver marched to the police headquarters, which also housed the jail, grateful that Vera had thought to bring his uniform.

He found stocky, powerfully built Abrik Singh—a sergeant he and Kwai had served with in Mombasa—on duty. Singh put a hand to his Sikh turban in a salute. "Sergeant Libazo is very down in the mouth," he said.

"I'll talk to him," Tolliver said. "In the meanwhile, send a runner to Jodrell and ask if I can meet him in half an hour. Tell me if he says no."

Singh saluted again, and Tolliver went to Kwai's cell.

Tolliver had never seen the man so diminished. He rose when Tolliver entered his cell but slowly, lethargically. He did not salute. There was bandage on his upper left arm.

"I will not let them punish you," Tolliver said though he held no certainty of keeping such a promise.

"I do not care what happens to me, sir." Kwai was the picture of the Europeans' belief that a native would die if imprisoned. Tolliver understood that more than the threat of rotting here troubled him.

"I care," Tolliver said. "And you have a child to think about." The words were out before Justin realized he had no idea if the baby was a boy or girl.

"She needs a mother, and she has none."

Tolliver tried to look in his eyes, but his head hung over and his shoulders slumped. For reasons Tolliver could not explain, his anger rose—not only for Kwai, but *at* him. The heat of it fired his words. "Stand up straight, sergeant," he ordered in a sharp voice.

No doubt out of habit, the man snapped to attention.

Tolliver faced him squarely. "Just because the Europeans who have come here call you boy, is no reason for you to act like one. You are a man, Libazo. You have always acted like a warrior. It is time you resume that role."

Kwai stiffened his spine, assuming the stance of a mahogany statue. His gaze did not meet Tolliver's eyes.

"That's better. I have seen you stand up to flying bullets, the flames of a burning building, and a black mamba about to strike. I am not going to watch you crumble now." Tolliver took a breath. "Look at me."

The glance that met his was pleading at first, and then defiant.

"Ah," Tolliver said, holding his gaze and wondering what he himself would do if he lost Vera. The very thought of such an outcome squeezed his heart. "That baby girl is all you have left of her mother. She belongs to no tribe. She has no sisters or brothers. You are all she has. She will need a father."

"I would have died to save her mother," Kwai said quietly.

"You could not have stopped her fate. No one could."

Tears glistened in Kwai's eyes. He bowed his head. "I am no Maasai warrior," he said.

"You have the capacity to be a leader."

"I have no one to lead."

Tolliver chewed his bottom lip. Kwai used to have something of a bright future in the police force. Now he might not have a future at all. "I am going to talk to Jodrell. Be of good heart. You do not know what he will decide."

"Yes, sir." It was a phrase Libazo had used in many different tones of voice with Tolliver over nearly three years. Today it sounded like resignation.

Tolliver left the police station for Jodrell's office in Government House, his head full of phrases to use in Kwai's defense. He was barely inside when he encountered the last person he wanted to confront—District Commissioner Cranford, the government's most powerful officer in this sector and one with whom he had been at odds for as long as they had known each other. This was the man who had made the investigation into the murder of Vera's uncle such a travesty. The D.C. measured right and wrong only by what would keep him out of trouble with the settler community and his own superiors. The biggest obstacle Cranford saw to his own comfort was what he called the savagery of the natives.

"So Tolliver," he said in that booming voice of his, "I see your favorite blackie sidekick has shown his true nature."

"Yes, sir," Tolliver said heartily, though he could not bring himself to raise his voice to Cranford's volume. "He acted the way any brave English gentleman would have, putting his family's safety ahead of his own." He did not know where the words came from, but he was proud of them.

Cranford sputtered. "Now see here—"

To Tolliver's utter delight, Cranford paused and allowed him to fill the silence. "I am glad you can see what an upstanding man he is."

Cranford harrumphed. "You do have a habit of getting above yourself, Tolliver. It's good that you are leaving the police force. You've been nothing but trouble." He turned on his heel and marched off in the direction he had been coming from when Tolliver encountered him.

Unfortunately, Jodrell's office was in the same corridor. Tolliver followed him, lagging behind, and was dismayed when Cranford entered the D.S.'s room before him. He stuck his head in before the door closed and said, "I am here for my appointment, sir. I will wait until D.C. Cranford is finished with his business with you."

The door fairly slammed in his face. He waited nearby, hoping to get something of an idea of what was going on between the district superintendent of police and the D.C. without actually putting his ear to the keyhole. They mumbled. He had no idea what they were saying. It occurred to him that it was better for him and for Kwai if Cranford held his temper, but then he realized that a cold Cranford was even more dangerous than a heated one.

Their exchange took less than three minutes. When he heard Cranford say a hearty, "See that you do," Tolliver backed to a safe distance from the door.

The D.C. stormed out and, seeing Tolliver, harrumphed again and pushed past and out into the stairwell.

Jodrell was standing when Tolliver entered the office. He did not give a moment for greetings. "I am sorry there is nothing for it, Tolliver, old boy. Cranford has given me a direct order."

Tolliver could barely speak the words that came to him. "To shoot him?" His mind went immediately to freeing him, to Kwai running free, carrying his native spear and that sword—the one that had killed the black mamba.

"Not that," Jodrell said. "Cranford wanted it. Said he must be made an example of. But I managed to convince him that commanding armed natives to shoot their own officer was not a good precedent."

Tolliver breathed. "Thank heavens."

"You won't say that when you hear what he extracted in exchange for clemency."

Tolliver steeled himself again, but as hard as he tried to chill his nerves, they could never have been cold enough to tolerate what he heard.

Jodrell nearly whispered his response. "He wants him humiliated in front of the entire Nairobi contingent. He must be flogged, forty lashes, and you must do it yourself."

"I cannot do such a thing. I will not." Tolliver whispered too.

"I can give you no choice because I have none. If you do not do it, I must inflict the greater punishment the law prescribes: execution."

A picture fell into Tolliver's mind of Cranford in chains and himself holding his service revolver to the D.C.'s head.

An eternity seemed to pass before he could say anything. Finally Jodrell took a step forward and laid his hand lightly on Tolliver's shoulder. "It is my role to make sure you do what the D.C. calls 'a proper job of it.'"

"When must this happen?"

"The faster we get it over with the sooner he will be free."

"Free to do what?" Tolliver did not want an answer, and Jodrell did not give one.

"Tomorrow morning," Tolliver said, having no idea what he would do, knowing he could not take a whip to Kwai. Wishing he had the courage to die in his place.

Vera convinced Justin to let her remain with him overnight in town. She went off to find them a room, while Denys stayed with Justin at the club—the perfect companion, who would not insist on talking.

With the flood of new settlers taking up all the available accommodations, Vera was forced to beg a room from her father's friend the Reverend William Bennett, the rector of St. Phillip's Church. Her strongest memory of Dr. Bennett was from her mother's funeral, the thought of which twisted her heart. Then suddenly she realized that she and her father had never finished their conversation about what to do about Aurala's body. Even in the cool highland climate, they could not wait much longer. She and Denys had both tried to see Kwai to ask him what he wanted to do, but the men guarding him said they had strict orders not to let anyone see him.

In the end, at Dr. Bennett's suggestion, he took her to the small mosque near the Indian bazaar. They asked the Muslim priest, who told them that the ritual must be performed by the devout of his religion. When Vera told him there were none such near the dead woman, he balked at giving her any advice. In the end, the reverend managed to get a description of what a devout Muslim would do, if they were able to find one.

As she and Dr. Bennett walked back to the manse, he surmised, "Perhaps they think it sacrilege for anyone but one of their faithful to perform the rite."

"Still we must do our best. I will tell my father, Nurse Freemantle, and Wangari. They will wash her and wrap her in white cotton, and bury her with her head facing Mecca. That much they can do."

She wrote it all out to her father, and then, along with a note that she and Justin were staying the night in town, sent it by runner to the Mission. After that, she went to fetch Justin.

On the way back to the manse, he was silent. As they approached the church, he suddenly hissed through clenched teeth, "Bloody Cranford. I want to see him devoured by a lion."

She reached out to put a hand on his shoulder, but he shrugged her off. "He is insane," he said now in full voice. "What he insists that I do is mad. I will not."

"What is it that he wants you to do?"

"I cannot say it."

She grabbed his arm and held him back.

"Stop it," he snapped.

"You will tell me, or you will have to drag me along bodily."

His teeth clenched again. He refused, and she insisted until finally he relented.

She had all she could do not to retch into the gutter. She pulled him away from the front of the manse into the deserted cemetery on the other side of the church.

He kicked the wrought-iron fence.

She had no idea what to say. "Darling—"

"Don't darling me," he bellowed. "I cannot bear this." He was stalking now, back and forth between a headstone that said *Stephenson* and a Celtic cross that bore strange carvings and no name at all. "Bloody monster. How can he? I want to tear off his arm and beat him to a pulp with it."

Vera had never seen Justin like this. He stopped in front of a low grave marker and for a moment she feared he would stomp on it. She held her tongue. Speaking her mind would only enflame him more.

"The bastard. The bloody bastard. How can Britain have such a man in such a position of authority? It's monstrous."

She agreed. Cranford was just the type to want to whip a man himself. To whip a black man. "And he calls himself civilized and Kwai a savage." The words fell out of her in a whisper.

Justin turned on her, his eyes burning. "What?"

"Nothing," she said. "No name you can call him would be evil enough." Her throat ached with his pain.

He slammed his fist into his palm. "I swear, one day I will find a way to make him pay."

She reached toward him but did not touch him. "In your own good time, I know you will."

He paused and looked at her for a long time, breathing raggedly at first. "When he least suspects it," he said.

She held his glance.

Tears came into his eyes. "He's arranged it so that I have no choice. I must do it or see Kwai executed."

The tears overflowed. "I can't see how I can do it. How will I ever bring myself to do it?"

She could not breathe. His pain seared into her heart.

"I would rather have Cranford whip me," Justin said, softly now.

"I know you would. You really would."

They stayed there in silence for several minutes.

He took her in his arms, and with her head to his chest she could hear his heart still pounding.

When they went into the house, she took Dr. Bennett aside and told him what Justin must do. That good man did not force Justin to talk about it. He gave them dinner, which neither Vera nor Justin ate. They did not speak.

Before bed, Dr. Bennett told them that silent prayer was their best way to deal with it. Vera had no idea if Justin was praying. She was not.

Tolliver went over his whole life in his mind. Never had he ever had to do anything remotely approaching the difficulty he would face in the morning. Vera sat near him all evening, and during the night held his hand and did not sleep. But she did not fuss. She stayed quiet, asked him no questions.

He saw that he had to calm his temper when the time came. He felt the danger of getting overwrought. He imagined the whip in his hand. He must be in control of himself when he did it. Yet he could not picture himself striking Kwai Libazo. Every drop of his blood rebelled at such a thought. His nerves were not up to it. Not up to it at all.

His mind went over and over the same territory until the sky was beginning to lighten. He could not imagine finding it in himself to carry out this bloody order. Who could do such a thing?

Lovett had said he had had to amputate the leg of a man who had been attacked by a lion. He had found the courage to do that—to save a man's life. Tolliver wanted to think he could perform such an operation to save Kwai's life. It would be intolerable to have to do it. It would inflict incredible pain. But it would save his life. He had to look upon what he would do this morning in such a way. Lovett had described getting the man drunk.

Tolliver reached his arm around Vera and drew her to him. He kissed the top of her head. "I love you," he said. "You are the best wife a man could hope to have."

She kissed his cheek and soon fell asleep. As he watched the dawn light the windows, he lay awake planning precisely how he would comport himself that day.

He slipped out of the bed. When carefully shaved and groomed, dressed, and ready to leave, he made his way to the parlor of the manse, where he expected to purloin a bottle of the reverend's excellent whiskey. He found the man waiting for him.

"I wanted to see you off, my boy," he said. "I will pray for you while you carry out this dreadful business."

"Thank you, sir. I very much appreciate your intercession. God knows I will need all the help I can get."

"God knows your goodness," he said. "A lesser man would not suffer so, and an evil one would take pleasure in it and never think of it as the sin it is. But the sin is not yours."

"I am going to save his life. It is how I have begun to think of this. But I wonder if I might ask you: May I take some whiskey with me? I want to spare him the worst of the pain."

"That is a capital idea." He went to take a fresh bottle out of the sideboard. He also handed Tolliver two small, thickly made glasses. "Put these in your pocket." He held up the bottle. "I have an old leather bag here that you can use to carry this item."

He then went out with Tolliver and bid him good-bye at the door of the church.

Marching to the jail, in the early hours when few were on the streets, Justin thought of Bennett kneeling before the altar of his church, of the differences that man of God saw between goodness and evil, of how the Protectorate contained both the best and the worst of what was England. He tried to think of himself as part of the former, but he knew full well that being a policeman put him on the cusp between the two.

To his horror, the sergeant at the desk that morning was Kang—the very one who had arrested Kwai and started this dreadful sequence of events. Taking no trouble to ingratiate himself to the dolt, Tolliver used his most commanding voice: "I am going to talk with Sergeant Libazo," and strode past him, asking no quarter and giving none.

In the cell, he found Kwai sitting on his cot, his head in his hands. He did not rise. Tolliver did not order him to.

"They have told you what is going to happen?"

"Yes, sir. I do not care. You cannot hurt me any more than I already suffer."

"Look at me, Sergeant Libazo."

"I am no longer a sergeant."

"You will always be a sergeant to me," Tolliver said. "We have been through much together. I have been thinking about how we will get through this." He sat beside him and took out the whiskey bottle and withdrew the glasses from his pocket. "I have brought you something to deaden the pain."

"I have been thinking about this too, sir," he said. "I have my own plan. I have told you that I was denied the rite of passage by my father's people. When I still thought the Maasai might accept me, I tried to train myself to bear the pain that would come with circumcision. My ability to do that has never been tested."

"The pain of your heart is testing you now," Tolliver said.

"Yes." Kwai paused for a moment, and then continued. "This is the day I will bear pain in my body that I have never borne. This is the day I will become a man. I do not want your whiskey. Your whip will be my *emurata* knife. It will be the test of my manhood. I do not intend to flinch under the lash. I do not intend to dishonor my ancestors."

Tolliver turned away, not to let Libazo see tears glistening in his eyes. "Prepare yourself then, Kwai Libazo. When this is over, I will take you home to your child."

He then went out behind the station and downed two quick swallows of whiskey. He felt its warmth all the way to his empty stomach. He smiled ruefully. Kwai was trying to follow the way of his ancestors. Justin Tolliver was certain his own ancestors would be reaching for a whiskey bottle at a moment like this.

He left the satchel with the bottle in it on what used to be his desk.

He ordered Sergeant Kang to march the askaris out to the small staging area between the back of Government House and the river. The men of the Nairobi police battalion lined up in silence. Tolliver positioned himself and Kwai so that if Cranford looked out of his window, he would see the evil thing he had wrought.

Kwai stood, naked to the waist, his hands bound in front of him.

"There is no post here, sir," Kang said. "We should tie him to something so he does not run away."

Tolliver looked to Kwai, who shook his head almost imperceptibly.

"He is too much a man to run away," Tolliver announced so that everyone might hear him. He stared into Kang's eyes. "You may leave if you care to."

Kang opened his mouth, but had at least enough intelligence not to speak.

"Are you ready?" Tolliver asked Kwai.

Kwai knelt down and bowed, offering the bare skin of his back.

Tolliver steeled his nerves. It took all the determination he could muster to force his arm to raise the whip. He bit his lip till he tasted blood. He must do this. He would. His eyes clenched shut. God help me, he prayed. Save his life. He brought the lash down, and began to count the lashes. He thought of poor Lovett.

Justin squinted his eyes and pictured himself saving the life of the man with the mangled leg. Lovett would have had to look. Justin opened his eyes and kept them open for as long as he could, feeling the pain. The guilt. Hating Cranford. Hating himself. Holding in the hate so that it would not cause the lash to hit harder. Telling himself he must. How many strokes of Lovett's saw did it take to remove that man's mangled leg? Ten strokes? Twenty? Thirty? Forty minus one.

26

Two weeks later, on the veranda of the Scottish Mission, Vera and Tolliver sat sipping tea and saying nothing. Baby Will stood beside his mother's chair, holding on to her hands and rocking on his chubby feet. A dozen zebra were drinking from the river. A herd of kudu grazed out on the plain, off toward the outcrop where the Mission family often took picnics. At midmorning, the air was warm but cooled by a gentle breeze. White clouds sailed above the blue hills in the distance.

Nurse Freemantle appeared from the direction of the hospital and crossed toward them. Tolliver stood when she neared, a gesture of respect that men of his class seldom afforded a woman of hers. Vera smiled up at him.

"Kwai Libazo is safe from infection," she said in that businesslike way of hers. "If the wounds were meant to suppurate they would have done so by now."

"Oh, that is good news," Vera said. Little Will let go of her hands and sat down with a gentle thump.

"There will be considerable scarring," the nurse said. "His back looks like an American slave's."

Tolliver shuddered.

The nurse made an erasing gesture. Her lips disappeared into a thin, angry line. "Do not take any guilt upon yourself, Mr. Tolliver," she said. "Libazo is alive. He understands full well where the decision for the flogging came from."

"And his baby? What does he say of her?" Vera asked.

"He has found the heart to see her. She is to be called Lalo. It is a name the boy Haki made up from the ends of Aurala's and her sister's names. It's not a Christian name, but then again, she is not a Christian child." Again those disapproving lips disappeared.

"I think it is a lovely name," Vera said.

Nurse Freemantle did not voice her obvious disagreement. "I must go back, I have a badly burnt child and a woman with a terrible rash of some sort in the native wing." She marched off.

Tolliver took Vera's empty cup and put it on the table behind her chair. He was about to retake his seat, when he noticed two riders cresting the hill of the horse path from Nairobi. "Ah, here are Denys and Gian Lorenzo. That will cheer up my sister. From the way she has been moping, you would have thought their two weeks in Mombasa had been two years."

Vera picked up Will and was cooing and talking to him, telling him what a good little boy he was. Sometimes, from the way he looked at her, Justin thought that his son understood every word.

"I'll go tell Constance," he said. "No use postponing her joy."

Vera carried the baby with her toward the stable where she welcomed the arrivals. Gian Lorenzo leapt down, tossed his reins to Haki, said but a brief hello to Vera, and strode off toward the house and his ladylove.

Denys chuckled. "I thought he was going to lame his horse trying to get here as soon as possible. He has news."

"He has heard from King Victor Emmanuel?"

Finch Hatton's bright eyes filled with skepticism. "That decision is responsible for his ill humor. His king is withholding permission until her father grants his first. Then he says he will consider it, provided she converts to Catholicism."

Vera was vexed. "I would have thought that the daughter of an ancient British family would look like a catch to the king."

"I said as much to Gian Lorenzo," Denys said. "According to him, his cousin is a king, and as such, he doesn't want to be put in a position of saying yes and then being snubbed if her father, who is only an earl, says no. Gian Lorenzo sees his king's point and is sorry he did not think of that himself. He worries that his king was insulted at being asked in that way."

They walked toward the veranda. "My father expressed a fear that there would be more difficulties with it than the couple deserve to have. He so wants Constance to be happy."

"I have said this before—your father is the least likely Scots clergyman I can imagine," Denys said with a laugh.

"And I am just as happy about that as you are," she said.

By the time Constance and Gian Lorenzo emerged from their private conversation, luncheon was about to be served. From the way they leaned their heads together, they seemed determined to go forward no matter what anyone said.

As they took their places, Justin offered some jocular encouragement. "A man ready to attempt Everest must not be daunted by my papa," he said.

Constance wrinkled her nose at him.

"I have already booked passage to see him," Gian Lorenzo said.

"I will marry you whatever my father has to say," Constance declared.

Denys raised his glass. "To the *promessi sposi*," he declared.

He then turned the talk to the latest grist from the Protectorate's hardworking gossip mill. Baron Bror von Blixen-Finecke's fiancée, Karen Dinesen, was on her way to B.E.A. "We can expect another wedding of nobility before the year was out."

Gian Lorenzo raised his glass. "To Bror and his bride." He turned to Constance. "And to my future bride. May all the powers we need to support our love see the light."

"To seeing the light," Vera echoed.

They passed the afternoon playing music and listening to Gian Lorenzo's tales of the Arctic.

At sunset Justin said to Denys and the duke, "I think you must stay the night. I can lend you a couple of dinner jackets."

When they had gathered on the veranda for cocktails, Denys sipped his drink and plied them with a rumor he had picked up that morning at Afghan Ali Kahn's stable about fisti-cuffs breaking out last night in the men's bar at the Mombasa Club between a German and an Englishman over the political situation in Europe. "The contentious relationship between our king and his cousin the kaiser is beginning to affect us and our less than amicable neighbor to the south."

"Whatever is it all about?" Constance asked.

No one had an answer.

Denys shook his head. "I don't like to further mar the evening," he said, "but there was also an inquest in the High Court about the murder of Ruth Van Slyck."

Justin put down his glass. "And?" he said.

"You won't like it," Gian Lorenzo said.

"It was all over yesterday's edition of *The Leader*," Clarence McIntosh put in. "I have kept it from you not to upset you, but I have it. It's on the desk in my study."

Justin's mind roiled with possibilities. He could not prevent Vera from following him into the house, standing behind him, and reading over his shoulder. What was written in the news-paper was exactly as he feared.

The medical evidence did not support the charge of rape but the victim's body had been deliberately mutilated using a tribal knife employed in a common form of tribal operation. The victim was known to have opposed this tribal ceremony and had been in conflict with the natives over her opposition. Agitators on both sides of the question have tried to use the situation to their advantage. The verdict of the inquest was willful murder by person or persons unknown. No arrests were made.

Vera put her hand on his shoulder. "I am so sorry, dearest," she said.

"You are the last person on earth who needs to apologize to me, but good God, what is the editor of this rag thinking, printing gossip?"

Will, who had been napping in the next room, began to cry.

Vera went to him, lifted him from his cot, and held him to her.

Justin took her in his arms, the child between them. "Hush, darling," she said, kissing the top of the little head. "Hush. Hush."

He kissed the boy and the arms that held him. The child settled.

"The number of wrongs done. The number of falsities. It is maddening," Justin said once Will was back to sleep. "I am so very happy that in a few weeks I will have no responsibility for justice in this country."

She kissed him. "You will be responsible for apples and pears and peaches," she said. "What can be more benign than that?"

"I never want to read the newspaper again."

"Oh, I think when we are off up in Ngong, you will want to know how your old mates on the cricket team are faring."

He took her in his arms again. "You are right, as ever." He released her. "Before we go back to the others, I want to ask you something," he said.

"Yes?"

"Kwai and I haven't—we haven't been able to resume our old ways with each other."

"I noticed that," she said. "It pains me. But I don't think he blames you. Not really."

"It's not about blame." Justin could not say what the cause was. Was it shame? It was something like shame. "At any rate," he said, "I want us to take Kwai and Haki and Lalo with us. Kwai is very clever, as you know. I hope that eventually he will want to work with us up there. But I think you need to be the one who talks to him about it."

"I would not want to go without them," she said. "Do you think he will say yes?"

"I hope so." He knew he sounded completely unsure.

"Have you talked to him about—about what happened?"

"I have not had the spine. He has suffered a great deal of pain. He may have changed his thinking about what I did."

Vera doubted that, but she did not say so.

"Do *you* think he will say yes?" Justin asked.

"I do," she said, and she prayed it would be true.

When they rejoined those on the veranda, Clarence was showing them photographs of Will's baptism. Vera went off toward the hospital. Less than half an hour later, she returned with Kwai carrying his child and Haki trailing along. Kwai was wearing his policeman's shorts and a white shirt, open at the front, no doubt to keep it loose against his back.

"I wanted to come to thank you, Bwana Finch Hatton," Kwai said, "for sending Irungu to take my place on the night of the attack, so that I could go to the hospital to defend my child. Without you, I would have been under guard and who knows what might have happened to my baby girl."

Denys shook his head. "You owe less to me than to that little chap." He indicated Haki. "When the reverend and I returned from the station, I went to where the porters were camped behind the hospital. He came to find me. It was his idea to put someone in your place."

They all looked at Haki with disbelief.

"You walked around in the dark alone?" Clarence McIntosh said. "How many times have I told you that it is too dangerous with all the animals?" His words were scolding, but his tone was not. He turned to the others. "He grew up in

Mombasa where there were no hippos and lions prowling about in the night."

The boy put his hand on the baby wrapped in a white blanket in her father's arms. "My sister needed our father," he said. "And I have told you, Reverend, sir, that Mombasa does not have such animals, but it is a dangerous place too. I am not afraid."

"Right you are," Denys said with a laugh. "You are a brave lad. I commend you."

"We all commend you," Vera said.

"Hear, hear."

Dusk was falling fast.

The duke looked across the lawn and exclaimed, "Look. Look at that!" The place where the lawn met the darkening woods was filled with fireflies.

Haki ran to them. They all stepped away from the lamp-light and stood together on the grass.

"They come every June," Kwai said.

Hundreds of tiny lights winked among the trees.

"Oh, how lovely! How very lovely!" Constance exclaimed.

"They are magic," Haki shouted as he danced away toward them, arms outstretched. "They are magic."

Kwai went and caught one for the boy to hold in his hand.